Landon had never felt so out of control, so fiercely protective for another in his life

He scooped Kaitlyn into his arms. Somewhere along the way, he'd connected with her, not just from a protector's viewpoint, but from a pack-member's perspective. He thought of her as one of his own…one he also wanted with a deep, abiding desire that knocked him in the gut.

But he didn't trust himself not to hurt her if things between them heated up. His inner beast was always there, just under his skin, growling for him to take action. Adding sex to the mixture would only heighten his primal senses, making it very easy to forget just how breakable she was.

But she would have his loyalty. There was nothing quite like a wolf's dedication to his packmates.

And Landon knew he'd defend her with every last breath in his body.

Books by Patrice Michelle

Silhouette Nocturne

*Scions: Resurrection #31
*Scions: Insurrection #40

*Scions

PATRICE MICHELLE

Born and raised in the Southeast, Patrice Michelle gave up her financial calculator for a keyboard and never looked back. Thanks to an open-minded family who taught her that life isn't as black and white as we're conditioned to believe, she pens her novels with the belief that various shades of gray are a lot more interesting. She's a natural with a point-and-shoot camera, likes to fiddle with graphic design and, to the relief of her family, strums her guitar to an audience of one.

Visit Patrice's Web site at www.patricemichelle.net to learn about her upcoming books, read excerpts and sign up for her newsletter.

SCIONS: INSURRECTION

PATRICE MICHELLE

Silhouette Books

nocturne™

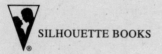

SILHOUETTE BOOKS

ISBN-13: 978-0-373-61787-6
ISBN-10:   0-373-61787-9

SCIONS: INSURRECTION

www.silhouettenocturne.com

Printed in U.S.A.

Dear Reader,

Welcome back to the intriguing, dark and sensuous SCIONS world! This second book in the trilogy, *Scions: Insurrection*, continues with Landon Rourke and Kaitlyn McKinney's story.

Landon is one of my favorite heroes because he's not perfect. He's tortured and flawed, but possesses a strength of will and a sense of duty and honor that I hope will make you cheer for him as he searches for his place within his pack and wins the heroine's heart.

Strong-minded and courageous, Kaitlyn McKinney has many obstacles to overcome in order to find her way to happiness. Loyal to the core, Kaitlyn's capacity for love, along with her compassion, are the qualities that will make her path to falling for Landon both heart-wrenching and heartwarming at the same time. She truly is Landon's perfect match.

Open your heart and fall headlong into Landon's and Kaitlyn's lives as they embark on an emotional adventure about past mistakes, ingrained loyalty, intense passion, forgiveness and, ultimately, deep, abiding love.

All the best,

Patrice Michelle
www.patricemichelle.net

To my family, thank you for always believing in me!

Acknowledgments

To my amazing agent Deidre Knight for believing
in my writing and finding a home for my books,
to my editor Ann Leslie Tuttle for her astute
editorial input and endless enthusiasm,
and to Charles Griemsman—a wonderful
point person all the way around. Thanks also
for answering my obscure questions about
New York with infinite patience.

And to fabulous author Linnea Sinclair for her
willingness to share procedural information with
fellow authors.

Prologue

I'm being hunted.

Nearly imperceptible vibrations rumbled underneath Landon's bare feet as he lifted the ax.

Cool fall wind whipped through the forest, drying the sweat that coated his naked chest and soaked the top of his jeans.

He scrunched his toes in the damp underbrush, feeling, sensing the pulse of the predator. The tiny hairs on the back of his neck and along his arms stood on end as his senses went into overdrive. Without turning, he sniffed the current in the air and waited for his sense of smell to catch up with his supercharged hearing and heightened tactile abilities. Filtering out the strong scent of oak, pine, decomposing leaves and earth surrounding him, he homed in on new scents and listened for movement.

Behind him. Six o'clock. Coming in fast. Landon pinpointed his hunter's stealthy approach.

His biceps flexed and he swung the sharp tool. The ax split the wood with ease, and twin pieces fell onto the stack of wood piled around the stump. With unhurried movements, he replaced the splintered wood with another log and lifted the ax once more.

The predator was closer. Seventy feet away and closing. Fifty feet. Close enough that he caught a whiff of its sweat.

Landon's lips curved in a predatory smile. He brought the ax around in a sharp arc at the same time he twisted his spine.

"Holy shit!" Caine drew himself up short, less than a yard behind Landon. Frozen in place, he stared wide-eyed at the pointed triangular blade that now hovered a quarter inch from his throat. "You almost took off my head!"

Landon lowered the ax to the ground. "When are you going to learn you can't sneak up on me?"

Caine's white teeth flashed. "The wind was in my favor."

"You know I don't depend on my nose," Landon growled, annoyed with the younger were. His sense of smell might not be as acute as those in his Lupreda wolf pack, but Landon's other senses had adapted, taking over where his nose left off. "Why are you here, anyway?" he asked as he lifted the ax.

"All three zerkers have disappeared."

Landon slammed down the ax, splitting not just the single log but the tree stump underneath it.

Leaving the ax buried in the split stump, he curled his hands into fists and faced Caine. "Why tell me this? I'm no longer a member of the pack."

Caine's hazel gaze locked with Landon's. "The Omega asked me to seek your help."

Landon's chest constricted as fury and resentment swept through him. Each year the Omega board ruled that his sub-standard sense of smell disqualified him from the annual

Alpha challenge—which was more than a test of physical endurance, it was proof of a were's leadership ability and combat strategy—yet they didn't have a problem coming to him for help. He ground his teeth and gritted out, "Nathan is their chosen Alpha. Let him find his lost werewolf zerkers."

"Nathan doesn't know."

Landon scowled at Caine. "As leader of the pack, Nathan should've been informed."

Caine crossed his arms over his chest. "You know damned well why he wasn't. Nathan would go to war with the vampires. The Sanguinas are the only ones strong enough to overcome a zerker."

"The vampires don't know zerkers exist!" Landon hissed. "How do you know the three weres didn't leave on their own? It's not like they were welcomed in the wolf pack." Landon might not be caught between shape-shifted forms like the zerkers, but he definitely understood what it felt like to be ostracized.

Caine's gaze narrowed. "Something happened to them. Blood was everywhere. Werewolf blood."

What a helluva mess. Landon ran a hand through his hair as his mind raced through the ramifications of the news Caine had just dumped on him. "What does the Omega want from me?"

Caine's shoulders visibly relaxed. "They know you have a tenuous truce with the Sanguinas' new leader, Jachin Black. They want you to talk to him and find out if the vampires had anything to do with our zerkers' disappearance."

And how the hell was he going to do that without revealing the zerkers' existence to the Sanguinas? Landon set his jaw and gazed into the woods around him.

"The Omega are trying to avoid a war, Landon. Wouldn't you do this for your pack?"

He glared at Caine, giving him a low, threatening growl. The bastard knew better. Landon would do anything for the Lupreda. The pack's well-being had always been his top priority.

"They sent you on purpose." Landon jerked the ax from the stump. Gripping the wood handle tighter, he stalked away, heading toward his cabin.

"Probably true." Caine's low laughter caught up to Landon as the younger were fell into step beside him. "They know you have a soft spot for me."

Landon slanted his gaze at Caine. "I would think *you'd* have a vested interest in the pack's concern over the zerkers' disappearance. If you don't, you should."

"That was way below the belt."

Landon paused and glanced over his shoulder at the pain underscoring Caine's tone. The younger were had halted. His fists were curled by his side, his eyes slitted and his lip lifted in a snarl.

Gripping the bullet slug that hung from a silver chain around his neck, Landon rubbed his finger across the partially crumpled metal. "Yes, it was, but you need to be reminded how closely you ride the line. Past mistakes linger with you."

Caine's angry expression melted away as he approached him. Clapping his hand on Landon's bare shoulder, his lips straightened to a firm line. "Yeah, I know."

Their gazes locked—a lifetime of support reflected between them.

"I'll see what I can do." Landon finally broke the silence.

Caine smiled and punched Landon's arm. "I've already insisted they reinstate you."

"Nathan will love that—the Omega undermining him." Landon snorted.

Caine followed him up to the cabin's wooden porch. "Nathan's an idiot."

"On that we definitely agree," Landon said with a grin.

"Nathan will never forgive you for kicking his ass in front of a captive audience of weres *and* vampires."

Landon shrugged. "I did what needed to be done to protect our pack from an all-out war with the vampires. Jachin will make a fair leader for the Sanguinas."

"I think it's rich Nathan can't oust you completely since your property butts the edge of Lupreda land." Caine's eyes lit with feral intensity. "By the way, fair warning, ever since you so thoroughly trounced him three months ago, he openly spouts-off about how much he hates your guts and if he runs across your traitorous ass, he'll rip your heart out."

Landon welcomed the primal need for a rematch that rose up inside him. He gave the younger were a calm, deadly smile. "Tell Nathan I said, 'Bring it on.'"

Landon glanced up from talking with a police officer and nodded to Jachin when the vampire entered Jamie's Pub in New York's Lower East Side. Jachin looked healthier than Landon had ever seen him. Apparently, mated life suited the Sanguinas' leader well.

"Gotta meet with a friend." Landon stood up from the table.

"Later, Rourke." The burly officer with a red-veined nose picked up his mug, saluted Landon and then knocked back his entire beer in one big gulp.

Clapping the man on the back, Landon smiled. "Make sure you take the subway home, Mike."

"Yeah, yeah, I hear ya," Mike called after him. Smoke clung to Landon's skin as he wound his way around small café tables and headed toward the bar. The scent of peanuts and alcohol, intertwined with the patrons' sweat—heavily loaded with varying emotions, from depression to euphoria—reached out and yanked at his heightened senses while he passed through the crowd. Out in open air, his sense of smell wasn't as acute as his werewolf brethren, but in close quarters…the onslaught left him a little dizzy and reeling. Landon snorted, blowing a gust of air out his nose to clear it. He needed his senses on full alert around Jachin.

Jachin's deep blue gaze watched him with predatory wariness as Landon approached the bar. He lifted his shot glass in salute. "It's been a while."

"Three months." Landon settled on a tall barstool and called to the bartender, "I'll have a Guinness."

After the bartender set his draft in front of him and walked away, Landon took a deep drink. The thick beer tasted good going down. Eyeing Jachin, he wondered how Jachin's human mate was faring living among the vampires. "How's Ariel? She's a resilient human, surviving that bullet wound like she did."

Jachin frowned. "If it hadn't been for my sister's medical knowledge…" He paused, then shook his head and chuckled. "My mate's tough. She's finally feeling herself again. She's pregnant and has been throwing up like a champ for several weeks."

A child? While a smile tugged at Landon's lips, a burning sensation spread through his chest. Was that jealousy? Probably indigestion. Damned raw steak he'd had for dinner a few hours ago.

"How are things with your pack?" Jachin rolled his empty shot glass along his cupped palm and his gaze turned serious.

Tension whipped through Landon, knotting his shoulders

at the center of his spine. He gripped his mug's handle tight and stared at the dark liquid in the glass. "The Alpha kicked me out for challenging him at the sacrificial circle."

"Attacking your Alpha was ballsy."

Landon's gaze snapped to Jachin's. "Nathan was too caught up in you trespassing on Lupreda land. He would've called for the entire pack to kill you, no matter the losses on either side. I had to give you enough time to move the ascendancy chalice and claim your leadership. With you as the new vampire leader, peace between our races might one day be a reality."

"You shouldn't be separated from your pack."

Landon shrugged at the anger in Jachin's tone. He knew he'd eventually kill Nathan. Was it justifiable homicide if the man deserved to die from sheer, arrogant stupidity? But dammit, if he did take the bastard out, Landon didn't know if there was anyone with enough balls to lead the pack. Nathan had brass ones. Unfortunately, the shithead didn't have the brains to go with the role.

After a few tense seconds passed, Jachin said, "There's a reason you called me here."

Landon met Jachin's steady gaze head-on. "The Omega want to know if the Sanguinas have anything to do with the disappearance of three of our weres."

Jachin's easy smile faded. "The Lupreda think the Sanguinas are responsible? Why?"

"Because our men are missing."

The vampire's deep blue eyes narrowed and his angular jaw hardened. "You'd better have more than that if you're going to accuse the Sanguinas, my friend."

The tension levels between them increased considerably. Landon heard Jachin's heart rate lower to a deadly slow thump and smelled the vamp's testosterone levels increase. The primal scent hung heavy and thick between them…as if the man was intentionally waving a red flag in front of Landon just to rile him.

The posturing smell made Landon's nose hairs burn. He snorted and pinched the bridge of his nose to keep from reacting. A good brawl was probably exactly what he needed, but it wouldn't be conducive to his reason for being there.

"The weres weren't taken unharmed," Landon said in a cold tone.

"And who could've done that, Landon?" While his black eyebrows drew downward, Jachin's expression held sincerity. "What Sanguinas would be able to walk into the middle of a wolfpack and take three weres without being detected and attacked by the rest of the pack?"

The hairs on the back of Landon's neck rose in defense. "The weres weren't living with the pack."

A lethal calm settled over the vampire's features. "Why would these other weres be living outside of the group? Did the Alpha kick them out, too? The Lupreda's best defense is their cohesiveness."

"No humans could've taken these men," Landon said, evading Jachin's question. "So I'll ask you again…are the Sanguinas responsible?"

Jachin's fingers cinched around the shot glass, shattering it. Shards of glass scattered across the bar top as he growled in a low voice, "Have you considered the possibility one of your own might've attacked your missing weres?"

Landon's chest tightened at Jachin's comment. He didn't want to think an insurrection was possible—that a Lupreda could be responsible, but Nathan had been the one who'd wanted to eliminate the weres once they went zerker. Only the Omega's humane ruling had saved the young weres' lives…even if the zerkers had to live away from the pack. Had Nathan won others to his side and taken out the zerkers, despite the Omega?

When Jachin opened his hand and pieces of glass fell to the bar, Landon saw the vampire's cuts heal right before his eyes. Obviously Jachin had fully recovered from the sickness that had almost destroyed the vampires twenty-five years ago when human blood mysteriously turned poisonous to vampires, forcing the vampires to withdraw from the human world. When a human woman wrote a book about vampires three months ago, Jachin knew she was the one to fulfill his father's dying prophecy of a better way for vampires to live. He took over the clan and claimed the human named Ariel Swanson as his mate. From the fast healing Landon had just witnessed, Ariel's blood was indeed viable.

Landon's gaze jerked to Jachin's furious one, his concern growing for his pack's safety. If the Lupreda ended up going to war with the Sanguinas, fully recovered vampires would have a definite advantage. "There have been reports of a few homeless humans who've gone missing the past couple of months. Have you discovered that other humans' blood is viable as well?"

Jachin nodded. "Apparently the sickness is being bred out of the humans. The younger ones' blood isn't poisonous."

Landon clenched his fists. "Have other vampires been feeding then? Missing humans isn't a very humane approach, Jachin."

Jachin's gaze narrowed before he finally answered in an even tone. "There are some vampires who deserted the clan when I became the Sanguinas' new leader. Our Sweeper unit hasn't located all of the rogue vampires yet. A few still remain at large, evading our detection. It's possible they've discovered how to tell which humans are no longer poisonous."

"If that's true, your rogue vampires could've taken our weres." As Landon stared intensely at him, the vampire's jaw began to tic. They each were weighing the other's sincerity. "No matter your and my goals for peace, hatred still runs deep between our races," Landon finally said once his temper had settled to simmering tolerance.

Jachin smiled then, his white teeth flashing in the bar's dim light. "Then it's up to us to set a positive example." He inclined his head slightly. "Though I don't see how the rogue vampires could've attacked and taken your weres without leaving their scent behind, if they did take your brethren, their actions wouldn't be condoned by me or any member of my clan."

Landon nodded. "The Omega won't like the answer, but they might understand it."

Jachin brushed the last bits of glass from his palm, then ran his credit card through the payment machine on the bar counter in front of him. As he slid the card into his leather coat pocket, he said, "We'll step up the Sweeper unit presence in the city. I have no idea what the rogue vampires would do with weres, other than enjoy battling with them. Their food source is in town, not in the Shawangunk mountain range." Stepping down from the stool, Jachin continued, "You never did tell me why the missing Lupreda weren't living with the pack."

Landon made his payment and stood up, the wooden stool scraping the hard floor behind him. He was slightly broader in the chest than Jachin, while the vampire had at least an inch on Landon's six-foot-two height. The men faced one another, each measuring the other with steady, assessing stares.

Landon inhaled, posturing instinctively. Decades of distrust still smoldered between them. Like dying embers in a fire, the slightest whiff of aggressiveness would ignite the blaze once more.

Old habits died hard.

Trust had to be earned…over time. "They didn't walk in line with the Alpha," Landon said. As he turned away, he mentally grunted at the double meaning behind his honest response.

Chapter 1

"I heard you were awesome with the kids at Handleburg Hall tonight."

Kaitlyn snorted into the cell phone and peered out her car window into the dark parking lot. "For cripe's sake, Abby Brooks, I haven't even left the orphanage yet. Who's your spy and is he old enough to work for the NYPD?"

"I have my ways," Abby's smug purr came across the line. "I hear you're coming back next week. Are you getting hooked on these kids like I told you you would?"

She'd had a great time tonight. "Yeah, you could say that." Kaitlyn might've grown up in a loving home, but she had one thing in common with Handleburg's troubled teens. The sobering realization had hit her tonight when one of the kids had challenged her during her speech on working for the police. He'd told her she knew nothing of what his life was like.

That was true enough. She hadn't grown up in a drug-riddled home or had to worry about gang shoot-outs happening in the middle of the night or day. But in the not-too-distant future, just like these young men and women, she'd be parentless, too. Then her police coworkers, Abby and the "Hall" teens would be the only family she had. If nothing else, she hoped she could give the teens the support they needed to know that they didn't have to follow the same path their parents had.

"Thanks for hooking me up for the lecture. Oh, by the way, they want me to help demonstrate in your tae kwon do class next Thursday," Kaitlyn said as she turned the key and started the car. "And drum roll…I've decided to commit at least one night a week to Handleburg."

"That's wonderful, Kaitlyn. But what about your mom?"

Kaitlyn turned up the heat to ward off the chilly fall air. "Mom has a lot more bad than good days now. When she's having bad days, she doesn't want company. The pain medicine makes her sleep a lot. I thought spending time with the kids would keep my mind off her. Otherwise, I just…" She paused. Worry for her mom clogged her throat.

"That makes sense to me, hon. Did you get the gift I sent to your new digs?"

Kaitlyn laughed. "Yes, thank you for the congratulations gift. I've already attached the small voice recorder to my key chain."

"I figured you could dictate during boring stakeouts, but hey, I'm not done. Let's go to Fuel and celebrate your promotion to detective."

Kaitlyn pulled out of the parking lot and drove down the road. "Not tonight, Ab—"

"You really should celebrate and cut loose. Not to mention, it's been a while since you've been out on the 'scene.' Mr.

Right could be there at the bar, waiting to sweep you off your bonnie Irish feet."

More like the guy'd be ready to jump into the sack with the first woman who said yes. She knew Abby's suggestion that she help out at Handleburg and now this invitation to the bar was her best friend's way of helping her find someone to care for in her life, yet Abby's casual "Mr. Right" comment caused thoughts of her last boyfriend to flit through Kaitlyn's mind. She hadn't dated anyone since she'd broken up with Remy two years ago.

She'd initially been attracted to his clean-cut charm and understated bad-boy edge. After dating the guy for a little over a year, they'd grown apart, seeming to have less in common than she first thought. The man's obsession with being a Garotter like his father finally became more than she could deal with. Remy chose to live in the past. She didn't.

She wasn't surprised when she heard Remy had joined up with the old vampire hunter group. The Garotters had reinstated themselves three months ago in response to a woman's kidnapping. Ariel Swanson had been abducted right after her fictional book about vampires was released to the public. Sheesh, it was just a book! While it was true vampires had cut a murderous path through the human population in their past, the monsters had been extinct for a good twenty-five years.

"Sorry. I've got an early day tomorrow. Along with my new promotion, I was assigned my first case. I have a good bit of research ahead of me."

"So dedicated." Abby gave a resigned sigh. "You know your father would be proud of you."

Would her father be proud? Kaitlyn wondered as she rolled to a stop at a stoplight. She hoped so. She missed his gravelly voice and lilting accent.

Blinking back the moisture in her eyes, she pushed on the gas pedal when the light turned green. "Thanks for the congrats and for your friendship. I don't know what I'd have done without you these last few years. Call me tomorrow and tell me how Fuel went."

"How'd you know I was going anyway?"

Kaitlyn laughed. "This is *you* we're talking about. I'll talk to you later. Bye." Once she closed her cell phone, out of habit, Kaitlyn turned on her police scanner instead of the radio.

While listening to the calls coming in and the police officers responding, she considered the biggest crime situation facing the force today. Other than drugs, gunrunning had always been an issue for the city.

A couple months ago, a Tacomi vehicle loaded with pulsar guns had been hijacked on its way to a government warehouse. The laser weapons had been created to give the police an advantage over criminals now sporting Kevlar. Apparently, the thugs had wanted the pulsar weapons the police were carrying, but when rumors had come through that the Garotters were active again and carrying pulsar weapons, most police officers had turned a blind eye. Except for her boss.

Kaitlyn's headlights sliced through the darkness as she took a side road that led to the interstate.

Her boss had set his sights for a bigger role and he wanted a juicy "win" to bring to the table when promotion time came around. His informants had told him this new self-funded Garotter regime had ties to the Mafia, which fell in line with the greater number of pulsar weapons being carried by well known Mafia men, too. Kaitlyn's first assignment was to ferret out the Mafia connection, if there truly was one. Hence, the major research she needed to do tomorrow.

A crackling call came across the scanner, capturing her attention. "Lady reports yelling and a flash of bright lights in Morningside Park."

Without hesitation, more out of habit than anything else, Kaitlyn punched in her badge number and hit the call button. "This is Detective McKinney. I'm in the vicinity. I'll check it out."

"Copy, McKinney. Backup is on their way. ETA seven minutes."

"Copy, dispatch."

Heart thumping a little harder, Kaitlyn reached into her glove compartment. Once she'd pulled out her gun in its leather holster, she clipped the holster to her belt. Securing a palm-sized comm unit beside her gun, she then turned her vehicle down another road and headed toward Morningside.

Just like her father…there was no such thing as "off duty" in her mind.

Kaitlyn pulled into the darkened, pothole-riddled parking lot. She scanned the abandoned park's broken picnic-shelter roof and the graffiti on the restroom building next to it.

A lone streetlight provided little illumination for the park area that backed up to the woods. Under her coat, the tiny hairs on her arms began to stand up, warning her.

Turning off her headlights, Kaitlyn reached beneath her seat and withdrew the NYPD-issue flashlight. She wrapped her fingers around the cool, heavy-duty metal and got out of the car.

Kaitlyn closed the door with a quiet click and took slow, even breaths. Pulling her coat out of the way, she rested her hand over her gun, tucked in its holster, as she scanned the shadowed playground.

Adrenaline pumped through her veins and she turned her flashlight toward the merry-go-round slowing to its final spin at the same time she unsnapped the holster, removing her weapon. Backup would be there soon, she told herself as an invisible force seemed to pull her toward the play equipment.

An owl hooted; its deep night call sliding icy fingers down her spine. She gripped the gun's handle, while cool air, laced with the faint scents of home fires and pine, kissed her cheeks.

"Police officer. Come out now!" She moved across the parking lot, and puffs of frosted air plumed in front of her with each breath she took.

As soon as she stepped out of the streetlight's glowing circle into the darkened playground, a grating, nails-on-a-chalkboard sound echoed in the darkness, skidding all the way to her bones.

She froze in place. Her breath caught while she listened for the source of the sound. Another piercing squeak echoed before the equipment came to a complete halt.

The merry-go-round.

Her flashlight swept the monkey bars, the play hut and slide. Whoever it was must be gone now. The tension in Kaitlyn's stomach eased and she began to breathe again. Confidence restored, she started toward the shadowed equipment with assured strides.

A gust of wind rushed past her, so strong, so specifically directed—as if someone or something had dashed right past her at a rapid pace—it flapped open her coat, sending frigid air straight through her cotton button-down shirt underneath.

Her skin prickled and Kaitlyn halted. Cinching her grip around the gun, she quickly traced the wind's path with the light.

Not a soul. Only leaves floating in the air and her car sitting in the dimly lit parking lot behind her. *I'm losing it.*

Shrugging, she faced forward once more. This time she

tuned into every little sound. Broken glass and leaves crunched beneath her shoes' hard soles, and tiny pebbles scattered out of her way as she approached the merry-go-round.

She could go back to her car and wait, but an underlying "need to know" drove her forward.

Once she reached the merry-go-round, she shone the beam of light on the base. Faded, chipped blue and red paint created pie pieces on the round wooden floor. An empty beer bottle sat in the middle.

Kaitlyn sighed and gripped the merry-go-round's cool metal handrail with her gun hand, while she scanned her flashlight across the open field behind the playground and then into the dark forest beyond.

Other than a blanket of low fog hanging a few inches above the cool grass, nothing was there.

Shaking her head at the boondoggle call someone had made to the police, she turned to leave, but something caught her eye in the open field behind the playground. The wind must've blown the fog away, exposing what had been hidden underneath.

Glowing embers. Fiery orange.

Beckoned by an unseen force, she ran toward the bits of burning ash.

As she moved closer, the smell of burned hair and flesh permeated the air, making her stomach roil.

When she reached the area and the full ashy sight came into focus, the need to retch grew so strong, she gagged. Surrounding the ashes left behind, a glowing, aura-like outline remained where a body had once lain. The aura revealed arms and legs in a straight-out position, as if the victim had been staked to the ground.

Her pulse raced out of control and she began to shake all

over. She knew most people didn't see auras, especially of dead people, like she did. A detailed outline always surrounded the bodies. It was as if, at the moment of their death, each victim left a strong energy signature behind—a signature to give her clues. And this time it was a neon-purple color. Purple meant the death had been brutal.

Death always upset her, especially violent murders, but what frightened her most was the shape of this outline surrounding the ashes.

While she scanned the forest with her flashlight to make sure no one was lurking in the woods, she contemplated what she'd tell her fellow officers once they showed up. The aura wasn't like any human she'd ever seen. She knew the other police officers wouldn't be able to see the energy signature she did, but she hoped the lab might be able to lift the DNA of the victim from the ashes.

Lights flashed behind her and her insides jerked to attention. Kaitlyn turned to see a vehicle pulling into the parking lot. It wasn't a squad car.

"Damn," she whispered and crouched to quickly turn off the light. This wasn't the best area of town and she was alone. Even though Abby had trained her to red belt level in tae kwon do and she had a gun, she wasn't taking any chances.

She had no idea who was in that black truck, yet the distinctive grille across the front looked familiar. As she racked her brain, trying to remember where she'd seen the vehicle, a tall man stepped out.

Landon Rourke.

His wide shoulders looked even broader covered by a leather jacket that stopped at his thighs. The streetlight shone on his light brown hair and highlighted his strong jaw as he started across the lot toward the playground.

Breathing a sigh of relief, Kaitlyn stood up slowly. She tucked away her gun and stared at the man approaching.

Landon had offered his P.I. expertise to the police from time to time in the past, most often in the field. Hence the reason she'd seen him only a couple of times at the station while she interned during her last year in college. His dominant presence wasn't easy to forget. From his confident bearing to his aggressive stride, the man was definitely an impression maker.

She'd heard that he'd stopped working with the police a few years ago. Rumors abounded; the most popular was that he'd had a falling out with the now-retired chief.

What was he doing here?

Landon made his way across the playground toward Kaitlyn McKinney. His teeth were clamped so tight, he thought his jaw might shatter. He couldn't believe it when he'd pulled into the parking lot and her car was there.

It was bad enough the bastard who'd called him on his cell phone twenty minutes ago had told Landon to come to this particular park. The fact that Kaitlyn was also there sent a warning through his body, while guilt slithered a slimy, winding path through his conscience.

"If you want your missing pack members, go to Morningside Park. They might be a bit steamed when you get there."

The line had gone dead. All Landon knew, until he could have the phone number traced, was that the caller was a man. It wasn't a voice he'd ever heard before.

When he was within thirty feet of Kaitlyn, Landon bit back a howl of fury. His chest tightened with the need to roar. He scented burned flesh—Lupreda flesh—floating through the air toward him. The need for revenge rippled through him, contracting every muscle in his body. *Sick bastards.* Fisting his hands, he mentally vowed to rip apart whoever was responsible for murdering his pack mates…zerkers or not.

He approached Kaitlyn as the last ember on the ground changed from orange to black.

"It's Landon Rourke, right?" Kaitlyn held out her fine-boned hand to him. "Detective Kaitlyn McKinney."

Detective? When did she get promoted? Landon glanced at her outstretched hand. Shoving his hands in his jeans' front pockets, he gave a curt nod. The last thing he needed was to touch her. "Nice to meet you, Detective."

"Call me Kaitlyn. What are you doing here?" She lowered her hand and her eyebrow rose, lips quirking slightly. "Don't tell me you were just out for a stroll."

He didn't miss her sarcasm, even as he wondered, *Why the hell had the killers done it* here *of all places?* He swept his gaze across the burned remains of his brethren. The wind began to pick up, stirring the ashes. Rain's thick moisture carried heavily in the air. A downpour was imminent.

Who would be so twisted as to bring both Kaitlyn and him to this very park? His heavy conscience beat a staccato thrum against his skull. The bullet on the chain around his neck seemed to burn, branding his skin.

"Did you hear the call over the comm?" she prompted, drawing his attention.

"Yeah, I was near the area." *Lucky break on my excuse for being here.* He stared at the ashes. "What do you think? Kids burned some animals or something?"

Kaitlyn's auburn eyebrows rose. "Um, more like one *something.*"

Landon's heart jerked. There was no damned way she could tell what had been burned from looking at the ashes.

Could she? He kept his expression carefully neutral and gestured to the pile of remains dissipating with each windy gust. "What else could it be? You don't think this was a person, do you?"

She shook her head and tucked a thick auburn strand of hair that had fallen from her clip back behind her ear. "No, I—" She paused and glanced down at the remnants, looking perplexed. "I think this was something humanlike but not quite human."

He froze. "Humanlike? What are you talking about?"

She gave him an uncomfortable look. Her teeth snagged her bottom lip and she scouted the edge of the ashes, pointing with her flashlight. "The victim was lined up with his…its head facing north. It was at least seven feet tall with elongated jaws, more like a muzzle." Moving to the opposite side, she pointed to another area. "And its legs and feet were bent at an odd angle, as if…well, as if it walked on the balls of its feet."

Every word that came out of her mouth cinched Landon's chest tighter and tighter. Her accurate description was like a vise screwing closed around his lungs.

Damn. She'd just accurately described a Lupreda zerker.

But he couldn't tell Kaitlyn how right she was. He gave her a hard look and spoke in an even tone. "Halloween's not for another two weeks, Kaitlyn. I smell burned fur." He kicked at the ashes, hoping to disturb the image she was seeing. "We'd better make sure this fire is completely out. Whatever the accelerant was, it took care of any bones, but its presence might leave these ashes more likely to flare up again. That concerns me, being so close to these woods."

"Wait! Did you just feel a rain drop? There won't be any evidence left if it rains." She handed him the flashlight. "Hold this for me."

She quickly pulled the clawlike clip out of her hair, then bent to scoop up some of the ash with her hair clip. "I saw some bits of silvery stuff along the edges of the ash where the hands and feet were. I want to have a sample analyzed."

"That clip's like a tainted evidence envelope with holes." He squatted down to give her the light she requested.

"Yeah, but it's the best I've got under the circumstances," she said as he bent close.

Her gorgeous blue eyes, flecked with swirls of golden brown, peered at him through her auburn hair. The silky-smooth curtain had fallen out of its twist to lie over her right shoulder. When she tucked her hair behind her ear, her action let loose the most appealing smell…woman's musk and violets.

Their gazes locked and in that instant he knew. He saw the slight tremble in her hand movements, heard her heart rate kick up and felt her heat level rise as the scent of her arousal flooded her body.

She was attracted to him.

Something about her alluring smell leaped at him, grabbing him by the throat in a tight fist. When the beam of light bounced off her hair, revealing several shades of red, from deep auburn to burned amber, Landon gripped the flashlight tightly to keep from reaching over and running his fingers across the colorful strands. The urge to experience the fiery silk sliding along his skin grew stronger. Even as his chest constricted with his internal battle, her aroused scent imprinted itself on his hunter's memory. His blood thickened and his groin hardened instantly.

Landon gritted his teeth to suppress the overwhelming desire to grasp the back of her head and crush his lips to hers. He'd never wanted a woman with this much ferocity, this much savage intensity.

He wasn't built for this kind of denial. Lupreda followed their primordial instincts without reservation when it came to coupling.

But she wasn't Lupreda.

For fifteen years, he'd watched over her, protected her since she was six years old, since she'd lost her father.

Yet over the past few years, as she'd moved into adulthood, his protective feelings for her had changed, felt more… personal. Landon had distanced himself from her, giving up his connection to her through the police. He hadn't worked a case for the NYPD in three years.

Tonight he saw just how much she'd grown up. Now twenty-four, she'd matured into a desirable woman, complete with curves and a sexy, kissable mouth. Her fine-boned stature should've dissuaded him, but instead her human fragility only attracted him more, despite his fear he could crush every bone in her body with the slightest touch.

All it would take was one moment of primal lust, one slip of unconditioned control and he could kill her.

He'd always kept his distance from Kaitlyn, but now…his closeness to her began to unravel the rigid lock he'd held over his senses whenever he was around her—the attraction that he'd refused to acknowledge in the past exploded within him in primal certainty, demanding he claim her, mark her…as his.

Clenching his hands into tight fists, he quickly stood to put some distance between them.

She gave him a triumphant smile and held up the claw clip. "I'm using the hinge to hold a chunk of the ashes."

Landon swallowed the lump in his throat. The woman had no idea she was staring raging need directly in the face. He should never have gotten so damned close to her.

"Tell me how you came up with such a fantastical description from a pile of ashes?" he asked before he thought better of it.

Kaitlyn almost said, "Dead people communicate with me," but she figured the intense man staring down at her with a skeptical expression on his handsome face wouldn't believe her, anyway. Even if it were true.

The deceased's energy signatures were especially brilliant, usually a bright violet if the people died violent deaths…as if they were calling out for help via a spiritual connection. The one she had seen tonight was neon-purple, different from all the ones she'd seen in the past.

She wasn't sure why she had initially told Landon what she saw. Maybe she was looking for affirmation of what she'd seen because the aura had been beyond bizarre, even for her. Or maybe it was because something about Landon just felt…trustworthy. But the fact remained her unusual ability definitely put her in the weird category. None of her coworkers knew. If they did, they'd have recommended her for a psych visit instead of a promotion to detective. The fewer people who knew, the better.

"I have an overactive imagination." A definite drop of rain hit her on the nose. Then another cold droplet followed, saving her from feeling the need to respond to his doubtful look. Cupping the claw clip carefully, Kaitlyn stood and held out her free hand. "Thanks for your help. I'll take my flashlight now."

Landon laid the flashlight in her open palm at the same time several more drops of rain hit her face.

When they started to walk away from the sight, he asked, "You going to call this in?"

Kaitlyn had totally forgotten that her police backup

should've been there by now. Casting her gaze back to the dark pile of ash, she froze. Without the flashlight shining against the ground, she saw several partial human handprints. In the darkness, they glowed in fluorescent iridescence on top of the flattened, singed grass surrounding the ashes. It wasn't an aura image. This was different.

"Do you see that?" she asked as she fully turned to stare.

Landon halted and stared at the ashes for several seconds. "All I see are ashes."

Kaitlyn's stomach knotted at his calm tone and the odd look he shot her way. The man must think she was a complete loon. She turned forward, and when the rain began to fall in a heavy downpour, she quickly tucked the clip in her coat pocket. In no time, her hair and clothes were completely soaked. Chills rushed throughout her body from the frigid, pounding drops.

She knew she'd be lucky if she made it to her car with any of the ashes still intact in her hair clip, and yet she had a feeling Landon was curious as to her answer to his question. He didn't strike her as the "idle conversation" type.

"As for calling this in…it'll be considered an illegal burning of an animal. We'll see if the lab can get anything from my clamp." When her teeth began to chatter, she picked up her pace.

Before she stepped into the light in the parking lot, Kaitlyn peered through the rain, scanning the field and the playground one last time. For what, she didn't know. Maybe a sense of closure? Something that would give her an answer to the questions running through her head? Had she imagined what she'd seen tonight?

She paused and her breath caught in her throat. The same fluorescent, sparkling glow she'd seen around the ashes radiated from one of the merry-go-round's metal bars. That hadn't been there when she'd investigated the equipment earlier.

Or had it?

An eerie shiver started in her shoulders and shimmied all the way down her back.

"Kaitlyn, are you all right?" Landon's deep voice made her jump.

Pulse racing, she glanced over his broad shouldered, six-foot-plus stature. He stood a good seven inches taller than her. While her gaze traced the water that ran off his thick eyebrows and strong jaw to the small cleft in his chin, her stomach did an entire gymnastics routine, including the floaty ribbon dance.

She was glad he hadn't moved close enough for her to get a whiff of his musky scent again. When he'd bent near her with the flashlight, she'd lost all sense of time. His alluring smell had surrounded her like a warm, cozy blanket, seducing her senses, muddling her thoughts.

Red and blue lights flashed behind Landon, causing her to blink back to reality. As the squad car pulled into the parking lot, she took a calming breath. "I'm fine. Better go tell the officer we're done here. Thanks for the backup."

"No problem." Landon turned and walked over to his truck. After he drove off, Kaitlyn approached the squad car.

Charlie Johnston rolled down his window a couple inches, squinting up at her. Cold rain bounced off his patrol car window, hitting his ruddy face. "Sorry, McKinney. Lady had a blowout right in front of me. I saw Rourke was here with you. Haven't seen him around the precinct in a while. Everything okay?"

She nodded. "It appeared to be an illegal burning of some kind of animal."

"You're not gonna bother with that, are you?"

She'd have Ryan look at the ashes for curiosity's sake. "No worries. I'll write it up." Rapping his window with her knuckles, she smiled. "Have a good night."

Charlie waited for her to get in her car and start the engine before he drove off. Kaitlyn shivered uncontrollably and cranked up the heat. She started to pick up her flashlight and set it back underneath the passenger seat when she felt deep ridges along the metal handle.

Frowning, she switched on her inside light to get a clear look at the barrel. Four deep impressions curved along one side while another dented the opposite side.

Kaitlyn's heart began to race all over again as she laid her hand on the metal and curled her fingers around the indentations on the barrel. Her fingers and thumb slid easily into the much bigger impressions on the thick metal casing.

The thought of Landon crushing the heavy-duty metal with his bare hand turned her on just as much as his intoxicating smell had. Something was going on under that calm persona he presented to the world…something deep and intense.

And incredibly intriguing.

Chapter 2

Two hours later, Landon entered his cabin located deep in the Shawangunk mountain ridge. Caine was laid out full-sprawl on his brown leather sofa. "Make yourself at home, why don't you?" Landon said as he tossed his keys on a side table.

"You said to meet you here." Caine grinned and spread his arms wide. "Never say I don't jump at your beck and call."

Landon snorted. "You listen when it suits you. That's your problem."

"Thank you, Doctor, for your astute assessment." Caine's sarcastic expression quickly shifted to anticipation. "What was so important you wanted to see me in person?"

He met Caine's steady gaze. "I got a phone call on my cell earlier this evening directing me to Morningside Park if I wanted to find some missing weres."

Caine scowled and sat up to grip his knees, his knuckles white. "Who called you?"

"I don't know. The trace from the call to my cell came from a pay phone across town." Clenching his fists, he continued, "I got to the park to find a pile of ashes. I definitely smelled Lupreda."

"Son of a bitch!" Caine hissed. "I should've been there. I might've picked up a scent."

Landon narrowed his eyes at the younger were's unintended insult. "I smelled nothing! My sense of smell may not be as acute or track at great distances like the other Lupreda, but this…this nothingness disturbs me."

Caine's brow furrowed. "How can there not be a scent trail at all?"

"Exactly." Landon sat back on the couch, his anger settling in his belly. "It goes from bad to worse. Kaitlyn was there, and she described in intricate detail the outline of what had been burned."

The color drained from Caine's face. "She didn't go nuts over what she described to you?"

Oddly, she hadn't. Which made Landon wonder why she *hadn't* freaked if she believed what she had described. At the time he'd been too busy trying to get her mind off what she saw in the ashes to worry about her reaction one way or the other. "She did try to collect evidence for analysis, but it started to rain hard, washing most of it away."

Caine blew out a breath of relief. "Lucky for us."

True, but a part of Landon, the "werewolf" residing within him, had been pleased that Kaitlyn hadn't gone all wiggy at what she "thought" she saw.

"With Kaitlyn's accurate description, she did tell me something I wouldn't have known otherwise. The remains were only of one Lupreda," Landon began when his phone buzzed on his hip. Pulling his cell from the clip, he eyed the caller

I.D. and mumbled, "Not what I need right now," then flipped open his phone. "Rourke."

"Finally my call goes through! You must be back in the mountains. I've been trying to get in touch with you for two days," Jachin said. "No more bullshit. I want answers. Now!"

Jachin's tone ignited Landon's anger. "What the hell are you talking about?"

"I found one of your weres…or what's left of him," Jachin grated out.

Landon sat up, gripping the phone tightly against his ear. "Where? I want to investigate the scene—"

"We disposed of the body."

Landon bristled, his shoulders knotting all over as tension heightened within him. "He's my pack member. I had a right—"

"He was left at my front door, half burned, but intact enough. He was in partially morphed mode. I want an explanation."

The ramifications of Jachin's comments spoke volumes. There was no question in Landon's mind now—the Lupreda weren't involved in the zerkers' disappearance. The werewolves had tried for the past twenty-five years to discover the location of the Sanguinas' home, but they had always been unsuccessful. If they had been able to find it, they would've gone to war a long time ago.

"If you want my cooperation, you'll start talking," Jachin cut through his thoughts in a harsh tone.

Landon felt Caine's avid stare. The younger were's keen hearing allowed him to pick up everything Jachin said. "We call them zerkers. When we convert from human to wolf form, this half-man, half-wolf mode is part of that conversion. We figured out we have the ability to stay in that form for stints of time. It became an addiction for some, like a drug. Several of the younger weres morphed every chance they got, especially during dominance battles."

"In other words, they thought they could fight vampires in that mode." Jachin spoke in a cold tone.

Neither confirming nor denying Jachin's statement, Landon continued. "The more they did it, the longer they could stay in that mode, but it came with a price. Their immature brains were eventually affected as well. In a few…it resulted in their inability to change back to human shape."

"You're saying they were permanently stuck in that half-morphed form?"

Landon exhaled to alleviate the weight pressing on his chest. "Yes. Knowing they could never shift back really messed with them mentally."

"That's why they lived away from the pack." Jachin mumbled.

"One of our weres' ashes was left in a park in the city tonight. You've found another one. One more zerker is still missing."

"We'll keep a watch out. It's obvious now that the Lupreda didn't do this nor did the Sanguinas."

Landon's insides jerked. "I assumed it had to be one of your rogue vampires taunting you. They're the only ones who know where your clan resides."

"I didn't sense any other vampires around, nor did I smell Lupreda, other than this one. What's odd is the fact I couldn't smell anything. It's as if a trail doesn't exist."

"It was the same in the park. No scent," Landon admitted even as he considered the strange glowing stuff Kaitlyn had tried to point out surrounding the edges of the ashes. He'd seen the substance, too, much to his unease. "Did you see anything around the were's remains? Footprints or anything?"

"No, nothing but his half-burned body. Rain washed any footprints away." Jachin paused and continued, "I think it's time you consider the prophecy. My father spoke to Ariel in a dream right after I took over as the new vampire leader. He told her the rest of the prophecy and said it wasn't just about the vampires like the Sanguinas had originally interpreted."

"Tell me." Landon prompted.

A human will speak of our demise.
Her purity and intelligence will help us survive.
A mate she becomes to the leader of Vampires.
Joining our races, fulfilling our ultimate desire.

The hunted becomes the hunter, no longer the prey.
An enemy in your midst is less dark and more gray.
Examine your failures and there you will find
the answer to all your questions in time.

A leader is needed, you know this is true.
Look not to one, but two.
A lesson was the goal you sought.
You too must learn from what you taught.

Layers of deception must be unveiled
for three to become one and peace to prevail.

Once Jachin finished relaying the entire prophecy, he said, "Think about the prophecy as a whole now that you know the rest. The words might shed some light on what's happening. Someone or something is trying to pit us against each other. Whatever it is, it was strong enough to ambush your zerkers. Watch your back."

"Are you out of your effin' mind," Caine shouted the second Landon closed his cell phone. "Our Musk form was our best 'surprise' defense against the Sanguinas if it ever came down to an all-out war, Landon."

Landon narrowed his gaze and growled. "Watch it."

When Caine took a couple of calming breaths, Landon said, "We can still shift to Musk mode, but right now there's something out there. It's just as strong, if not stronger than Lupreda and possibly stronger than the Sanguinas. One thing's for certain…it's very cunning."

"Why are you putting so much belief in a prophecy, especially one espoused by the very creatures who created us for hunting stock?" Caine asked with a snarl.

Landon understood Caine's cynicism. He'd felt the same way until he'd heard Jachin's ideals on peace.

Pinching the bridge of his nose briefly, Landon started from the beginning. "I'm sure you're probably wondering how I ended up having a tentative truce with a vampire in the first place."

"I figured you'd get around to telling me at some point," Caine snorted.

The one thing Landon had always appreciated about Caine was that the younger werewolf maintained his unwavering faith and loyalty.

"Jachin and I ran into each other one night at a bar. By the time we saw each other, we were both wasted." *We were each living in our own personal hells at the time,* Landon mentally added. "We went out back in the alley and almost killed each other. In the end we were so damned tired and worn out from our fight that we found ourselves propped up against the back wall of the pub, bleeding and talking. Jachin started rambling on about some prophecy he hoped to fulfill. The idea of peace between our races appealed to me, just as it did to Jachin. We forged a kind of truce that night.

"Jachin truly believes in this prophecy, and so far the beginning of it has come true with his human mate, Ariel."

Landon thought about the final lines of the prophecy and the last sentence struck a chord within him. *For three to become one and peace to prevail.* What did that mean? "I don't know if the 'three to become one' part is referring to the vampires, weres and humans all learning to get along or not. I seriously doubt the general human population would welcome vampires and werewolves with open arms. Hell, they've had a hard enough time getting their minds around the vampires' existence. Can you imagine if they learned about us?"

Caine nodded. "True enough. If you really believe this prophecy has something to do with us, maybe the number 'three' refers to something else…like what's going on with our zerkers. Is there another race out there stronger than the Lupreda or the Sanguinas? A race that doesn't leave a scent behind? Who or what would want to pit the Lupreda and the Sanguinas against each other?"

"Not the human government." Landon shook his head. "They had to have learned their lesson once their Scions project fell apart and left vampires terrorizing the city."

Landon's wolf pack had endured a lot from the vampires in the past, yet the Lupreda weren't lily-white, either. They had their own mistakes to bear. As far as Landon knew, there was only one other unique "race" beyond the vampires and weres. But…they hadn't survived. Had they? He pushed the thought to the back of his mind at the sheer implausibility and met Caine's curious gaze.

"Good theory about the zerkers' attackers being the 'third' mentioned in the prophecy. At least now you might understand how this prophecy could lead you down a path for answers. The prophecy allowed Jachin and me to find common ground, a place where we could talk without killing each other. Those few words, the power and promise they conveyed, were the only thing that kept Jachin going. He'd been kicked out of his clan for a few years when I met him. Can you imagine being a vampire and forced to live among humans, their poisoned blood constantly tempting you?"

"It's no more than a vampire deserves," Caine sneered.

"Peace takes cooperation, Caine," Landon reminded him.

Caine expelled a heavy sigh. "Fine. I'll bite. I know Jachin took over the Sanguinas with hopes of changing their future, but I had no idea true peace was his goal. How do you think the prophecy plays into all this?"

"I'm not sure yet." Landon stood up from the couch. "For now, don't report anything to the Omega. If pushed for answers, just tell them I'm working on it. We need to find the other zerker first."

"Understood." Caine followed Landon's lead and walked with him to his front door. He stared at the partially crushed silver bullet on the chain around Landon's neck. "What are you going to do about McKinney's daughter?"

Not what I want to do with her. "I'm going to pay her a visit."

Caine's eyebrows rose. "To find out if she's going to leave the zerker thing alone?"

"To see if she can help."

"Involving a human?" Caine smirked. "And you say *I* like to play with fire—"

"She won't know we exist," Landon said in a final tone.

When Landon opened his front door, Caine walked through the entrance, then turned to face him. "Sometimes I swear I still feel the vampires' damned silver collar around my throat." He tapped the silver chain around Landon's neck. "With something out there strong enough to bring down a zerker, you might want to take that off in case your Musk form is necessary."

When Landon didn't comment, concern and regret flickered in Caine's gaze. "Landon—"

"Good night." Landon shut the door, cutting off any more discussion.

As he headed upstairs to his bedroom, he fisted his hand around the bullet—a constant reminder of how important it was to control his savage urges.

Landon's pulse raced as he ran through the dark woods after Isabel. Free of clothes, her fair skin seemed to glow in the pale moonlight. She dodged around a tree, sexy laughter following in her wake.

"Come on, Landon. Show me your Musk form." Isabel cast a quick, teasing gaze over her shoulder. Her long blond hair trailed behind her as she faced forward once more, doubling her speed. She was one of the few female weres who drew his attention.

His chest tightened and his body shook with the need to shift. The chase always made him ready to take her while she screamed in sheer pleasure.

"I'll bet Caine's already in his Musk form for Margarete. Shift for me. It turns me on." Her provocative voice bounced through the air, enticing him, seducing him…stirring his primal needs to irresistible levels.

The seduction of the hunt, the cool fall wind blowing across his face…. He wanted to feel it against his entire body, to experience her soft skin under his hands, his chest, her curved rear pushing back against his hips.

His skin began to itch even as his breastbone started to

crack and pop. Landon's jaw and nostrils burned and ached while his facial structure morphed and stretched, and his legs shifted and bent midstride. He vaguely heard his clothes rip. Growling, he tugged the rest of the material off with his clawed fingers.

Wind brushed against him, lifting the light fur that coated his body, like a promising whisper of pleasure to come. His vision grew sharper, switching to a heat-seeking mode. He saw Isabel in colors, red heat radiating off her body as she jumped over a stump, like an agile gazelle. She dodged around a tree and stopped, throwing herself against it, breathing heavily. The wind blew harder, bringing with it the scent of rain. He felt the moisture in the air.

His jaws widened in a predatory grin. He closed the distance between them, the impending rain notching his excitement higher.

When he rounded the tree and slammed his claws into the trunk, blocking Isabel in, she gave a husky growl. Margarete's excited screams reached them from somewhere in the forest.

Isabel raised a blond eyebrow, amusement and desire glittering in her gaze. "Tell me you don't want—"

A loud boom echoed through the woods, jerking Landon's attention.

He let out a battle howl. Pulling his claws from the tree, he took off, dodging around trees as he headed toward the noise. The need to protect his pack members beat a thrumming pulse in his brain.

As he neared the edge of the woods, he saw a human. The man stood on the playground at the edge of the forest, holding a gun. More shots exploded from his weapon.

Landon's gaze followed the direction the bullets had taken. Caine stumbled into the forest's edge while Marga-

rete darted farther into the woods, calling Caine's name, her voice full of fear.

The rain started then, falling in heavy sheets. Landon returned his line of sight to their human attacker. He wore a determined look on his face as he raised his gun to fire again and mumbled, "I won't let you hurt her."

The Alpha need to protect his own rose up inside Landon, building in his chest like a bomb ticking toward detonation. He howled his anger and exploded from the woods, rushing toward the man.

The human turned to see Landon in full Musk bearing down on him. He got off one shot before Landon reached him.

The bullet connected and fire lanced through Landon's shoulder, making him see red. He roared and swiped his clawed hand at the man, sending his puny human body flying toward the playground equipment.

The human hit the monkey bars with a dull thud, then fell to the ground, slumping over.

Landon's whole body shook from the intense fire burning from his wound. Never had he felt such vicious, excruciating pain.

Gritting his teeth, he jammed his claws into his wound, digging at the muscle and sinew. Blood coated his claws as he sought the offending bullet that felt as if it was searing him in two.

With a pained groan, he ripped the bullet from his shoulder and snarled his fury at the unconscious human before he rushed to Caine's side.

Fear gripped Landon's gut when he saw Caine lying on his back, writhing and shaking all over. When the young were began to convulse, his eyes rolling back in his head, Landon scanned his injuries. Blood poured from three wounds, one *on Caine's thigh, another on his chest and the third near his stomach. Landon moved quickly, ripping muscle and tissue first on Caine's shoulder to remove the bullet. Then he moved to the were's left thigh to dig out the next bullet.*

Caine moaned as Landon attacked the gaping hole in his abdomen, searching for the last remaining bullet. The rain didn't make his job any easier.

Once he'd removed all three bullets, tension eased from Landon's shoulders and back. He let out a sigh of relief to see the young were's features settle before he passed out.

Caine would survive.

At Landon's mental call, Margarete and Isabel rushed forward and he instructed them to take Caine back with them to Lupreda land.

Once his pack members were gone, Landon shifted back to human form and sloshed through the wet woods, collecting their clothes and the bullets he'd pulled from Caine's body. He knew their blood couldn't be deciphered since it broke down in sunlight exposure, but the bullets might carry bits of their skin or muscle. He wasn't certain what, if anything, lab experts might glean from a Lupreda tissue sample. Better not to leave it behind. Steam rose off his body as he made his way over to the unconscious man.

When he didn't hear a heartbeat or sense a pulse, Landon's chest constricted with regret. He squatted next to the human, noting his own bloody claw marks across the man's thick barrel chest. Rain had washed away some of the blood. He knew his Musk mode made it harder to control his savage urges, but the wound he'd inflicted didn't look deep enough to have killed the human.

That's when he saw the pool of blood soaking the pebbles underneath the man's head. His gaze traveled up the play equipment to see a bloody smear along one of the metal poles.

Nausea roiled in Landon's belly. Guilt crept through his chest like a black vine quickly veining through his lungs, choking his breath.

He hadn't intended to kill the man, but he was responsible for his death, nonetheless. After he'd collected the bullet he'd pulled from his own body, he glanced over the man's clothes—his jeans, button-down shirt and windbreaker— looking for anything that would give him the human's name.

His gaze settled on a brown wallet a few feet away from the body.

Nudging the wallet open with the side of his foot, Landon's heart jerked and he softly murmured, "Son of a bitch."

On one side of the wallet, a silver shield flashed accusingly at him. The other side identified the man. He'd killed a police officer named James McKinney.

"Landon?"

His heart skipped several beats at the sound of Kaitlyn's voice.

She approached from the parking lot, carrying an umbrella to shield her from the rain, an "all business" detective's look on her heart-shaped face. "I just got a call from dispatch. What do we have?"

Landon jerked awake to a sitting position, his lungs burning with each breath he took. Sweat rolled down his naked chest and his hands were fisted at his sides.

He kicked the tangled, soaked sheets off his legs and put his feet on the floor. Settling his elbows on his knees, he jammed the heels of his hands against his eyes and took deep, steadying breaths.

After a few seconds, the gentle sway of his necklace drew his attention. The night after he'd accidentally killed Kaitlyn's father, he'd attached the bullet he'd pulled from his body to a silver chain and placed the chain around his neck.

Landon stared at the chain, hating how it made him feel—trapped. Once the vampires had started dying from the sickness and they'd gone into hiding, he'd vowed he would never allow silver to be placed on his body again. He squeezed his eyes shut, his chest burning over his guilt—he'd never expected he'd kill a human with his Musk strength. The irony that he was the one who clasped the silver chain around his neck in a form of punishment didn't escape him.

Crossing paths with the police officer that fateful night eighteen years ago had passed on some invaluable information Landon wouldn't have known otherwise. The bullets McKinney had used were specially made—mostly silver with enough metal to allow the bullet to withstand being shot out of a gun.

Landon learned silver didn't just prevent werewolves from shifting during a full moon. Apparently, the Lupreda had developed a deadly allergy to amalgams with high silver content. Once the silver entered his body and mixed with his blood, it began to poison him with fiery intent. He had no doubt that if he'd left the silver in their bodies, both he and Caine would've died.

But one man did die that night. Because of Landon's primal instincts to protect his own, Kaitlyn's father had paid with his life.

Thoughts of Kaitlyn invaded his mind, making his gut clench with remorse while his groin swelled in arousal. The constant conflicting emotions that had warred within him for years had increased tenfold the moment he'd crouched down next to her in the park earlier that night.

Her sweet floral scent still clung to him while her inviting face, her perky nose, rosy cheeks and soft pink lips slammed through his mind.

Taunting him, torturing him.

She was the one woman he could never have, never touch.

For many reasons.

Chapter 3

Kaitlyn sat in her car a block down the road from the Tacomi office building and warehouse.

She'd spent all morning digging up everything she could find on Tacomi. The company was the pulsar gun manufacturer whose shipment of pulsar guns had been hijacked. After much cross-referencing, Kaitlyn was able to link several indirect connections between Tacomi and the Mafia. In other words, no illegal money filtered through this business, no loans, nothing, but the ties were there—through a few employees who were close blood relatives to well-known Mafia members. She could dimsiss one Tacomi employee having ties to the Mafia as being random happenstance…but four? She didn't believe in that many coincidences.

Then she ran across a name on the Tacomi board that surprised her, Kenneth Duvoe. Kenneth was Remy's father, who she knew was a member of the old Garotter regime. And now

Remy was part of the newly formed Garotters. Yet another connection in the triangle that tied the Mafia to the gun manufacturer and the manufacturer to the Garotters.

She wanted to get a closer look at the building, especially the warehouse, but security was tight with a fifteen-foot tall chain-link gate around the perimeter of the company's two acres of land. Her stomach growled, reminding her she hadn't eaten anything today. She'd spent her lunch hour trying a direct approach—to get a tour of the Tacomi facility by telling the man at the front desk she was writing a paper for her NYPD night class on the new pulsar weapon.

"Although I know how to use one, I wanted to delve into the manufacturing process," she'd said, giving the young, blond-haired guard behind the desk her sincerest smile.

"Only authorized employees allowed," the guard told her after he'd walked away to call management to see if they would give an NYPD officer a tour.

The sunshine warmed her car as Kaitlyn eyed the other buildings adjacent to Tacomi's property. She nibbled her fingernail and considered various ways she might get inside.

A tapping sound on her passenger window made her heart jerk. She glanced at the person standing outside her car, ready to tell him she didn't have a dollar to spare.

Landon peered in her window. Tapping again, he gave her a stern look and gestured for her to unlock the car so he could enter.

Kaitlyn hit the unlock button.

Landon quickly opened the door and slid into the passenger seat. He brought with him the cool fall air, the smell of soft leather and his own earthy masculine aroma. The appealing scents seemed to perfectly complement each other, devastating her senses.

"I'm trying to be inconspicuous here," she said as he pulled the door closed. Even though his amazing smell made her stomach do several somersaults and his arresting green eyes caused her heart to trip in her chest, she stared at him with a suspicious gaze. "What are you doing here? And I'm not buying that you were just in the neighborhood."

"I tracked you here," he said simply.

She glanced in her rearview mirror to the street behind her car. "Last I looked I didn't leave a trail of bread crumbs for you to follow."

He chuckled, his teeth a splash of white against his tanned skin. "I used the GPS tracking built into every NYPD-issue vehicle."

Kaitlyn shook her head. "Great, big brother truly is watching. Why are you looking for me?"

"I want to talk to you about what you saw last night."

"What? Last night I was off my rocker and today I'm probably back on my meds, is that it?"

His lips quirked upward. "I had no idea you were so sassy." Sobering, he continued, "It's important, Kaitlyn."

She blew out a breath and stared at the Tacomi building. When her line of sight landed on a tall red oak tree that butted against the fence, its limbs thick and wide, she followed the tree to the old warehouse currently being used as a haunted house.

She met Landon's steady gaze. "I'll tell you if you'll do me a favor."

"Name it."

She smiled. "I want you to go out with me tonight."

Landon felt like she'd slammed a two-by-four against his chest. He coughed to ease the pained sensation cinching his lungs. "You uh, want me to take you out?"

She nodded and her pink tongue darted out, swiping across

her bottom lip. It took every bit of control he had not to lean over and kiss her, to lay her down in the seat right there in broad daylight. In the close confines of the car, the afternoon sun highlighted her gorgeous hair. The warmth heated her fair, peach-toned skin, making her seductive floral scent float all around him, seeping into his pores. He was acutely aware of every swallow she took, every breath, every thump of her heart. The closeness wreaked havoc with the primordial werewolf inside him.

She pointed to the warehouse adjacent to the Tacomi building. "That's my way onto Tacomi property. I'm going to buy a ticket into the haunted house, slip out the back of the warehouse and use the tree to get over the fence."

When she finished speaking, she turned to him and waited for his answer. Fringed with long, auburn lashes, her hazel-blue gaze made him want to stare at her all day, to get lost in their mosaic color. No murkiness or darkness hid in their depths, just honest sincerity.

Eyeing the Tacomi building and the tall fence all the way around it, he set his jaw. "Why do you want to check out this building?"

She followed his line of sight. "Just following a hunch."

He cupped her chin, turning her face to his. "Kaitlyn, I want to know why."

Her gaze dropped to his hand touching her chin and he heard her intake of breath. Landon quickly released her, but not before he registered how soft her skin felt underneath his fingers.

"I'm investigating a connection between the Garotters and the Mafia." She swept her hand toward the Tacomi building. "All of this is in relation to illegal pulsar gunrunning."

Every muscle in Landon's body tensed in fear for her. If there was a connection and they found out she was sniffing around, the new Garotter regime and the Mafia wouldn't hesitate to eliminate a threat to their livelihood. He narrowed his gaze. He wanted to protect her, to tell her to go home where she'd be safe, but Kaitlyn was a police officer…a detective. The need to serve for the betterment of the community was in her blood. "I highly doubt your boss would approve of you being here or in there alone."

She stiffened, her lips thinning in a stubborn line as she leaned against her window. "I'm fine. I'm just researching."

"But you plan on going in there without backup. It might be a wild goose chase—then again it might not be."

She sat up straighter and crossed her arms, her action pulling her blue blouse tight against her pert breasts. "But I'm not checking out the place alone. You'll be with me."

Her trust surprised the hell out of him. "Is that so?"

A perplexed look crossed her face. "I don't know why, but something about you makes me want to trust you." She grinned. "Plus, you didn't tell my boss I needed a psych evaluation after last night's adventure in the park. That gives you extra points."

Landon snorted even as he recognized the obstinate look in her eyes for what it was. She would go through with her plans whether he helped her or not. Tenacious, stubborn woman.

He let out a heavy sigh and nodded, knowing that—for many reasons—he'd end up regretting his agreement to help.

The brilliant smile she cast his way slammed him hard, pummeling the air from his lungs. That little leprechaun on the Lucky Charms cereal box had nothing on Kaitlyn McKinney's charm skills.

She cast a quick glance at the haunted house a block down the road. "I'll meet you outside 'Scream Central' at seven."

He resisted the urge to grunt his disgust at the idea of

traipsing through screen sets of all the made-up "bullshit" horror humans concocted to scare the piss out of each other. At least the place would be dark so she wouldn't see him rolling his eyes as they walked through it.

He gave her a curt nod, then addressed what he'd come to talk to her about. "About last night—"

"Ah, yes, my delusional moments." Her lips lifted in amusement.

He smirked. "What did you see as we walked away? You never did say."

Pushing her hair over her shoulder, she turned to face him, her expression all business. "I saw a phosphorous iridescent glow in the shape of handprints on the flattened grass surrounding the ashes." She paused and her brow furrowed as if she were puzzling through the scene in her mind. "It was like whoever left the images behind had squatted beside his captive and had touched the ground a few times." Then her eyes opened wider. "Or maybe there was more than one person at the site."

What she described was much more detailed than what he'd seen. He knew his werewolf vision and ability to feel vibrations beyond other weres was enhanced due to his muted olfactory senses, but he'd just seen iridescent sparkles, not a specific pattern. Maybe whatever special ability she possessed that allowed her to accurately describe the zerker in the ashes also gave her the ability to "see" the entire handprint signatures left behind.

"Thanks for describing it to me," he said.

"Did you see it, too?" Her eyes were bright with a hopeful look.

He might not want her to know about his were abilities, but for some reason he didn't want her believing she was crazy. He shook his head. "No, but I was curious if there was something we could follow up on using special lighting or something."

She blew out a frustrated breath and rested her wrist on the steering wheel. "The rain came down even harder as we were leaving. I'm pretty sure there's nothing left to check out."

He nodded in agreement. Silence descended between them, leaving him with little to focus on other than Kaitlyn. His fingers itched to cup the back of her neck and pull her close. His nose burned with the need to glide along the column of her throat and experience her scent up close and personal. His body craved hers…like—he suddenly realized with startling clarity—like he craved the hunt. The excitement of hunting his prey, stalking it, taking the animal down…the exhilaration and adrenaline that rushed through him during a hunt felt startlingly similar to the way he felt right now.

Yet with the hunt, he felt no physical connection to his prey. With Kaitlyn, he felt intimately connected, and an entirely different kind of hunger raged within him where she was concerned. She wasn't prey, but she was deeply, powerfully…coveted.

He closed his eyes and laid his head back against the headrest, trying to calm the primal instincts claiming his thoughts. The irrepressible sensations rode down his spine, tightening his groin in unfulfilled, arousing knots.

"Are you okay?" Kaitlyn asked.

He jerked away from the feather-light touch of her fingers across his brow and narrowed his gaze so she wouldn't see his eyes had changed color with his arousal. Many Lupreda females had told him that the unusual green shade was enticing, mesmerizing and entirely irresistible.

"I have all my rabies shots. Honest." The melodious pitch of her laughter rolled over him in teasing, seductive waves.

"I just have a headache," he grunted as he gripped the door handle and opened the car door.

Once he got out of the car and was about to close the door, she leaned across the passenger seat and called out, "Seven o'clock sharp, Rourke. Got it?"

"Don't go sniffing around on your own. *You* got it?" he responded in a stern tone.

Giving a mock salute, she cast him a half smile and sat back against her seat. "I'll wait for my escort."

"*Dictionary of Wolves, The Lupine Encyclopedia, Supernatural Phenomenon.*" Abby ran her fingers across the spines of the books on the built-in bookshelves behind Kaitlyn. "Interesting collection. I can't believe I've never been in your dad's office before now," she mused before she put her hand on the high-back leather chair Kaitlyn sat in.

Kaitlyn tapped on the keyboard. "You're the one who insisted on coming over to learn more about my trip to a haunted house."

"That's what best friends do, silly. We're nosy like that," Abby said with a snort. "Plus, I had a couple hours to kill before my next lesson starts."

Kaitlyn glanced up from the laptop to the multitude of books lining the bookshelves and shrugged. "As far as the books go, for as long as I can remember my dad had a thing for wolves. He was a research nut. I guess he just glommed onto the subject matter and really got into it."

Abby raised her dark eyebrows, accentuating her vivid green eyes. "I'm surprised your mom didn't pack his stuff away years ago. I mean, it's not like either your mom or you took up the interest, right?"

Her friend's mention of her mom made Kaitlyn's heart ache. Even though she was following her mom's wishes not to be disturbed on her down days, she felt as if she was being shut out of her mother's life. She hoped tomorrow was a better day and she could go to the hospital for a long visit.

"Some of my dad's stuff is packed away, but Mom doesn't want his office touched. Dad was very particular about his 'space.' Everything in its place and all that." Kaitlyn glanced past the laptop to her father's Spartan oak desktop underneath. The polished surface sported a banker-style lamp, a beer mug doubling as a pencil-and-pen holder and a glass "howling wolf" paperweight. She'd played with the wolf figurine on the carpet beneath his desk countless times while he did research for work. Pulling on the long, delicate silver chain around her neck, she touched the tiny silver wolf charm and smiled. Her father had given her the charm on her sixth birthday, saying, "He'll keep a watch over you when I'm not around." She'd never gone a day without wearing the charm since the day her father had died.

Returning her attention to the computer screen, she tucked her necklace back into her shirt. The charm fell into place, nestled between her breasts, as she typed, "Landon Rourke" into the database and clicked on the search button.

Abby moved to stand beside her. "Don't you think it's a little odd to do a background check on your man *after* you've made a date with him?"

A date? As the search icon spun on the screen, Kaitlyn shook off the depressing realization that it had been twenty-four months since she'd been on a date, let alone had sex. She gave Abby a pointed look and replied with annoyed sarcasm, "Don't you have a class to teach or a six-foot-five Conan to subdue or something?"

Abby's lips spread wide in a Cheshire grin. "You really should've come last night. Willie and I hit it off right away. He's taking me out to that new cool restaurant in town tonight."

"Willie?" Kaitlyn laughed out loud. "You just mentioned the hulking guy you'd met, not his name before. It's a good thing he's a big man. I'm sure that name has gained him his share of ribbing over the years."

"He's definitely large all-the-way around, my dear. Now back to your man. Tell me about—"

At that moment, a photo of Landon, in all his sexy glory, popped up, rendering Abby speechless for all of two seconds. "Holy mother of—*that* man inspires deep green envy. Haunted house, eh? Now I get it. It's a great excuse to get up close and personal."

Rolling her eyes, Kaitlyn scrolled past Landon's picture and stats. "This is business, Abby. I hate haunted houses with a passion and the damned place is my only way to get to Tacomi's warehouse."

Abby crossed her arms over her big breasts, which were precariously held back by a V-neck Lycra workout top. She gave Kaitlyn a knowing nod. "Uh-huh, and that's why you're checking up on Mr. Too Hot for Words, because you want to make sure he's not some psycho, right?"

Kaitlyn tabbed down the screen. "Honestly, that's pretty much the truth. If this man is going to back me up tonight, I do want to know a bit more about him." *Even if his appealing smell leaves me feeling slightly dizzy and out-of-sorts whenever he stands near me.*

Leaning close, Abby examined the screen. "Do you think that database lists how many women he's left satiated and panting? I imagine it's a long list."

A small spasm twisted deep in Kaitlyn's gut at her friend's

flippant comment—it felt strangely painful and unsettling. She frowned at Abby. "This database is a list of his work history with the police, projects he has worked on with the officers, etc."

Abby hit the down button until the information stopped. "It looks like he has helped out the NYPD for fifteen years, but hasn't been active these past three years." She glanced at Kaitlyn. "Wonder what happened?

Kaitlyn shrugged. "I don't know. The database still has him listed as a credible resource."

"How old is he?" Abby scrutinized Landon's face. "He looks like he's in his early thirties."

Kaitlyn scrolled back up and read Landon's stats. "It says here that he's forty."

Abby scowled. "It sucks how well men age compared to women."

After Kaitlyn skimmed over the cases Landon had worked in conjunction with the police force, she felt confident the P.I. could handle just about anything that might come their way.

As Kaitlyn closed the database and clicked through the shutdown sequence on her laptop, Abby said, "Once your clandestine jaunt with Mr. Wonderlicious is over, I think you should put the man through his paces for the rest of the evening." Ignoring Kaitlyn's frown, she continued, "You *know* you wanna take him for a test-drive and see just how well his pipe's ring."

"Give it a rest, Ab." As much as the idea of getting up close and personal with Landon Rourke made Kaitlyn's stomach tumble in excitement, she needed to stay focused on her case. Other than that eerily strange connection thing they'd seemed to briefly experience in the park, the sexy P.I hadn't shown the least bit of interest.

Intensity, maybe, but not interest.

* * *

At seven o'clock Kaitlyn drove from her house in the suburbs to the haunted mansion. As she pulled into the gravel parking lot, she was amazed at how full the lot was. Once she turned off her car, she could hear the muffled screams of the people inside the warehouse filter through her window.

Lovely.

After checking the safety on her gun, she slipped it back into the holster secured at her waist and snapped the holster closed. Buttoning her fitted black blazer over her turquoise fine-gauge sweater, she climbed out of her warm car, locked the doors, and then headed across the gravel lot.

Her steps slowed when she saw a long line of people snaking through the zigzag cordoned-off area near the haunted house's entrance.

Landon stood near the crowd, waiting for her. As Kaitlyn stepped next to him, he fell into line behind the last person.

He glanced at her thin blazer. His eyebrow rose and his breath frosted in front of him. "Where's your coat?"

Kaitlyn shivered and tugged her jacket's skimpy lapels up around her neck. She stared at Landon's buttery leather jacket with envy. "I didn't expect the line to be this long. My overcoat is wool. I figured I'd get hot once we were inside. I, um…have a tendency to get light-headed if I become over-heated too quickly."

His steady gaze slipped over her body in a slow, blatant perusal. "Good to know."

She laughed and rubbed her hands together to keep warm. "What about you? Got any quirks I should be aware of before we face the monsters?"

"Just my intensity." His tone seemed to go beyond his simple statement.

Snickering, she wrinkled her nose. "You're so-o-o-o blasé, Mr. Cool." She gestured toward the haunted house. "Don't tell me this doesn't get your blood pumping."

Landon shoved his hands in his jeans' front pockets and gave her a sinfully dark smile. "I'm far scarier than they'll ever be."

The way he looked at her, as if he wanted to jump her bones and feast on her body, caused a flash of electric heat to shoot straight to her belly, temporarily warming her from the inside out.

But as quickly as it appeared, the look of ravenous desire in his gaze faded, making her wonder if she'd imagined it. A sharp, cool breeze whipped through the crowd, evaporating the warmth that had begun to flicker within her. She shivered, and chill bumps formed on her skin. The crowd moved up several steps, and Kaitlyn followed the group, stomping her booted feet to warm them. Damn, she was cold. She glanced at Landon, who appeared to be unaffected by the frigid air. *Bet he's all toasty warm in that jacket.*

Landon fought his attraction to Kaitlyn with every fiber in his being. Her flushed cheeks and ready smile made him ache to touch her, to experience her soft skin under his fingers…her naked body pressed against his, under him.

A mental roar of sexual frustration echoed in his head. He set his jaw and jammed his clenched fists deeper into his front pockets to keep from running his fingers across her chilled cheeks.

As if his own torture wasn't enough, Kaitlyn suddenly stepped in front of him, pulled open his jacket and backed her luscious rear against his groin, surprising the hell out of him. When she tried her best to tug his jacket closed around her body, yanking him against her, he tensed and tried not to breathe. Her musky, violet scent floated around him, stirring just outside his nose…waiting for him to inhale.

She had no idea how close she was to being abducted.

"What are you doing?" he spoke in a calm tone, ignoring the beast growling inside him, demanding he grip her waist and bury his nose against her neck; insisting he clamp his teeth in that soft spot between her throat and her shoulder, marking her as his.

"I'm freezing my ass off," she shot back, glancing up at him with unapologetic eyes. Turning forward once more, she wiggled her sweet ass against him, destroying his ability to suppress his primal urges.

Consciously aware he could break her bones with his crushing strength, Landon used the lightest touch he could and gripped her hips, ceasing the excruciating torture. Resisting every savage urge that pounded through his veins, making his stomach knot and his erection swell to marble-hard proportions, he growled, "Hold still."

Kaitlyn froze and then said in a low tone, "That'd better be your gun."

"Why yes, I always pack my gun where it'll blow my balls off."

"Smart-ass." Amusement laced her tone and he heard her heartbeat trip, then ramp up several notches.

A feral smile tilted his lips as he leaned close to her ear. "That's the real deal, sweetheart. Since I can't take my jacket off to let you wear it without revealing my gun, I suggest you make like a statue if you want to stay warm."

"You mean stiff and hard like you."

He let out a strained chuckle.

They were almost to the ticket booth. The shrieks and

screams and eerie howls and growls from inside the warehouse grew louder as a new group of people walked through the front door. Kaitlyn leaned back and then whispered in his ear, "I have a confession to make. I *really* don't like haunted houses." She shivered. "I don't watch horror movies or anything else to purposefully scare me. My job is fraught with enough danger without adding fantastical scenarios to the mix."

"Says the woman who described fantastical stuff in the park as easily as reading a shopping list," he teased at the same time his gut wrenched at the confession she'd made. What the hell would she think if she ever saw him in Musk mode or in his wolf form engaged in full battle with a Sanguinas? She would never understand what he was. And he never planned for her to find out.

He grunted from the strength behind the elbow she jammed into his ribs.

"Very funny. Just stay close," she murmured, stepping away from him once the vendor with long, greasy black hair beckoned them to the ticket booth.

While Landon slid his credit card through the reader to pay for their entrance fee, the salesman grabbed Kaitlyn's wrist then slid his long, bony fingers across her skin as he stamped her hand with a fluorescent stamp.

Without a second thought, Landon pulled Kaitlyn's hand out of the man's groping grasp. He set his own clenched fist, fingers down on the wooden counter with a heavy thump and glared at the man.

The ticket man sneered and stamped Landon's hand with more force than necessary. Landon curled his lip in a snarl, then followed Kaitlyn up the wooden stairs.

As they stood under the rickety roof decorated with blood

and hanging bones and waited for their turn to enter the haunted house, Kaitlyn jerked her head back toward the ticket guy. "What was that all about?"

I didn't want his dirty paws on you. "I'd waited in line long enough."

She smirked. "It's good to see you're excited to get in there. Just don't forget to help me look for an exit that'll lead us to the back of this warehouse. And stay close."

The doors opened and Kaitlyn stepped into the pitch-dark hall that flashed every few seconds with a white strobe light high above the narrow plywood maze coated with splattered fake blood. Landon barely heard her last comment over the deafening roar rushing toward them.

As tough as she had to be for her job—she really wasn't kidding about her dislike of this "monster" stuff, he realized. A rush of protectiveness sent his libido to the backseat. He took one stride forward and stepped flush against her backside, placing a comforting hand on her shoulder.

Kaitlyn's small hand grabbed his and squeezed. The tension eased from her shoulders underneath his fingers, sparking a deep, abiding possessive streak that built inside his chest with each step they took.

Landon's werewolf eyes quickly adjusted to the darkness as they followed the narrow hall-like maze. Ahead of them he saw holes in the plywood where haunted house workers were reaching through and grabbing the unsuspecting patrons around the waist…eliciting screams of terror mixed with hysterical laughter.

As soon as Kaitlyn neared the grope fest, he couldn't help himself. He wrapped his arm around her waist and hauled her against his chest at the same time he grabbed the people's hands coming through the wall, halting their fun. He had to be careful not to accidentally snap the workers' wrists while he and Kaitlyn walked past.

Kaitlyn's breathing came in short little pants, and her hand laced with his around her waist. Primal satisfaction rumbled in his chest, and he found himself rubbing his nose against her silky hair right before he set her feet on the floor and propelled their locked bodies forward.

When they started to turn a corner in the maze, a sad-looking woman dressed in antique lace hovered next to the wall, reaching out to them with transparent fingers. The "ghost's" cries made Kaitlyn's hand cinch tighter around his. He chuckled and brushed his lips against the back of her head while directing her down the next section in the haunted house maze.

Every once in a while they would pass special rooms to their left and right. The first open room they came to was an insane asylum scenario with torture equipment and "patients" screaming out during an electric shock session. The second was an eerie cellar with jars of body parts in a clear liquid on a wooden shelf. Meat hooks hung on the far wall and a crazed "killer" with stringy hair and a scarred face yelled as he swung a bloodied ax toward the crowd. They all jumped back at the same time his ax hit a Plexiglas wall between them.

Kaitlyn's pulse raced and he could smell her fear rising above the others around them. Even though he knew this was all pretend and her fear was superficial, not life-threatening, his wolf's protective instincts still reared up within him.

He had to stop himself from literally lifting Kaitlyn in his arms and carrying her the rest of the way through the damned freak show.

They shuffled along with the rest of the patrons down another hall. This time the wooded park scene before them made his throat close—and his heart pound. Wolf howls echoed from the speakers on the floor and a huge gray anima-tronics wolf pushed his head and the front part of his body through thick shrubbery in the left corner. His eyes glowed a bloodred color, while his bared teeth and sharp canines dripped bloody drool.

When Kaitlyn didn't flinch or tense at the scene before them, Landon's chest swelled with pride. Just as he was letting out a sigh of relief, a different howl ripped through the loud haunted house, its pitch so feral and piercing, he winced.

Another creature stepped out from behind a thick tree in the park, baring down on the unsuspecting female actress who'd screamed in fear as she'd passed the wolf emerging from the bushes. She'd run deeper into the forest to get away from the animal. The humanlike werewolf's body was covered with a coating of light fur, and he stood well over six-and-a-half-feet tall with black evil eyes, pointy ears and a wolf's snout.

He displayed a whole set of razor-sharp teeth as he stalked the female, walking on his toes. His alien-looking elongated fingers sprouted deadly claws and he emitted vicious, blood-thirsty growls. Out of everything Landon had seen that night, this actor's mannerisms, costume and makeup were by far the most convincing.

Kaitlyn began to shake in his arms. "Too hot," she said, right before her legs collapsed and her body went limp.

Landon's concern for Kaitlyn spiked. He gripped her waist and lifted her off the floor and against his chest, while he scanned for an exit sign. Shouldering his way through the crowd, he burst through the exit door at the end of the blackened hall.

Cool night air rushed toward them, freezing his lungs. He quickly swept Kaitlyn's unconscious body into his arms. Carrying her to a wooden bench to the right of the exit, he sat down and cradled her against his chest. Regret and worry bunched his shoulder muscles. He'd never felt so out of control, so fiercely protective for another in his life.

The sensations slammed into him in unrelenting waves, battering his defenses. He slid his trembling fingers up her waist to her rib cage, careful to touch her gently. Kaitlyn's strong heartbeat thumped under his palm as he stared at her slack features. The entire experience in the haunted house and the protective streak hammering in his head made him realize just how much he'd come to value this human.

Somewhere along the way, he'd connected with her, not just from a protector's viewpoint, but from a werewolf's pack member perspective. He thought of her as one of his own…one he also wanted with a deep abiding desire that knocked him in the gut. Running his nose along her temple, he drank in her unique smell of violet and musk.

And ached.

It was painful, wanting a woman he couldn't have, but he didn't trust himself not to hurt her if things between them heated up. Whenever she was near, he had a hard time keeping his wolf side at bay. The beast was always there, just under his skin, growling for him to take action. Adding sex to the mix would only heighten his primal senses, making it very easy to forget just how breakable she was.

But she would have his loyalty. There was nothing quite like a wolf's dedication to his pack mates. Landon knew he'd defend her with every last breath in his body. Just as any Alpha would.

"You smell good, too." Kaitlyn's warm hand cupped his jaw and her languid voice sent a jolt of heat rushing through him.

Landon's insides rocked at the pleasing feel of her soft

touch on his skin. His groin instantly tightened, his body craving more. Fighting his instinctive response, he quickly set her down on the bench and stood. "Glad to see you're back to the land of the conscious."

Chapter 4

The condescending undertone in his curt comment made Kaitlyn feel like the world's biggest wimp. She sat up straighter and gripped the rough edge of the bench, thankful for the brisk night air to clear her head. Waking up cradled in Landon's strong arms, his hand resting on her ribs mere inches from her breast while he inhaled and groaned, caused her heart rate to hitch and her body to react in unprecedented, painful throbs.

God, the sexy man did it for her, hitting every single nerve ending. Something about his masculine scent, heavy with musky notes, rattled her brain whenever he was close.

She met his cold stare and tried to reason through his obvious need to keep his distance from her. Business. He wanted to keep their relationship purely professional.

Fine.

She gave a half laugh, hoping he couldn't see the color she

knew had to be spreading across her cheeks. "I guess the body heat finally got to me." In truth, the werewolf actor was so close to the outlined body she'd seen in the ashes, filling in the blanks with a visual 3-D representation, she seriously began to question her sanity. Werewolves didn't exist.

Glancing behind her at the dark Tacomi building and warehouse, she mentally shrugged off her musings about fantastical werewolf imaginings and sexy P.I.s and turned back to Landon with a forced smile. "Great job finding the back exit. We're where we need to be."

"I think we should bag this idea. You're not up to it."

Resentment blossomed in her chest. How dare he assume she couldn't go through with their plans. She jumped up and pulled open the two buttons on her jacket with quick jerks so she could get to her gun if she needed it. "Let's go," she said in a clipped tone before she climbed through the split-rail fencing that curved around from the back to the front side of the warehouse.

She didn't look back as she ran toward the huge full-limbed red oak tree that sat up against Tacomi's high fence. Once she reached her destination, she stood staring up at the tree's massive trunk.

"I see how you plan to get over, but how do you plan to get back out?" Landon spoke next to her.

Damn, how had he followed without my hearing his foot-falls? She batted her lashes and gripped his bicep through his leather jacket. "Don't you know that's why you're here, you manly man, you? So you can give me a boost up with your Herculean muscles."

His eyebrow elevated. "And how am *I* supposed to get back over?"

She eyed the low limbs on the other side of the fence. "You're taller. You can jump up and reach that lowest limb."

"Do I look like I have springs in my legs?"

She let out a huff of impatience. "If you can't reach it by jumping, then you can climb the fence to get to the limb." Before he could respond, she released him and stood on her toes to grab hold of a low-hanging limb. Her muscles strained, but she managed to hitch herself up to a sitting position on the thick branch.

"You're certifiable," he muttered as she gazed down at him.

Kaitlyn flashed an appreciative smile. "Just very determined. Come on," she said before she grabbed another branch above her, climbing higher.

A few minutes later, her heart raced as she inched across a thick limb that grew horizontal to the ground and crossed the fence's edge, encroaching onto Tacomi property. Her palms burned slightly from the rough bark as she lay on her belly, then swung her legs down and gripped the limb on either side of her body. Landon waited on another limb and snapped his disapproval. "Insane woman."

She ignored his comment and ever-so-slowly lowered her body until her feet hung toward the Tacomi property at least seven feet below her.

Taking a deep breath, she let go and prayed the shock to her legs didn't sprain anything.

When her feet hit, a sharp pain radiated from her right ankle, making her gasp, but she was more surprised by the fact that Landon landed next to her two seconds later. She shook off the pain and scowled at him. "How'd you do that so fast?"

He lifted his right arm and curled his fist in a body-builder pose, his white teeth gleaming in the dim light. "My manly muscles."

She rolled her eyes, then started toward the Tacomi warehouse with a quick, crouched down stride. As she made her way across the thick prairie grass, she gritted her teeth from the dull pain throbbing in her right ankle.

"Spoilsport," he called in a low voice as he shot past her. Even though he was in the same hunched pose, the man moved with a stealthy grace she couldn't help but admire.

A couple minutes later, her lungs working hard from her dash across the field, Kaitlyn leaned up against the side of the warehouse next to Landon and whispered, "Now to get inside."

"With a fence like this you know they'll have a security system," he reminded her.

"I have a 'Get out of Jail Free' pass." She gave a triumphant grin and pulled an I.D. badge out of her back pocket. She'd taken it earlier that day while the security guard had left his post.

"Where'd you get tha—" he cut himself off with a heavy sigh. "Never mind. I believe there's an entrance just around the corner of this building."

Landon stayed next to the building and she did the same, following him. Once they'd turned the corner, they had only a few more feet to go to get to the entrance. The cool night air whipped around the warehouse, stirring scents of axel grease and other unknown manufacturing fumes into a heavy cocktail. Her eyes started to water from the strong smell, and she pinched her nose.

Landon was almost to the door. He reached behind him for the security I.D. card, but as she started to hand it to him, his hand dropped, returning to his side. He halted outside the entrance and reached toward the handle.

Kaitlyn stepped beside him. "What's wrong—" she started to ask, when her gaze locked on his thumb, rubbing the metal handle. He had a curious look on his face as he stared at the substance beneath his hand. It radiated like a warning beacon and was the same bright iridescent glow she'd seen around the ashes in the park. This time the handprint was even more defined against the smooth metal surface.

Landon could see it, which meant…the shit had to have seen the handprints in the park. Kaitlyn felt as if she'd just been slapped in the face. She clenched her teeth and curled her hands into tight fists. "You lied to me," she said, punching him in the arm.

Landon scowled. "What are you talking about?"

Kaitlyn gestured to the door handle. "You can see the handprint on there just as clear as I can. Which means you saw what I saw in the park."

"It's a handprint?" Landon rubbed the sparkly substance that had come off the door between his fingers.

"No more lies, Landon. You can see it."

He shook his head. "I don't see a handprint, just an oil-based, iridescent substance—"

"Which you saw in the park, too," she interrupted, frowning. She could tell by his expression she had him there.

"I wasn't sure what I saw."

"Stop being evasive." Swiping the I.D. badge through the reader on the wall next to the door, Kaitlyn pulled open the door. "I'm doing what I came to do."

Damn, Landon had never seen her so pissed. The sight of her narrowed gaze and red cheeks both excited and riled his own temper. He grabbed the heavy metal door before it shut and locked him out. As he entered through the back entrance, Kaitlyn had just turned out of the darkened hallway, entering an office marked Manager.

Landon eyed the lights farther down the hall. He could

smell the machinery oils and hear the equipment pumping and pistoning along with the ching of scrap parts falling to the cement floor. Some voices rose above the loud factory noise off in the distance. They didn't have much time.

He picked up his pace. When he walked through the office doorway, Kaitlyn pointed to the jacket hanging on the back of the chair sitting in front of the manager's desk.

Landon's gaze locked on the white *G* with a dagger slashed through it emblazoned on the back of the black coat. Garotter.

Anger tightened his chest. First the sparkles on the door handle to this warehouse, linking someone associated with Tacomi to whoever had murdered the Lupreda zerker, and now a Garotter jacket was here…not a good combination. He glanced at Kaitlyn, who was rifling through a filing cabinet, and motioned for her to leave.

She shook her head at the same time she pulled out a file and set it on the desk in front of her.

Landon's sensitive hearing picked up footsteps coming closer. Shit.

He burst into speed, moving at a pace he knew would freak Kaitlyn out if she'd been paying attention. He jerked the folder out of her hand and slipped it back in the file cabinet before he shut the drawer.

"Someone's coming. We don't have time to get out of here before they reach us," he said in a harsh tone next to her ear. Tugging her toward the double doors in the corner of the room, he opened the narrow doors and shoved Kaitlyn in the supply closet, stepping in behind her.

Complete darkness engulfed them once he closed the door. The closet was only a few inches wider than his shoulders, and the supply shelves jutted out, giving them just enough space to stand face-to-face.

When he pressed his body flush against the front of Kaitlyn's in order to shut the doors behind him, her small hands landed on his waist, making a knot form in his throat. Damn, it was a tight fit. Not to mention the small space left him little choice but to take in her appealing smell.

The sensation of her soft breasts pressed against his chest, her heart thudding against him, her thighs entangled with his, made him want to roar. His gut clenched and his groin tightened. He reached above her head and gripped the edge of one of the shelves to keep from sliding his hands down her feminine curves and claiming her sweet mouth with his.

The sound of feet shuffling and a door opening outside distracted him from his lustful thoughts.

Landon tensed. If the closet door behind him popped open right now, he was prepared to fight a potential Garotter. Granted, his body springing from the closet's tight confines would be surprise enough to give him the advantage, but he knew he would take anyone or anything out in order to keep Kaitlyn safe. He was ready.

Kaitlyn gripped his waist tighter and she pressed closer, yanking his libido to full-on attention. He scented her excitement, felt her heart rate ramp higher. Landon fought his primal urges. Flexing his jaw, he swallowed a growl. His shoulders bunched and the wood shelf dented under the pressure of his fingers.

"We need another shipment," a man's voice demanded.

Chairs scraped the floor and a drawer opened. The men must have sat down at the desk.

"It's too soon. There was a female cop here today, asking for a tour of the factory. You know I support what you all do, but I don't need this kind of shit right now," a gravelly-voiced man responded.

"I know a cop was asking to see the facility. That's why I'm here tonight. We're working the government angle to allow us to purchase pulsar weapons, but you know how slow that red tape bullshit is. We've got a situation *now,* Carl."

Kaitlyn's body tensed against him and she whispered, "Remy."

Her murmured comment knocked Landon in the gut. Every moment she'd dated that guy, Landon had wanted to take the man out, out of her life…and her bed. But Carl's rough voice broke Landon's possessive train of thought. "I need a guarantee I won't be investigated."

"Done."

"I don't want the same scenario that happened last time. It's got to look like an accident where some guns went missing, not a hijacking."

A chair scraped across the floor as if someone stood. "Understood. Let us know when you're ready. We'll be there."

"I don't want to know when." A filing cabinet opened and closed, followed by the sound of a copy machine running. "Here's the delivery schedule and the routes our drivers take. That's as far as I go."

"That'll do."

The men's voices faded as they walked out of the office. Kaitlyn started to reach for the door handle, but Landon grabbed her wrist, stopping her. "No, they're still in the hall. We must wait," he whispered in a harsh tone.

"I don't hear them anymore." She tried to pull her hand free of his.

He had to concentrate not to squeeze too hard when he applied pressure to her wrist. She was so very breakable. "Trust me, Kaitie."

Kaitlyn tensed as if she were going to defy him. Landon

began to rub small circles along the soft skin with his thumb, hoping to distract her.

The swift uptick of her pulse under his thumb told him he'd succeeded. He could see her face as clear as day. The look of sheer surprise mixed with desire in her eyes tore him apart, making his erection instantly swell with blood.

Landon cupped her head and slid his fingers through the silky hair trapped by her clip. Her smell was quickly dissolving his rigid control, crumbling his iron-fisted reserve as tendrils of violet and woman's musk filled his nostrils.

He ran his thumb up the side of her throat until he reached her jaw, applying just the right amount of pressure.

Kaitlyn tilted her head and whispered his name as he lowered his mouth to hers.

The soft feel of her lips under his ripped down his reserve. Landon's chest tightened and his heart rate ramped upward. Tilting her head, he groaned against her mouth and brushed his lips against hers in an encouraging caress.

When her lips parted, his control unleashed. He slanted his lips across hers and thrust his tongue into the warm depths of her mouth, reveling in her sweet flavor. She tasted like pure fantasy, and he drank in her essence, taking everything and demanding more.

Kaitlyn slid her tongue alongside his. Her full and avid participation, her complete surrender to their attraction blew him away. It was one thing to know she wanted him, but erotically intoxicating to feel her desire washing over him with its seductive, alluring pull.

He wanted to fill her body with his, rough, soft—in every position and every way possible. He thrust his tongue deeper and locked her body against the shelves behind her, barely holding back the growl of dominance rumbling in his mind.

The sensation of her hands frantically tugging his shirt out of his pants, then her palms sliding up his bare back tempted his wolf. Her fingers curled inward and her nails dug into his muscles and skin. Her arousal waved all around him, like a red flag, beckoning his beast. Primal heat arced between them—building with each swipe of their tongues against each other.

She tasted so good. She tasted…like his. The wolf part of him roared silently in his head, scratching deep grooves in his chest, demanding to get out. The need to bury himself deep inside her body while he clamped his teeth down on that sweet spot between her shoulder and her throat seized his mind, refusing to let go.

He couldn't tear his lips away, so he put his hands on the shelf once more, trying to rein in his primal instincts. The smell of her lust nearly overwhelmed him, spiking his desire more than he could've ever imagined. He didn't trust himself to control his strength around her. He'd kill her.

She rubbed against his erection, encouraging him as she babbled almost incoherently against his mouth, "The way you smell leaves me dizzy and confused and so damned aroused I can't think straight. Touch me again."

Her sultry tone slammed into his gut. Landon dug his fingers into the wood shelves. The hard material turned to sawdust under the pressure of his fingers. He shook deep inside, felt himself spiraling out of control.

"I can't touch you," he grated out against her lips.

Her soft fingers brushed his, and she pulled his hand down. "Yes, you can," she said in a breathless voice as she cupped his hand over her breast.

Landon fought the desire to clinch his fingers around the soft mound under his palm. He watched her face as he slid his thumb across her nipple. The peak turned hard against her thin bra and her hitching breath drove his lust straight through the roof. But her face, the pleasure reflected there almost undid him. His fingers flexed with the need to grab hold of her hard. Instead, he clenched his jaw and slowly slid his thumb across the sensitive peak once more.

She moaned and pressed her breast fully into his hand as she planted a soft kiss on his neck.

Mine! The thought echoed like a ritual drumbeat, over and over in his head, knotting his stomach, vaulting his desire to a heightened pitch like his wolf's long howl on a moon-filled night.

His hands began a slow descent, inching toward the waistband on her pants. Landon's body raged. He gripped the loops on her jeans waistband to try and calm himself down, but Kaitlyn chose that moment to nip at his neck, and his tight rein on himself evaporated.

She gave a small gasp when a ripping sound punctuated their heavy breathing.

Landon froze. He'd barely pulled on the loops, yet he'd ripped them both completely from her jeans.

Quickly tucking the bits of material into his jeans pockets, Landon palmed her face and laid his forehead against hers. His breathing came in ragged pants, while he tried to get a handle on his arousal. He was so on the edge, he feared he might not be able to subdue the wolf howling within him, fiercely demanding that he claim her.

Here. Now. In many various ways.

"Well, that was a first," she said with a low laugh as her soft hands covered his. "Landon?"

He tilted his head back and squeezed his eyes closed, trying to shut out her evocative smell, her melodious voice and her heated curves pressed against him. Her ripe body, emitting its evocative, arousing scent, was locked against his rock-hard erection. Such sweet, jaw-grinding torture.

"That shouldn't have happened," he murmured.

Kaitlyn's rapid pulse rushed in her ears, while her heart thumped a rampant staccato against Landon's hard, muscular chest. She swallowed to slow her breathing and hide her disappointment that Landon had halted their heated session. She'd never been so caught up in a man in her life. His masculine scent, mixed with leather, washed over her, hanging in the air, mocking her. Making her throb from her breasts to her core.

She had no idea what came over her. Why she'd kissed him back. Why she'd encouraged him. She was supposed to be pissed at him for lying to her. And she still was…but there was something magnetic and irresistible about Landon. He exuded a primal dominance that called to her. The tension emanated off him as if he were a live wire vibrating with dangerous coiled energy.

The moment he touched her wrist…she was a goner. She'd fallen under his spell and pressed her body full against his hard one. She wanted him with an achy need that went bone deep. Her desire for Landon held a primal intensity that went beyond anything she'd ever felt for another man.

And it really freaked her out.

Now that her head wasn't fogged with lust, she was glad Landon had shut them down. At least one of them had some sense in his head. Damn, she needed some space and fresh air. Landon's appealing smell was overwhelming her.

Without bothering to ask if he felt it was safe to leave the closet, she opened the door behind them and shoved him away from her.

As he stumbled back and nearly lost his balance, she narrowed her gaze on him. "You're right. That was a mistake. Let's get out of here."

"Kaitie."

Landon tried to reach for her as she brushed past him, but she stepped out of his reach. "Don't."

Kaitlyn quickly hit the copier's button and made another copy of Tacomi's shipment itinerary that Carl had left in the copy machine. Folding the piece of paper, she slid it into her back pocket as she walked over to the closed office door. She placed her ear against the cool metal door. Nothing but the sound of machinery in the distance reached her.

Landon's strong presence loomed behind her, while she cracked open the door and peered out, staring down the hall toward the factory. Once she saw the hall was clear, she opened the door and headed toward the exit.

Landon made no sound behind her, but she knew he was there, protecting her back. No matter their differences, she intuitively knew he would keep her safe.

As soon as she walked outside, Kaitlyn took off running toward the fence and the oak tree. Her ankle still smarted at little, but the pain wasn't enough to keep her from trying to put some distance between herself and Landon.

For some reason, Landon must've held back because she reached the fence a few seconds before he did. Since she damned well didn't want his help getting back over, she decided to climb the fence to get to the limb.

She was about to reach for the chain link when Landon called out, "Kaitlyn. No!"

At the same time, something whizzed past her head and hit the fence with a sizzling pop.

Kaitlyn's stomach dropped when the charred rock landed

on the ground next to her foot. The fence was electrified. Landon had just saved her ass.

She cut her gaze to his as he stepped beside her. "How'd you know?"

He nodded toward the fence. "I heard the low hum." Bending at the knees, he laced his fingers together. "Step into my hands. I'll give you a boost to the tree limb."

Guilt nibbled at her conscience. "What about you?"

His intense gaze locked with hers. "I'm taller than you. I'll make it."

She eyed the limb a good eight feet above them and worried her bottom lip with her teeth. "I could try to pull you up once I'm on the limb."

He gave her a doubtful look. "I'm double your weight. I can make it."

Kaitlyn sighed and put her hands on his shoulders, then stepped into his cupped hands.

"Get ready to grab the limb," he said.

Before she could balance herself, she was sailing through the air. Her upward momentum took her slightly past the limb, and she tensed her stomach muscles when her belly landed on the limb instead. An *oomph* whooshed past her lips, but she quickly grabbed the limb on either side of her to keep from sliding off.

"You okay?" Landon called.

She peered down at him. "Apparently you don't know your own strength, He-man."

He grinned. "Just saving you muscle strain."

Kaitlyn straddled the limb and was careful to tuck her legs away from the fence while she scooted toward the tree trunk on the other side of the fence.

Once she reached the trunk, the limb under her jostled a bit.

She glanced back to see Landon hoisting himself up on the limb just as she'd done a minute ago.

How the hell had he made that leap to get to the limb, she wondered.

"Get a move on, unless you want this limb to break with both our weights bearing down on it."

Landon's comment spurred her into action. She stepped onto a lower limb and began to make her way down the tree.

As soon as she let go of the last tree limb, Landon landed on the ground beside her.

The smashed bullet slug on the silver necklace around his neck drew her attention. The chain must've come out from behind his shirt while he climbed. She was curious as to what it meant, but personal questions were out. "How'd you beat me?"

He shrugged. "I was a tree-climbing champ as a kid."

Exhaling a huff of irritation, Kaitlyn turned away and headed toward the haunted house.

Landon fell into step beside her, his hands tucked in his jeans front pockets. "What are you going to do with what you've learned?"

She shook her head. "I'm not sure yet. I'm going to talk to my boss and see how he wants to proceed."

Landon stopped walking and grabbed her arm, halting her progress. "Kaitlyn. The Garotters are dangerous. I don't want you to get involved. You heard what was said in there. Do you really think that truck driver will survive the 'accident' they plan? They won't hesitate to take you out."

She deliberately stared at his hand on her arm until he removed it. "The only way the Garotters will be stopped is if they are caught committing the crime. We just need to set up an operation to catch them in the act."

Landon's mouth formed a thin line. "I don't like it. You

can't know for sure how deep this goes. You heard that Garotter. They've got people on the inside with the police, or at the very least, a way to control the situation."

She gave him an assured smile. "That's why the only person who's going to know is the one person who put me on this case. My boss. He'll handpick the team and only use people he can trust."

When she started to walk away, Landon's next comment halted her steps. "Kaitlyn, I'm sorry."

She faced him, her gaze narrowed. "Are you going to tell me why you lied to me?"

He shrugged. "All I saw was sparkles. That's why I asked what you had seen. I didn't see the detailed handprints you described to me in your car earlier today."

"The point is you saw *something,* yet you didn't say anything. Thanks for the support." She turned and walked away.

"About what happened…" Landon called after her.

Kaitlyn kept moving straight ahead. "Like you said, it was a mistake."

Chapter 5

The next morning on her way to the office, Kaitlyn stopped her car while a tractor-trailer in front of her backed up into a building. Her thoughts drifted to the meaning of the dream she'd had the night before. She'd dreamed she was standing in her old childhood bedroom as it used to be—pink walls, cloud-and-moon ceiling and all—getting ready for bed.

She'd taken off her necklace and set it on the dresser. As she started to walk away, she heard the chain slide off the slick polished surface.

Turning back, she bent to retrieve the chain from the soft carpet, but the necklace and charm were gone.

Then a low growl erupted behind her, causing her skin to prickle as she slowly turned around.

A lone wolf stood there staring at her, his hackles raised. Brown with silver markings, he looked just like the wolf her father had had an artist paint on her bedroom wall near the door. But when she'd turned to stare at the rendition, only an empty place remained among the tall green grass. The real wolf gave a low, warning growl once more. He was enormous. Twice the size of the painting.

Heart racing, her eyes locked with his dark ones.

"Easy, big guy," she'd whispered and slowly eased toward the door.

His growl grew deeper and his lips curled back, revealing sharp white teeth.

She froze, stopping her retreat. The wolf settled for a second, then glanced toward the doorway, his second growl a deep, primal rumble.

A sound in the hallway drew her attention. Someone was coming down the hall—a tall shadow moving at a rapid rate.

She gasped and took a step away from the door at the same time the wolf leaped into the air.

The animal changed position as he arced across the room. He landed in the doorway with his back to her…but he was on his hind legs, upright like a human.

Kaitlyn woke with a cry of surprise rushing past her lips.

Had the dream been caused by recent events? She touched the delicate chain around her neck and felt the wolf charm brush against her breast inside her shirt. A horn honked, drawing Kaitlyn out of her reverie. Tucking the thoughts about her dream's meaning to the back of her mind, she pushed the gas pedal.

When Kaitlyn was almost to the office, she considered the conversation she was going to have to have with her boss, Ronald Sparks, and wondered how he'd take it. Ronald hadn't mentioned a possible connection to the police department. After discovering Remy had gone on the wrong side of the law, and then Landon had lied to her, yet she'd still kissed the guy—damn his alluring smell—she really had a reason to question her judgment of people, especially men. There was one person she could trust to give her an honest answer about her boss's character before their meeting about what she'd learned last night.

Picking up her cell, she called her father's old partner, Hank Freely. They'd gone through police academy together. Hank used to visit from time to time to check on her mom and her. Since he'd retired, he'd sold his house in the city and moved to his mountain cabin and his visits had ceased.

"Hello?"

"Hey, Hank. It's Kaitlyn McKinney. How's retired life?"

He laughed. "Can't complain. I've taken up fly-fishing. It's a helluva lot harder than it looks. How about you and your mom. Is she doing well?"

Her heart jerked. "Mom's hanging in there. She was admitted to the hospital a couple months ago."

"I'm sorry to hear that," Hank said, his tone turning sad. "I've been bad about keeping in touch. How are you doing?"

"I got promoted to detective," Kaitlyn said, trying to lift her suddenly depressed spirits.

"That's my girl! Your dad would be proud."

Kaitlyn swallowed the lump in her throat. She wished her dad was here to ask this question, but Hank would be a non-biased resource. "I hope you're right."

"I know so. Why do I get the feeling this call was more than just a reason to shoot the breeze with an old man? What can I do for ya?"

She eyed the stack of stopped cars in front of her as they waited for the light to turn green. When they began to move, she pressed on the gas pedal. "I need an opinion from someone I can trust."

Hank's lighthearted tone completely vanished. "Shoot, Kaitie."

"What can you tell me about Ronald Sparks? I know you and Dad went to the academy with Ron, but I just wanted your opinion on his character."

Hank cleared his throat. "Ron's a straight shooter. Always has been. I'd stand beside him any day."

Hank's opinion confirmed her own, which made her feel a lot better discussing the direction of her case—where a cop might be involved or at the very least compromised—with her boss when she got to work.

"Thanks so much, Hank. You've really helped. Maybe I'll come up for a visit to your cabin soon. It has been a while since I've seen it."

He chuckled. "You do that. I don't get many visitors. By the way, now that I've moved here, I have a lot less storage space. I have some of your dad's stuff. When you come, can you take it home with you? I'm sure your mom would like to put it with the rest of your dad's things."

"Will do, and thanks, Hank."

"Take care, Kaitie."

Once she got to work, Kaitlyn spent the rest of the morning typing up an official report of her findings and the indirect connections she'd discovered for her boss. She knew she wouldn't be able to "officially" include the information she'd learned last night, but they could say they had a tip from an anonymous source and went to investigate another potential hijacking. Catching the Garotters in the act was the next step.

The smell of pizza wafting through the office overpowered the morning coffee aroma, making her stomach growl. Ignoring it, she hunched closer to her keyboard and typed faster, promising herself she'd grab something to eat as soon as she finished the report.

Ron had been in meetings all morning, so she hadn't been able to speak to him yet about the case. Her desk phone rang and she glanced at the caller I.D. to see who was calling.

Lab.

She'd almost forgotten about the trace "ash" from the park. Picking up her phone, she said, "Tell me you got something, Ryan."

"Good afternoon to you, too," he said in a dry tone.

Kaitlyn blew out a breath of patience. She was so tightly wound, her shoulders and upper back ached. "Good afternoon, Ryan. Tell me you've got something."

He chuckled. "Gotta love a woman who gets right to the point. If only you'd agree to go out with me, I think we'd be well matched…"

She pictured Ryan's handsome open face, his broad smile, his sweet Southern accent. He definitely had a certain charm about him, but she had a rule about getting involved with her coworkers. *So what does that make Landon?* she asked herself. *A sexy, melt-every-bone-in-my-body, mistake,* even if he hadn't worked with the NYPD in three years.

"Ryan, you know my rule—"

"Rules are like piecrust, darlin'. They're made to be broken."

Her lips quirked. "Quit flirting. Were you able to make heads or tails of that ash I gave you?"

"You're breaking my heart." Sobering, he continued, "Not really. The rain broke it down a good bit. I don't know what you were thinking handing me a hair clip. This evidence is as tainted as they come. I was able to decipher silver and DNA traces for male, female—presumably yours—and…" he paused. "Do you have a dog?"

"Why?"

"I also found DNA in this trace that resembles canine structure."

Kaitlyn's heart stuttered. "You did?"

"This is just conjecture, not definitive evidence. You never did say, do you have a dog?"

"No, I don't."

"Didn't you say you found this in a pile of burned ashes? It could've been a dog someone burned. The male DNA might've come from your boyfriend handling your clip."

Kaitlyn snorted. "Nice try, Ryan. I'm not divulging any juicy tidbits about my personal life."

"You can't blame a guy for trying." he said, completely unapologetic.

"Thanks for checking out the trace for me."

"Next time I'm going to be smart and ask for a date *first,* then I'll agree to undocumented evidence analysis."

"And now I've been forewarned." As soon as she hung up her phone, it immediately rang. Her boss was calling. She picked up the phone. "Hi, Ron."

"I've got a free minute. Come to my office."

Her stomach tensing slightly with excitement, Kaitlyn saved the computer file she was working on and locked her terminal before she picked up the case file folder and headed down the hall to her boss's office.

Rapping on the door jamb, she walked inside Ron's office. As she seated herself in the chair in front of his desk, he lifted his reading glasses up on his balding head and lowered the file folder he'd been reading.

"I'm glad you asked to see me. I was going to talk to you today about the case I assigned you."

"Oh?" Kaitlyn tried to sound as casual as she could, but her gut knotted. There was something in his tone. She had a feeling she wasn't going to like what Ron was about to say.

Lowering his glasses to the desk in front of him, Ron cleared his throat. "I'm reassigning you to another case that has a higher priority."

Kaitlyn's stomach pitched. "What? I thought this case *was* a high priority."

"There are other cases that need our attention. We're short-staffed as it is." He picked up the neat paperwork in front of him and stacked it neatly once more. The man was avoiding her gaze. That wasn't a good thing. What happened to that spine of steel he seemed to have? Those high career aspirations?

"Did someone get to you? Were you threatened?" she tensed and sat forward in her chair.

His gaze jerked to hers and his brown gaze narrowed. "No one threatened me, and I don't appreciate the insinuation that I could be intimidated."

She slid her report onto the desk in front of him along with a handwritten note at the top of the shipment itinerary she'd copied last night. "But we could have a solid case if we could just catch them in the act."

Ron quickly skimmed her writeup and the note. When he turned and slid the papers into his shredder, hitting the on button, she stared in shock. He closed the thick folder that had been sitting on the desk in front of him and handed it across the desk toward her. "We wouldn't have a solid case, McKinney. Here's your new assignment."

As the last of her report disappeared into the waste bin,

chewed to criss-cross shreds, pressure weighted heavily on Kaitlyn's chest. The itinerary was her only copy. Everything else in her typewritten report was just the research she'd collected. She tensed her jaw and her throat burned with the need to scream her frustration at Ron.

Apparently Remy *had* held up his end of the bargain with the Tacomi employee—he'd taken care of the police.

"But all we have to do is catch them in the act—"

"Let it go, McKinney." Ron gave her a direct stare. "You've been reassigned. You'll have a partner for this case, Kent Sloan. If you don't like it, go back to your old job. Am I clear?"

She set her lips in a firm line and stood, taking the folder he held out. "Crystal."

As she turned to walk out of his office, her spine stiff and her ego bruised, Ron said in a softer voice, "We can't win them all, Kaitlyn."

She paused in his doorway and glanced over her shoulder. "Hank was so wrong about you."

Without another word, she turned away and headed down the hall toward her desk, the overstuffed manila folder clutched in her hand. When she got back to her desk, she sat there for several minutes, numb and disillusioned.

General conversation buzzed around her. Three detectives were standing around the coffeepot, discussing last night's game. Nothing appeared out of the ordinary. But something was very wrong. Her boss had apparently been intimidated into inaction. Now what in the hell was she supposed to do?

The title of detective wasn't the be-all and end-all to Kaitlyn. It just gave her the ability to work and solve cases. That was the most important thing to her, not some badge. This was her first case, and it felt like a failure to her to be reassigned.

Her stomach growled again, reminding her she needed to eat. As her breathing came in rampant pants over her frustrating situation, she realized she needed to get some fresh air, too.

She grabbed her purse from her desk drawer and stood up, ready to head through the maze of cubicles toward the exit.

"Hey, McKinney," a male called out, stopping her. Kaitlyn turned as a tall, dark-haired man walked up and held out his hand. "I'm Kent Sloan. Looking forward to working with you."

She grasped his hand and stared into his deep blue eyes, wondering who she could trust anymore. Damn, she needed to get out of the office. She was seeing conspiracy everywhere. "Nice to meet you. I'm running out for lunch. Want to go over the case file when I get back?"

"It's a pretty thick case file. Why don't we start going over it now? We're going to be here for a while."

Kaitlyn glanced at the three-inch case file on her desk and released his hand with a heavy sigh. "Which desk? Yours or mine?"

It was dark outside by the time Kaitlyn arrived home. She and Kent had spent the rest of the day going through her new case. Tired and annoyed, she didn't even bother turning on the lights as she walked inside her house and set her purse and paperwork on the table in the hall. She started to walk down the hall, intending to change clothes and then go see her mother, when the tiny hairs on her arms began to stand up.

Something wasn't right. The air felt warmer...as if recently disturbed. Someone was here.

She quietly unsnapped the gun holster and pulled her gun,

her pulse tripping a staccato beat. Her breathing turned shallow as she started to pass her father's office. A man's shadowed outline sat in the chair at her father's desk.

She rounded the corner and cocked her gun, aiming it at the intruder.

"It never looks good to shoot your boss, McKinney," Ron's calm voice floated across the room

Relief flooded through her and she uncocked the gun, but she didn't lower it. "What the hell are you doing breaking into my house, Ron?"

"I found the spare key." The desk lamp came on and Ron held up a picture he'd removed from the wall. "We were so young and full of piss back then. Just like you." He chuckled as he laid the picture on the desk.

She glanced at the photo of her father, Hank and Ron. They all wore smug smiles and had their arms slung around each other's shoulders. Her mother had told her the photo was taken the day they'd graduated from the police academy.

Past friend of her father's or not, she didn't appreciate his making himself comfortable in her home, not to mention summarily dismissing her at work that day.

She narrowed her gaze and held her gun toward him. "What do you want?"

He heaved a tired sigh. "Put the gun away, Kaitlyn. I'm here to talk to you about the Tacomi case. We need to be very careful how we proceed. Obviously there's someone feeding information to the Mafia or Garotters from within our department."

She sat down in the chair across from the desk, dumbfounded, considering how he had treated her earlier. "Are you telling me you never were dismissing me from the case?"

Ron slowly shook his head. "But I had to make it look like

I was, since I have no idea how the Garotters and Mafia knew that you were on the case. You were right. I got a threatening call. They wanted you called off."

"Damn, Ron, you should've considered a career in acting. You were that freakin' convincing!" Rubbing her hands together, she said, "Okay, now here's my idea—"

He put up a finger to halt her enthusiasm. "You're on the case, but it'll be strictly behind the scenes."

"That's not fa—"

"Think about it for a minute, Kaitlyn. If someone sees you actively checking into things, they'll know we're still onto them—that you're still working the case. Because this might potentially involve a dirty cop, you'll still be in the loop in case I need backup."

Kaitlyn didn't like it, but Ron was right. Now that she'd been made, the Garotters and Mafia would be watching her. She wanted this win, no matter who was on the front line. "What do you want me to do?"

Ron smiled and got up from the chair to come around the desk. "You're so much like your dad." His expression fell a little as he mumbled, "Well, like he was in the early days."

The early days? What'd he mean by that? Kaitlyn started to ask when Ron plunged on with his plans. "I memorized the dates and Tacomi truck routes before I shredded your document. I'll pick a small three-man team of men I feel I can trust. We'll stake out each route on the different dates until we catch the bastards in action."

She stood and faced him, creasing her brow in concern. "I hate to state the obvious here, but if there's a snitch within the department, shouldn't we be calling Internal Affairs?"

He gave a half smile. "Yeah, and we will, but I don't want their investigation to impede this one. This is a small window

of time. We might not get another opportunity like this again."
A smug look crossed his oval-shaped face. "Anyway, it might
be a moot point. Once we catch the Mafia members and Garotters responsible, they'll probably roll over on their mole
in the department."

Before she could say a word, he pulled her close and
hugged her. "Your dad, Hank and I were like brothers. I want
you to stay safe."

"I want to help," she mumbled against his shirt before she
pushed away. "Don't coddle me, Ron."

He gripped her shoulders, his gaze locking with hers.
"You're important in this. You're my point person, Kaitlyn.
I'll keep you in the loop when things start moving."

Crisp fall wind, carrying exhaust fumes and the strong
aroma of bratwurst and sauerkraut from a side stand, whipped
around Kaitlyn. As she walked from her car up the street
toward the hospital, she was so caught up in thinking about
everything she and Ron had discussed, she didn't notice
someone step into place beside her until he spoke.

"We need to talk."

Kaitlyn's steps faltered slightly when Landon's alluring
masculine smell invaded her senses. "You following me?"
Oddly the idea excited her. Straightening her spine, she
gripped the vase she was carrying tightly in her hands and increased her speed.

Yet she was unable to get the appealing *Men's Health*-
worthy picture of Landon in a hunter-green T-shirt, his leather
jacket and faded jeans out of her mind. Before she'd glanced
away, he'd flashed her a brooding, "I want to eat you alive"
look that made her body scream all over in response.

Damn the man. She was still mad at him.

Landon shoved his hands in his front pockets, then took a deep inhaling breath and growled in her direction. "Who is he?"

Taken aback by his question, Kaitlyn stopped and faced him. "What are you talking about?"

Landon halted. A crowd of people leaving a nearby restaurant came down the sidewalk. He had to step closer, his chest almost touching hers as the crowd bustled around them. He sniffed near her neck. "The man who wears this cheap cologne."

Indignant rage filled her, but instead of giving him the satisfaction of seeing her anger, she said, "It was official police business."

When she started to walk away, Landon caught her arm and held her in place, his gaze narrowed. "Was this about the Tacomi case?"

Kaitlyn deliberately glanced down at his hand on her arm, then raised her gaze to his once more. She pulled out of his hold. "That's none of your business."

Walking away from him, she shook her head at the jumbled emotions pinging around inside her mind. She didn't know why she was so angry with Landon, but honest to God the way her heart ached and her stomach tumbled and knotted when she'd talked to him just now, you'd think they'd just had a lovers' spat.

Sure, they'd shared an electric, toe-curling kiss that had singed every part of her body, but Landon's professional betrayal was a tough lump to swallow no matter how hard her heart tripped whenever he came within a few feet of her.

Landon watched Kaitlyn walk away, his tense frame howling for him to claim her once and for all. He'd smelled another man's scent on Kaitlyn as soon as he'd stepped into her personal space. It was all over her…as if they'd been very close. The tips of his fingers tingled and his wereclaws threatened to unsheathe.

He fisted his hands and fell into step behind her, wondering how he was going to survive this self-imposed bodyguard assignment when the other party didn't trust him and pretty much wanted nothing to do with him.

But beyond keeping her safe, he knew he was there for another reason.

Her hips swayed with her quick steps and her floral scent wafted in her wake. His groin tightened in response and Landon mentally groaned.

He caught up to Kaitlyn. "I know you're mad at me, but I'm telling the truth. I didn't see what you saw the other night in the park. All I saw were sparkles, nothing as defined as a handprint."

She swung around to face him. "It's hard enough to do what I do—to have this strange ability—without being made to look a fool. No one on the force knows about my talent, but for some reason—like an idiot—I felt I could trust you. And then you threw it in my face."

Landon knew exactly what it felt like to be a stranger on the outside looking in. He'd been living partially in two worlds for a long time, but he couldn't tell her the whole truth. Instead, he came as close as he could. "Being a P.I. and working with the police for as long as I did…" he paused and raised his hands then let them drop to his sides "…I never felt like I fit in. I've walked a loner's path for a long time, Kaitlyn, so I understand a little of what you feel. I apologize for making you feel the fool. That wasn't my intent."

He stared into her eyes, his expression turning hard as any Alpha's would when addressing his pack member in matters of safety. "But seeing the same sparkles at both the park and Tacomi's means these two cases are somehow connected. I don't want you to pursue this. This is far more dangerous than you realize."

Kaitlyn squared her shoulders and tilted her chin upward. "It was some animal burning, right? What makes it more dangerous?" Her gaze narrowed in suspicion. "How are they connected? What do you know that you aren't telling me?"

Landon set his jaw. Hell and damnation, he couldn't tell her without exposing his pack. Instead he chose intimidation. Leaning close, he ground out, "I didn't see this outline you saw, but if what you saw really existed, then whoever took it out could probably tear you to shreds with very little effort. Let it go, Kaitie."

Her jaw flexed and she stood on her toes until her nose almost touched his. Her hazel-blue gaze was the brownest he'd ever seen; almost like a wolf's in full challenge mode. "You know more than you're telling me, and until you come clean, I'll continue to go about my *own* business."

With a determined look, she turned and walked away, her head held high. Landon stared after her. Damn, she'd make a fantastic female Alpha. The woman had more balls than most of his pack members.

Chapter 6

After she left Landon, Kaitlyn proceeded into the hospital and up to her mother's room.

"O-o-oh, look what you brought me tonight." Kaitlyn's mom called out in a soft voice as her daughter entered the hospital room.

Kaitlyn turned the vase all the way around so her mother could see the colorful marbles she'd carefully arranged in a pattern inside before she poured water over them. "I like to call it my forever bouquet."

"It's beautiful." Sharon's blue eyes followed Kaitlyn's hands as she set the vase down on the hospital table beside her bed.

"I've come for a nice long visit." Kaitlyn pulled up a chair beside the bed and laced her fingers with her mother's hand. Her heart tugged and her stomach knotted when her mother didn't squeeze her hand as tight as she used to.

"Good, I've missed hearing about your adventures. Tell me how your job is going."

Kaitlyn noted the dark circles under Sharon's eyes, and she lifted her mother's hand and pressed it against her cheek. She still hadn't told her mom about her new promotion. She wanted her visits to be about her mom, not her. "Uh-uh…you first. How are you doing?"

Sharon expelled a tired breath. "I'm so very tired all the time, Kaitie. The meds keep down the pain, but I feel like all I ever do is sleep. I miss your father."

The past month, her mother had spoken more and more about her dad. The bittersweet conversations made Kaitlyn's chest hurt. She knew her mother was pining, hoping for an end to the cancer eating away at her body, but talking about her father seemed to make her mother happy, to remember the good times.

That night Kaitlyn talked about their trips to the shore together, the carnivals, the Halloween trick-or-treating and holidays…all while her heart bled for the pain her mother suffered and the realization she'd be alone in the world in the not-too-distant future.

As she reminisced about her father, the dream she'd had the night before about the painted wolf in her room coming to life came back to her. She gripped her mother's hand tightly. "Mom, I've been meaning to ask you—why was Dad so into wolves and werewolf lore? Had he always had a fascination with them?"

Her mother shook her head and sighed. "No. It happened almost twenty-five years ago, before you were born. We were newly married and your father had gone for his evening run in the park. He came home covered in blood and said he'd been attacked by a big dog. He got thirty stitches on his calf that night." Her faded blue gaze took on a faraway look. "Ever since then, he became fascinated with wolves, researching them. Eventually, his interest turned to werewolf lore as well."

Kaitlyn frowned. "Didn't you think it was strange that he would become so interested?"

Her mother's gaze returned to hers. "Yes, I did. Then I read an article about shark attack victims and how they sometimes develop a fascination as a way to overcome their phobia." She shrugged and gave Kaitlyn a wan smile. "Your father used to have nightmares and wake up covered in sweat, but the dreams stopped once he developed his hobby. I guess I saw it as the lesser of two evils and was just glad to have my husband back…even if he did have an unusual hobby."

Kaitlyn smiled at her mom. "Thanks for telling me. Every time we talk about Dad, it helps me understand him a little bit more. I was just too young and wrapped up in myself to get to know him as a person and not just my dad before he died." Kaitlyn had never been told the details behind her father's death. Just that he'd been mugged. Now, the cop in her desperately wanted to know what had happened, but she didn't want to discuss it with her mother. Her mother clung to happy memories. She'd find out the details on her own.

Her mother squeezed her hand for the first time during her visit. "Don't think that way, Kaitlyn. You were only six when he died. You were our miracle child after a few years of trying. Your father loved you very much, and he knew you felt the same. He was very protective of you and only wanted the best. Even in his death, he came through for you. Thank goodness for that college scholarship for deceased police officers' children. It enabled you to go to the college your father hoped you could attend. He was determined to take out loans if he had to. Only the best for his Kaitie-girl," her mother finished in a perfect mimicry of her father's lilting Irish accent.

"Oh, Mom." Tears filled Kaitlyn's eyes and she bent to kiss her mother's soft cheek.

* * *

Three days later, Kaitlyn finally had some downtime from the case she was working with Kent. She tried to visit her mother that evening, but apparently Friday had been another bad day for her mom. She wasn't on Handleburg Hall's schedule until next week, so instead of going home in a depressed mood, Kaitlyn decided to head over to the library in town. Parking in a side alley, she followed the sidewalk to the front of the library and pulled open the glass door.

When the heavy door started to jerk closed, a jagged edge along the door's handle sliced her finger. Wincing from the pain, she immediately stuck her wounded finger into her mouth.

Several people were leaving as she walked in, including a thin, dark-haired man. He did a double take as she passed him, turned and came back inside, patting his hands on his pockets as if he'd lost something. Even as the library's warmth chased away the evening chill, she shivered and kept the man in the corner of her eye until he walked off toward the autobiography section.

Sheesh, now that I think there might be a traitor at work, I'm getting ultraparanoid. Still she'd feel better if…she brushed her hand across the empty gun holster under her jacket and sighed. Knowing how sensitive the library sensors were, she'd tucked her gun safely away in her car's glove compartment to avoid becoming the center of attention as soon as she walked in the door.

Forcing herself to relax, she took a deep breath, rolled her shoulders and approached the front desk. A young, dark-haired woman with an eyebrow piercing asked, "How may I help you?"

"Can you tell me where the microfiche for old newspapers dating back over twenty years would be located?" Kaitlyn asked.

The girl pointed. "Microfiche department is that way. Room 100."

Kaitlyn flipped on the light switch along the wall to her left as she stepped into the stuffy room. Fluorescent lightbulbs popped on with a zinging sound above her head, revealing rows of tall shelving. Each shelf held microfilm labeled bins.

After finding the film she wanted, she loaded it on a tabletop projector and sifted through all the articles until she found the one she was looking for: Off-Duty Police Officer Killed in Morningside Park.

Kaitlyn's eyes widened and her heart jerked at the name of the park. She had had no idea that was where her father had died.

Then she read the lead paragraph.

James McKinney was found dead in Morningside Park early this morning. Witnesses on the scene noted a clawlike wound on his chest, suggesting he was apparently a victim of some kind of animal mauling. The marks were too wide to be a dog's, but no other suggestions have been offered at this time.

Closing her eyes, she squeezed back the tears, and her chest ached. When she'd been old enough to understand, her mother had explained what had happened to her father. But she'd been told that her father had died from a head injury in an apparent struggle with the thief.

She continued to scroll through more papers until she ran into a later article.

In a follow-up investigation on Officer McKinney's death, it was determined that he died from a blow to the head. Bloodstains on the playground equipment indicate he must have been shoved or thrown against it, causing instantaneous death. There wasn't sufficient evidence to determine what kind of animal attacked the police officer.

Kaitlyn's mind raced with strong possibilities of who had been her father's attacker.

Eighteen years ago, the vampires had been extinct for a few years. Was it possible they weren't extinct? There was that one unsolved incident with author Ariel Swanson's kidnapping a few months ago, but nothing else had happened as far as she knew. Then there was that strange creature's aura she'd seen in the park? If it was real, and it lived in the woods near the park, could something like that have attacked her father? Did it have deadly claws? Her chest burned with rage at the thought. Suddenly, she didn't mind so much that someone had burned that thing to a crisp, leaving nothing but ashes.

She wanted answers now…and the only person who might have some was Landon. He was the one who'd suggested that whatever had attacked and burned that thing in the park could probably tear her apart. Setting her jaw, she flipped open her cell phone and dialed the precinct's number. Someone there would know how to get in touch with him.

"Hey, Sandra. Do you have Landon Rourke's cell?"

"We do, but he prefers his privacy. I'll call him and tell him you're looking for him and I'll give him your cell. Will that work?"

Kaitlyn sighed in frustration. "That's fine. I'm getting ready to leave the research library on Forty-Second in a few minutes. I might lose coverage going through the library. Tell him to wait fifteen minutes and then call me back. Thanks."

Once she hung up, Kaitlyn switched the phone to vibrate mode just in case Landon called while she was still in the library. Her stomach was all tied in knots. She needed to talk to somebody. Shoving her emotions to the back of her mind, she spent the next ten minutes in autopilot mode, putting all the microfiche in their bins and shutting down the machine.

Kaitlyn waved to the librarian, buttoned her jacket around her waist and pulled her car keys out of her pocket before she walked out of the library and into the frigid night air.

No one was about on the main sidewalk, but a couple cars passed, lighting her path as she turned to head toward the corner of the building and the side street where she'd parked.

As soon as she rounded the corner, Kaitlyn sensed a presence beside her.

Though she couldn't figure out how the person had come on her so fast, her gut told her it was the thin, dark-haired man. She could probably take him, but he might have a weapon. He was so close, her skin prickled, yet she didn't cast her gaze his way. Instead, she stomped on his toe with her boot heel and jammed her elbow into his ribs. She heard his grunt before she took off running toward her car, her heart pounding like a jackhammer.

The further she got away from the street corner and street-light, the darker it got, but Kaitlyn could still see her car's outline another fifteen feet away. Her chest heaved and her legs burned as she put all her efforts into speed.

Hopefully, her elbow in his gut had slowed him down enough to allow her to get to the ca—

The thin man zipped past her in a blur. He turned to lean casually against her car as if he'd been waiting for her all night. Stunned and suddenly terrified at how fast he'd moved, she came to a stop ten feet away. His speed was inhuman.

"Wanna play, bitch? I'm up for it." He cupped his fingers toward his palm, beckoning her. And then he smiled, his fangs gleaming bright white in the dim light.

Even with the night air cooling her face, Kaitlyn broke out into a swift sweat. She turned to run back to the safety of the library, but a hard force slammed into her chest, sending her sailing backward through the air.

Before she hit the ground, the tall thin man caught her and a low, evil laugh rumbled through the bony chest she'd fallen against. He might be thin, but his hold was like steel bars, locking her in place. Kaitlyn gasped, trying to regain her breath. Pain throbbed in her sternum, making it difficult to take deep breaths.

What the hell had she run into? she wondered, when another man, this one taller and broader with long black hair stepped into her blurred view. "Giving us a good run, little red?" he sneered. His fangs exploded from his gums at the same time he reached out and his long claws sliced through her thick jacket as if it were tissue paper.

She screamed in pain at the burning, tearing sensation that splintered down the center of her chest when he'd curled his claws inward to grip her jacket's button in a tight fist.

Pain and self-preservation kicked Kaitlyn's adrenaline to full throttle. She slammed her fist into his meaty face and lifted her foot with a jerking force, catching him in the crotch. "This meal is still kicking, vampire bastard," she gritted out through the fire spreading in a hot burn from her wounds.

The long-haired vampire released his hold on her jacket and crumpled over, howling in pain as he grabbed his groin. The vampire holding her growled his fury and tossed her through the air.

Kaitlyn landed on the hood of her car, hitting her head with a hard thud. She thought she heard her cell phone skid across the pavement, but dizziness and splitting pain radiated in her head, dimming her hearing. Her vision began to swim and the weight of her lower body hanging over the side of her hood caused her to slowly slide off the car.

So much pain racked her body, her legs gave out and she fell to her side onto the road. As warm liquid seeped down her brow, the asphalt felt both cool and rough against her cheek. She vaguely realized it had to be blood and shut her left eyelid to keep the thick fluid from blocking her vision completely.

Hard footfalls drew near. She tensed and her heart seized with panic, while she mentally prepared to be punched or ripped to shreds. Instead, a howling battle cry echoed across the alley. A hard thud sounded, followed by guttural growls and vicious, bloodthirsty snarls.

Hope bloomed in her aching chest. Had the vampires started fighting each other?

It was dark in the alley and she tried to look, but her vision kept blurring in and out, leaving nothing but tall, dark shadows moving with deadly lightning speed in her line of sight.

An eerie primal howl filled the air right before something wet and warm splattered across her arm and shoulder. Nausea filled her belly. It was blood. A lot of blood. Which meant one vampire had killed the other. He'd be coming after her next.

Kaitlyn began to crawl away. She bit back the moan of pain that racked her body from her efforts and tried to remain as quiet as possible.

Snarls and primal battle sounds started up once more, causing her to pause. Had the one vampire only wounded the other? Instead of looking, she decided her best course of action was to get away while they were distracted. But after she'd made it a few feet, the metallic smell of her own blood and the sound of her pulse rushing in her ears made her head throb with a blinding force that stole her ability to breathe.

She paused to take a couple of deep breaths, to keep herself conscious, when she noticed something silver on the ground underneath her. Lowering her head so the item came into focus, Kaitlyn recognized the smashed metal piece on the silver chain.

It was Landon's necklace.

Dear God, was he back there? Was that his blood she'd felt splatter against her? Bile rose in her throat. She swallowed several times to keep from throwing up at the idea of Landon with those two vicious vampires. She didn't want anything to happen to the man. Despite Landon's refusal to tell her all of the facts, instincts told her he was one of the "good guys."

She quickly glanced back to the dark shadows fighting in the alley, needing to know for sure. One figure stood easily a head taller than the other. He looked different somehow, but her mind couldn't mesh the shadowy image with coherent thoughts. She blinked, but her blurred vision began to tunnel, turning black along the edges.

"Landon?" she called out softly, gripping the necklace tightly. Shoving the chain in her pants pocket was the last thing she remembered before she passed out.

Landon heard Kaitlyn's faint call. He glanced her way and his wolf's vision displayed her in vivid clarity in the darkness. Her heart rate was strong, but she'd passed out, fueling his rage.

His apartment was close enough that he'd walked to meet her at the library when he got the call from Sandra. As he got closer, he sensed the danger. Then he saw Kaitlyn on the ground. He didn't think twice about using his Musk form the moment he realized Kaitlyn was in trouble. He'd lifted the silver necklace off his neck and shifted in mere seconds, attacking the vampires before they knew what hit them.

He'd killed the thin vampire with a fatal death blow across his neck that had sliced open the bastard's main artery. As the vampire bled out, Landon and the long-haired Sanguinas faced off. They circled each other while they each sized the other up for weaknesses.

"Unbelievable." The vampire's gaze traveled Landon's seven-foot-plus, half-human, half-wolf Musk form up and down. "This will make our fight a lot more interesting."

Landon could smell the vampire's sweat. He growled deep in his chest, relishing how much the man reeked with fear. Just like the other vampire, this one would pay with his life for his attack on Kaitlyn.

What's so hard to believe? How easily I'm going to kill you? Or how slowly I'm going to do it? Landon taunted the vampire mentally as he curled his clawed hands in front of him and snapped his sharp teeth together for effect. *You never could catch me in the past, but you're welcome to try again.*

The vampire gave a low laugh, his evil smile displaying his sharp fangs. "The only difference with this new form is that I don't have to dive after you and roll around on the ground like a *dog*. We can battle as men."

Landon slowly shook his head. *No, the difference is…now you're* my *prey.*

The vampire sneered and launched across the ten-foot space between them, claws extended, fangs ready to rip Landon to shreds.

Landon caught the Sanguinas in the air. Curling his claws inward, he impaled them deeply into the muscle and sinew in the man's shoulders. The vampire howled in pain as Landon twisted his fingers. He jammed his talons into Landon's forearms, shredding the furred skin with his claws. Landon gritted his teeth from the pain and hurled the man over his head, slamming his body against the library's brick wall.

The vampire fell with a heavy thud to the asphalt, brick shards and mortar dust showering down around him. He growled and launched across the space once more, but Landon was ready. Slamming his fist into the vampire's angry face, Landon sent him back against the wall once more.

As he started toward the Sanguinas, police sirens sounded in the distance. Landon knew he had very little time to dispose of the vampires and get Kaitlyn to safety without being discovered himself.

Before the vampire could recover, he pounced and landed on the man's chest. Air whooshed from the bastard's lungs with Landon's weight. Landon grabbed the man's head and narrowed his gaze on him. *Much as I'd like to return every single bruise, laceration, fang and talon mark you've inflicted, lucky for you I've just run out of time. This is for Kaitlyn,* he said mentally before he gave a swift, snapping twist.

As soon as the vampire's heart ceased, Landon jumped into action, hauling both vampires to the center of the alley. He was damned glad it was an overcast night and the streetlights above them hadn't been replaced.

So far no humans had shown their faces. Then again, what human would dare enter a dark alley with the growling, snarling, howling sounds he and the vampires had made during their fight? But the police were minutes away.

Shifting back to his human form, Landon grabbed the keys Kaitlyn must have dropped during the vampires' attack and unlocked her car. He popped open her trunk and saw she had some long bungee cords in the back. Once he ripped the hooks off the ends of the cords and tossed the metal back into the trunk, he then opened her gas tank lid, where he quickly fed each of the cords' ends down into the gas tank. After he'd soaked several of them, he threw the gas-soaked bungee cords on top of the dead vampires.

Gathering Kaitlyn's unconscious form, he carefully laid her in her car's backseat and climbed into the front seat to start the car. He pushed the cigarette lighter into the on position and moved the car a safe distance away from the vampires.

With the car idling, Landon walked up to the vampires and held the end of the lighter's heated coil to one of the bungee cords. Flames immediately leaped upward, sending heat rushing to his face and across his bare chest.

Landon backed away and watched the fire quickly spread to the other bungee cords and the vampires' clothes.

The smell of burning flesh filled his nostrils as he made his way back to the car and climbed in the driver's seat. Before he drove out of the alley, he glanced in the rearview mirror. He would've preferred a more thorough disposing of the bodies, but the police would be there in a couple minutes.

Landon turned the car away from the sound of the sirens and headed toward the Shawangunk mountains. He didn't know if the vampires had tracked Kaitlyn or not, but when he had come upon them they'd seemed to be toying with her. His chest ached with the need to know if Kaitlyn was going to be okay. If not, his truce with Jachin would be completely and irrevocably severed, rogue vampires or not.

Chapter 7

Landon tensed when Kaitlyn fought against him as if she were still in the throes of a nightmare as he'd carried her into his home. She passed out again right before he laid her on his bed. Setting his nose against the pulse thudding on her throat he held his position and counted.

It was steady. She was going to live.

He shuddered with relief and sat back to survey the damage the vampires had inflicted on her body.

Her jacket and shirt were shredded. Blood coated the material stuck to her chest.

Her blood.

Landon sat on the bed next to her, and his hands shook with fury as he slowly unbuttoned the bottom half of the jacket and the rest of her shirt.

He lifted a long silver necklace that lay between her

breasts, surprised the delicate chain had survived unscathed when her clothes, and even her bra, hadn't.

A tiny silver wolf dangled from the end of the chain. Landon's jaw flexed. His self-imposed responsibility to protect Kaitlyn twisted his gut with guilt. He hadn't done such a great job tonight.

He set the long chain on the bed beside her neck and peeled her shirt away from her blood-caked skin. Her bra fell apart into two halves, taking with it newly formed scabs that had crusted over the four deep three-inch-long gouges between her breasts. Her wounds welled with blood once more.

The sight sent Landon over the edge. He let loose a long, bloodcurdling howl. The deep, soulful baritone shook the rafters and rattled the windows of his home.

Once he'd exhausted his lung capacity, he quickly pulled the rest of Kaitlyn's clothes off to make sure she didn't have any more injuries that needed attention. When he was done, only the four wounds on her chest screamed at him to heal them.

Landon stared down at Kaitlyn's wounds and did exactly what a wolf would do for a pack mate who was too weak to heal herself—a pack mate he cared deeply for. He lightly brushed his lips across her temple and then her slack lips before he moved his mouth over her wounds.

Landon's frame shook as he ran his tongue in a long lap across the first gouge. The torn flesh moving under his tongue, combined with the metallic flavor of her blood, sent a strange mix of emotions zinging through him.

She tasted like…

His.

Like a Lupreda. Landon sat back, puzzled at her taste. He pulled the clip out of her hair and ran his fingers through its soft strands. "Do I wish our union so much that I'm convincing myself that you're like me, my little wolf?" he whispered, his heart tugging.

As if in answer, one of the wounds on her chest began to fill with bright red blood, highlighting her human body's inability to heal itself.

His lips thinned in a grim line and he leaned toward her chest once more. "You are mine, no matter the blood that runs in your veins," he vowed before he ran his tongue across her new wound, sending werewolf healing saliva into her wounds.

Before he laved at Kaitlyn's last wound, Landon grunted in satisfaction that the other three deep gouges had already stitched closed. He was surprised to see scabs already forming but glad of it.

During his ministrations over Kaitlyn's wounds, Landon worked hard to keep his emotions at bay, those primal urges that demanded he had every right to run his lips along each sweet inch of her skin. His fingers itched to enjoy the soft mounds of her breasts, her hips and the appealing curve of her rear. But he forced his mindset to the important task before him and kept his sexual desires firmly buried.

With a soft groan full of deep-abiding love, he laved softly and gently over the last wound on her chest. Crawling up beside her on the bed, he ran his tongue along her temple, healing the gash there. He leaned close to her neck and closed his eyes to enjoy her scent and savor the remnants of her alluring taste on his tongue. He considered pulling on clothes, but her soft skin felt too good against his. He didn't want to leave her side for a second.

An hour later, Landon froze when she moaned and rolled her body fully toward him, pressing her soft breasts against him.

The sensation of her fingers spearing in his hair, along with the pressure of her hands tugging his head closer told him her actions were intentional.

His heart thumped at the languid look in her eyes, the sound of her heart rate kicking up and the distinctive smell of her growing arousal.

"I don't know why I'm naked in bed with you, why my body feels used and abused…and *not* in the way I'd like to be." She sighed tiredly and continued as she ran her hands down his neck, sending tremors rocking through his body. "But right now I don't want to think. You make me feel safe. I want to feel your mouth against my skin."

"You're injured—" he tried to say, but she pressed her fingers against his mouth.

"Shh. I'm alive. That's all that matters. Touch me, Landon." She arched closer, then winced and whispered almost to herself, "Love me."

You have no idea how much I want to, he thought. His stomach clenched painfully as his erection swelled to throbbing fullness in a matter of seconds. A low groan rumbled in his chest. His fingers tingled as he ran his hand along the soft curve of her hip. In as gentle a motion as he could, he pulled her close. Inhaling her arousing scent, he slid his nose slowly and with reverence along the swell of her breast until his lips brushed her nipple.

She tugged on his hair and begged in a demanding yet sweet tone, "Kiss me."

Landon ran his tongue around her nipple and exhaled his warm breath across the hard, pink tip. He reveled in the keening sounds of anticipation she made, the clenching need her fingers in his hair evoked.

He was surprised at how much patience he had with this woman, how much he wanted to draw out her pleasure, to make her squirm and writhe for his touch, his kiss, but Kaitlyn was having none of it.

She dug her nails into his scalp. "Stop teasing me. I'm done waiting."

Landon's entire body tensed in heated response to her demanding, sexy tone. He clasped his lips tightly around her nipple and sucked hard, loving her taste, her mewing response and the scent of her full-on arousal filling the air around them.

His nostrils flared and he gripped her hips, pulling her body fully under him.

Her swift gasp was a much-needed reminder of her injuries. He immediately put his weight on his elbows and settled his body between her sweet thighs as he moved his mouth to her other breast.

When he lavished the puckered nub with the same, loving attention, Kaitlyn traced her fingers to his shoulders and dug her nails deep. Arching her back, she pressed her wet sex against his stomach and moaned.

Landon's fingers flexed on her hips as he slid his lips to her belly and brushed a kiss against the soft skin. "I smell your desire," he growled against her belly. Her rapid heart beat thumped against his mouth, teasing him.

He fought the urge to roll her over, lift her hips and drive inside her body, deep and hard. "Spread your legs, Kaitie. I want to devour your sweet body and hear your screams when you come."

Kaitlyn tensed. She stopped panting and raised her head to stare at him. "I—I've never been able to have it that way," she stammered, color rising on her cheeks.

He gave her a feral smile. "You will with me." He might not have the privilege of being her first lover, but he would damned well make sure he was her best…and last lover.

Moving lower, he ran his nose along the soft tuft of red hair covering her sex. Inhaling deeply, he growled his pleasure at her musky, sweet smell. His mouth watered with the need to taste, to lave at her body and make her call out his name in ecstasy when she came.

All mine!

Kaitlyn ached all over, both physically and sexually. She'd never throbbed in need for another as much as she did for Landon. His handsome face and intense green eyes captured her attention, while his broad shoulders and muscular chest made her feel very puny in comparison.

She started to glance down at her wounds, but Landon barked, "No, look only at me."

Her gaze snapped to his, mesmerized by his loving gaze. The way he held himself above her, he made her feel cherished and protected, like his only goal was to please her. She never expected Landon to be such an attentive, gentle lover.

The man's eyes held secrets she'd yet to unveil, but his body and his sharp mind attracted her down to her toes.

"Lay back, Kaitie…and trust me to love you the right way."

Sexual tension arced in the air, sending invisible molten sparks zinging down her body.

Kaitlyn had just laid her head to the pillow when a hot, wet tongue swiped deeply between her folds, touching every crevice.

She arched and cried out, surprised at how quickly her body responded to the purposeful pressure of his tongue.

"Relax and open to me, sweetheart," Landon mumbled against her sex at the same time his big hands gripped her buttocks and he tilted her hips upward.

"I don't know if I ca-a-a-a-an-n," she started to answer when his tongue began to tease her sensitive nub in knowing, purposeful circles. Kaitlyn's heart thumped and her pulse rushed in her ears like ocean waves slamming against the shore.

Her legs began to tremble and her entire body shook as her approaching orgasm built in steadily increasing spirals of pleasure within her.

"Landon..." she said as her hips began to move, rocking in her need to finally achieve that elusive pinnacle that had always been just outside her reach.

The added friction of his tongue applying constant pressure caused pinpoints of pleasure to ripple through her, while tears of wonder spilled from her closed eyes.

"Give yourself to me," he demanded right before his mouth latched onto the ultra-sensitive bit of skin.

"I'm going to—"

"Come," she heard him say in a rough rumble right before he slid two fingers deep inside her body. His tongue rubbed against her sensitive nub and turned slightly rough—the new sensation was a euphoric drag, plucking screams of pleasure from her sensitized body.

Kaitlyn screamed long and hard as her body convulsed around Landon's thrusting fingers. Intense pleasure swept through her body in heated shock waves that splintered to the tips of her breasts, her fingers, her toes, while sparks zipped up and back down her spine. She felt taken and shaken to the core in every sense of the word.

She was so lost in her own plane of euphoria that she came back down to feel Landon's bruising grip on her buttocks as he thrust his tongue possessively inside her. The deep guttural groan he made when he withdrew his tongue and swallowed, then went back for more, both surprised and thrilled her on a deeply primal level. He acted as if her flavor was just as erotic and sinfully satisfying to him as her orgasm had been to her.

When he went back for a third taste, she asked, "Landon?"

Without removing his mouth from her body he glanced up, shocking her.

His eyes held a wildness she'd never seen before…so very different from the intense calmness she'd always seen reflected in his face.

The color was the lightest green, most arresting color she'd ever seen.

She started to speak when a loud crashing sound exploded from another room in the house.

Landon was off the bed and leaping over the banister at the edge of the room before she could sit up and pull the covers to her chest. Kaitlyn blinked and shook her head. *I'm losing it.* From what she could tell from her position on the bed, the room she was in was a loft level. Surely Landon hadn't just leapt to the second floor below.

Landon had shifted to his Musk mode by the time he landed on the floor below. He snarled at the intruder, who was also in Musk form, ready to rip him to shreds.

The black werewolf turned toward Landon and familiar hazel-green eyes stared at him. The feral grimace that was curling his muzzle smoothed out as he tilted his big head in a curious look. *You appear unharmed. I answered your call as soon as I could.*

Landon took in the deep claw marks on Caine's chest. The blood had already started to clot and the wounds close.

"Landon?" Kaitlyn called from above.

Grabbing hold of Caine's arm, he hauled his pack mate into the kitchen and shifted back to human form. "Everything's fine, Kaitlyn," he called upstairs, "It's just my overzealous baby brother."

By time he returned his gaze to Caine, the younger male had also shifted to human form. Pulling free of Landon's hold, Caine crossed his arms over his naked chest and lifted an eyebrow in an annoyed expression. "Baby brother?"

Landon frowned at him. "How the hell else am I going to explain you crashing into my home? Not to mention, you do have a tendency to act like one. You know better than to overuse your Musk form. You're too close to the line."

Caine's face hardened. "I rushed over here to help as soon as I could get away, and this is the thanks I get?"

Landon let out a heavy sigh, guilt riding him. Glancing at Caine's partially healed chest, he frowned. "What happened to you?"

The muscle in Caine's jaw jumped. "Nathan."

Landon's chest burned with anger and thoughts of revenge. "Why?"

"Because I tried to answer your Alpha call."

A sudden stillness rushed over Landon. "My Alpha call?"

"You know damned well you're the rightful Alpha of our pack. Nathan knows it, too. We heard the anger in your howl. Several pack members started to come to your aid. Nathan went ape, attacking and slashing out at every wolf who dared to respond. I have a feeling when I get back he'll try to cast me out of the pack."

Damn, he hadn't realized his Alpha tendencies went so deep as to resonate with his pack, especially from such a distance. "No, the hell he won't," Landon shot back.

Caine laughed and clapped Landon on the shoulder, his gaze sparkling in feral satisfaction. "You going to kick his ass again? If so, then getting kicked out will be worth the front row seat."

Landon grunted at Caine's steadfast support. How many of the other pack members would follow him if he challenged Nathan outside of the annual "run"?

"I'm sure your call will have stirred the Omega's interest in your progress on the zerkers."

Landon set his mouth in a thin line. "Noted."

Caine suddenly grinned. "Care to share how your 'anguished and angry' howl fits in with the scent of a woman that permeates your home and is radiating off you like you bathed in it?"

Landon narrowed his gaze. "She was attacked by vampires in the city."

Caine's eyes widened. "Is that why you were in your Musk form when I came in? To protect her?"

Landon rubbed the back of his neck, tension riding up his spine at Caine's reminder that he had business to take care of. "Yes." His certainty about Kaitlyn hit him hard, surprising him, but he continued in a serious tone, "She doesn't know yet, but I will claim her as my mate."

Caine's eyes widened, concern etching his brow. "A human? The pack would never accept a human as their Alpha's mate."

Landon knew Caine was right. "Then it's a good thing I'm not their Alpha."

"Your pack needs your leadership, Landon, especially with the vampires making their comeback. Does this woman accept what you are?"

Setting his jaw, Landon shook his head. "She didn't act fearful or treat me like a monster when she looked at me. I believe she passed out before she saw me in my Musk form."

"Surely she would've known something felt different when you had sex."

Landon set his jaw, but said nothing.

Caine raised his eyebrows and then laughed out loud. "Did I interrupt?"

"You could say that," Landon said in a dry tone.

"I would apologize, but I'm a selfish bastard." A stubborn expression settled on his face. "You are our rightful Alpha."

Caine's comment drew on the painful longing within him, but Landon wasn't going to give up Kaitlyn. Ever. The woman jacked him up on so many levels. He'd never enjoyed pleasuring another or reveled in her taste as much as he did with Kaitie. The thought of finally sinking inside her and making her his set his entire body on edge.

Landon rolled his neck to relieve the pent-up sexual tension riding him. "I'll get you some clothes. I want you to guard Kaitlyn while I give the Omega an update."

He started to walk away when Caine grabbed his arm. "I don't want you to go back without me."

Landon narrowed his eyes on Caine's hand, then met the younger wolf's steady stare. "Your job is to keep Kaitlyn safe."

Caine's jaw flexed and he released his hold. "Got it."

He knew Caine wasn't happy, but Caine saw him as Alpha and would do as he was told.

When he walked back upstairs, Kaitlyn stared at him with wide eyes, her grip on the sheet tight against her chest. "What was that all about?"

"Long story." He walked over to his dresser and pulled out a new pair of jeans. As he stepped into them, he said, "I need to go take care of something. Caine will stay here and keep you safe until I return. Don't worry, he'll stay downstairs."

"Landon…"

Her voice shook a little and he noted the deep wounds on her chest had been replaced by angry red marks. His gaze met hers. "Are you okay?"

She bit her lip and nodded. "Just really tired."

Landon grabbed more clothes for Caine and a shirt for himself before he walked over to the bed and hooked his finger under her chin, tilting her face up. He pressed his lips against hers, then met her hazel-blue gaze. "Rest for a while. I'll be back soon."

She lay back on the bed and closed her eyes, her voice tired. "I'll do that…just rest for a bit."

He waited until her breathing was even in sleep before he walked downstairs.

As soon as he left his cabin, Landon pulled his backup cell phone from his hip and dialed Jachin's number.

"Any news?" the vampire asked in a crisp voice.

"I killed two of your vampires a few hours ago." He quickly described the two Sanguinas in the alley. "Were these two some of your rogue vamps?"

"Yes. That was Tomias and Ren." Jachin's tone was clipped, edgy. "What happened?"

"They attacked a human."

"They were feeding on her?"

Jachin's question made Landon pause as he entered the dense forest in the direction of Lupreda territory. His cabin bordered the edge of Lupreda land. The vampires had seemed to be toying with Kaitlyn. "No, they weren't feeding on her when I got there."

"I'll let the Sweeper unit know that two of our rogues have been eliminated. From now on, I'll take care of my vampires."

"If they're attacking me or my own, they're fair game." Before Jachin could reply, Landon closed the cell phone with a quick snap.

A half hour later, Landon entered the Lupreda's main house and immediately sought out Garius. While he made his way down the long hall, Landon didn't smell Nathan's presence at all in the big mansion. That surprised him. After what Caine had just told him, he'd figured Nathan would stay close to home, with his weres acting like they might mutiny at any moment.

The idea of a mutiny made Landon smile as he pushed through the heavy oak double doors and entered the elaborate library with its wall-to-wall shelving full of old leather-bound books.

"Landon," Garius called out from his seated position in a plush reading chair near a tall front window. The thick book he was reading closed in his lap as he beckoned Landon forward with a sweeping motion. "I'm assuming you have news."

Landon approached the older man. Short, slightly graying black hair framed his round, deceivingly innocent-looking face. The man's meaty hands could crush a six-inch steel pipe as if it were a piece of aluminum foil. Garius was the most respected Omega for good reason.

Landon seated himself in a chair. "I came to report on our missing zerkers."

Garius raised a dark eyebrow. "You didn't come to calm the weres you stirred up with your call earlier?"

Landon met his challenging stare with an unrepentant one. "That wasn't my intent."

"You know that's as good as an open challenge to Nathan. He has never been able to command the entire pack that way." An amused smile lifted the corners of Garius's lips. "Ever."

Before Landon could respond, Garius cleared his throat and got right down to business. "What is your news on the zerkers?"

"Two of them are dead. One is still missing."

Garius's expression hardened. "What of the Sanguinas' involvement?"

Landon shook his head. "It wasn't the Sanguinas. One of the zerkers was left, quite literally, on the vampires' doorstep."

Garius grunted. "Do you know who's doing this? Who would have the ability to find the Sanguinas' territory when we haven't been successful?"

He had an idea, but it was just speculation. He had no definitive proof. "Not yet."

"But you have some thoughts." Garius's blue eyes narrowed.

Landon shrugged. "I think someone or something is trying to ignite a war between the Sanguinas and the Lupreda."

Stroking his stubbled chin, Garius said, "And they would've been successful if you and the Sanguinas' leader hadn't forged a truce."

"Where is Rourke? I smell the bastard!" Nathan's imperious voice reverberated throughout the huge mansion.

Landon jerked his narrowed gaze to Garius. "Do not allow Nathan to kick Caine out of the pack."

"Tell him yourself." The Omega smirked and waved his hand toward the door at the same time Nathan burst through it.

"What the hell are you doing back in my home?" Nathan snarled. The pulse on his temple jumped a threatening beat when he stopped in front of them.

Landon stood. "Your home, Nathan?" He glanced to the weres, who'd crowded the doorway the Alpha had just come through. "This home belongs to the pack, of which Caine is *still* a member."

Nathan's hands fisted by his sides and he shook with suppressed fury. "As much pleasure as it would bring me to kill you on the spot for daring to invade my home and dictate who is or isn't a member, I have pressing business that needs to be addressed." Jerking his head toward the doorway, he finished through clenched teeth. "Get out."

Landon could feel the emotions emanating from the group of Lupreda standing in the background. They reeked of anticipation. He'd never felt so much hyped-up adrenaline mixed with concern. Something was very wrong. "What business?" he said in a calm tone despite his desire to rip Nathan to shreds.

Nathan's upper lip curled back to reveal his teeth. "That's none of your concern—"

"The other Omega are here. Speak this business now, Nathan," Garius cut in, his tone commanding and intense.

Nathan whirled around to see the weres had separated to allow the five other Omega to enter the room. Jerking his gaze to Landon, he gritted out, "I won't discuss pack business with outsiders present."

"Speak!" Garius slammed his fist on his chair's arm.

Landon jerked his gaze to Garius. While it was true the Omega were a council made up of retired Alphas, he'd never seen an Omega pull rank before. It surprised the hell out of him.

Nathan gnashed his teeth. "Someone left one of our zerkers on the edge of our property. His body was partially burned."

"Someone?" Garius raised an eyebrow.

Nathan's narrowed gaze darted between Landon and Garius. Landon could tell the Alpha truly wanted him gone. Dead would be preferable, he was certain. Nathan's news made his stomach knot. He knew what this meant. The Alpha would blame the vampires.

"The Sanguinas." Nathan spat, his tone spewing hatred and revenge.

"You smelled vampires?" Landon asked.

Nathan glanced at the group of weres watching their exchange. He cut his gaze to Landon. "Yes."

The son of a bitch would throw them into a war with the vampires all for what? The need to show his leadership?

"You're lying," Landon snarled. Rage sent his claws to the tips of his fingers, a stinging sensation rippling across every fingertip. A firm hand clamped down on Landon's shoulder before he could leap for Nathan's throat.

"Are the other zerkers unharmed?" Garius asked in a calm tone beside Landon as the five Omega formed a half circle behind Nathan.

Landon slid his questioning gaze to the pack's very first Alpha. Garius *knew* what had become of the other zerkers.

Nathan glanced behind him at the other Omega, then locked gazes with Garius. "We couldn't find the other zerkers. I don't believe they're unharmed."

"Until we find the others, who might shed some light on what happened, I believe it's not in the best interest of the pack to go after the vampires at this time." Glancing at the men behind Nathan, Garius continued, "Do the rest of the Omega agree?"

"We agree," Markson said, while the other four men nodded their assent.

Kaitlyn awoke with a jerk. As she stared at the white ceiling with exposed dark beams, it took her a second to remember where she was.

Landon's home. Which was *where* exactly?

She'd tried to get out of bed earlier when Landon had jumped over the handrail that led to the bottom floor, but dizziness had made spots form in her vision. She'd ended up falling back into bed and closing her eyes to overcome the spinning sensation in her head. She had briefly spoken to Landon, but the conversation was fuzzy. Something about his brother was all she remembered.

She let her eyes drift shut and tried to recapture her slumberous dreams. They'd been filled with Landon. She was locked in his embrace, begging him to make love to her. The euphoria faded from her mind, along with the dream. Rolling onto her side, she pressed her face into the soft, cotton pillow beside her and inhaled Landon's musky, masculine scent.

A light came on in the room below hers, filtering upstairs. Kaitlyn looked at her watch. Five-thirty. Was that a.m. or p.m.? *How long have I been out?* Her body screamed in protest as she turned to stare out the big picture window into the night sky. Ugh, she didn't want to think about the bruises her body must be sporting.

Kaitlyn gasped when everything came flooding back and she remembered her chest had been wounded by one of the vampires. Lifting the thick covers, she glanced down at her chest to see four barely perceptible pink marks where open wounds had been only hours before. "How did I heal so quickly?" she murmured, her brow furrowing in confusion.

"You're a fast healer?" A man's voice offered an answer.

Her attention jerked to the edge of the room. Kaitlyn grabbed the covers to her chest, her heart rate speeding up. "Who are you?" Reaching over to the bedside lamp, she fumbled with the switch and turned it on.

The man with pitch-black hair appeared to be in his late twenties. He leaned casually against the wall at the top of the stairs. "I'm Caine, Landon's younger brother," he said with an open, friendly smile as he folded his muscular arms across a New York Giants football shirt. Jeans and bare feet completed his casual look.

Feeling very exposed, Kaitlyn pulled the covers tighter around her chest. "Where's Landon?"

"He had to run an errand. He wanted me to stay and keep you safe." Tilting his head, Caine continued, "I heard you tangled with a couple of vampires."

She frowned. "More like they hunted and attacked me."

His eyebrows drew downward and he pushed off the doorjamb. "They hunted you?"

Nodding, she leaned back against the headboard. "From the time I walked into the library. One of them noticed me and waited for me to leave. They both attacked me in the alley where I'd parked my car. Then Landon came along and…I guess I passed out." Her brow furrowed as she tried to remember. She shook her head in amazement. "I don't know how he got me out of there without being torn to shreds himself."

Caine's smile turned smug. "My brother is very protective of those he cares about. I'm not at all surprised he came out unscathed."

"Even from vampires?" she asked, but Caine's comment warmed her all over, bringing back the memory of the amazing time she'd spent with Landon before she'd fallen asleep. It had been real, not some fanciful dream. Landon had shown her how much her body craved his…on the deepest level. Her body rang with the remembered passion.

When Caine's smile broadened as if he knew exactly what she was thinking, Kaitlyn's face burned. Running her hand through her messy hair, she said, "Um, how about I meet you downstairs once I get a shower."

After Kaitlyn showered, she tried to find her clothes and discovered them in the washing machine. Once she switched them to the dryer, she rifled through Landon's chest of drawers. Every pair of pants she tried on fell to her ankles, even his elastic-waisted lounge pants. Giving up, she shrugged into a white T-shirt that tugged at her heart a little when she read the bold black lettering on the front: Lone Wolf. She remembered Landon's comment about not feeling like he really fit in. As the large shirt fell to just above her knees, she inhaled his masculine scent and was surprised by the sense of belonging that washed over her.

She took in his loft cabin home with its contrasting white ceiling and dark beams and found it very welcoming. The bedroom, decorated in masculine browns and a gorgeous hand-carved wood bed frame, fit Landon's strong person-ality perfectly. Stepping over to the large picture window, she drew back the heavy drapes fully and gasped when she saw the mountainous outline of trees that went on for miles. Where exactly was she?

How had Landon not broken a leg or at least sprained something? she wondered as she walked down the carpeted staircase. Passing a painting of a wolf standing in the woods, howling at a full moon, she smiled when she saw Landon's living room was sparsely but warmly decorated. A large soft leather couch and side chair took up most of the room, while a soft area rug decorated the wood floor next to the couch, and a matching one was laid out in front of the stone fireplace across the room.

Sitting on the mahogany end table beside the couch, a stone wolf faced toward the front door as if waiting to scru-tinize any new guests who might enter the cabin.

She followed the strong, delicious aromas of bacon and coffee through the living room and down the hall toward the kitchen, where she stopped briefly in front of the wooden wolf statue sitting in the corner next to the kitchen doorway. As tall as her hips, the animal had been intricately carved out of a tree trunk. He sat in a regal pose on his haunches. Serious eyes stared right at her as if he were deciding whether or not to let her enter. "Nice doggie." She smiled and patted his head before walking into the kitchen.

"You like dogs?" Caine leaned back against the counter and lifted his coffee cup to his lips.

"Yes, though I don't own one myself. You'd think I'd have had one growing up as much as my father seemed to love wolves." She laughed and swept her arm back toward the living area of the house. "Like Landon, he had them everywhere in our home. That coffee smells divine. Got any more?"

Caine's gaze lingered on her T-shirt and his expression tightened before he turned to retrieve a coffee cup from the cabinet. Filling a mug with the rich brew, he said, "Have a seat."

Kaitlyn pulled out a spindle-style chair and sat down at the small, round wooden table.

Once he'd handed her the coffee cup, Caine then set a plate of eggs and bacon in front of her. "You should eat to regain your strength."

"Thanks for the food." She smiled her appreciation. When her stomach began to rumble at the wonderful smells wafting from her plate, she picked up a piece of bacon and bit into it.

Caine took another swallow of his coffee and locked his curious hazel gaze on her. "Why do you think the vampires attacked you?"

She shrugged and sipped her coffee. "They're vampires. Enough said." Though in truth, the vampires did seem to relish attacking her, as if they expected her to put up a good fight. "Speaking of which—" She glanced past the cherry cabinets to the walls in the kitchen, looking for a phone. She remembered she'd lost her cell phone in the alley. "I didn't see a phone in the bedroom. Is there one down here? I need to call the incident in. The police should be alerted that the vampires have returned."

"Those vampires won't be bothering anyone else," Landon's voice sounded from behind her.

Kaitlyn glanced his way, her heart jerking in surprise. She didn't hear him come in. "Law enforcement needs to be on guard, considering the Garotters are too busy stealing guns to help. That is *if* hunting vampires is still their main mission."

Landon walked into the kitchen and poured himself a cup of coffee. Leaning against the stove, his penetrating green gaze met hers. "The vampires are gone, Kaitlyn."

The man might look mouth-watering with his brown hair wind-tossed and an overnight beard shadowing his jaw, but she recognized the challenge in his eyes—the one that said, "It's over. Leave it alone."

Kaitlyn cupped her fingers around the warm ceramic mug on the table and met his gaze with a steady one. She wanted to argue with him, but since Caine was present she swept her gaze over Landon's body and asked the question that had been on her mind since she'd woken up. "I don't see a mark on you. How did you take out the vampires without being attacked yourself?"

"Yeah, bro. How'd you do that?" Caine echoed, turning to Landon, an expectant expression on his face.

Landon slitted his gaze on the younger were. "It's time you went home."

Caine's amused expression turned somber. "I can't."

Locking gazes with Caine, Landon's voice turned harsh. "Yes, you can. Now go."

With a grin of appreciation, Caine set his cup down and walked over to Kaitlyn. Grasping her hand, he bent and brushed his lips against her knuckles. "It was nice to meet you, Kaitlyn. Don't let my brother intimidate you…" Caine paused and cast his gaze back to him.

Landon mentally growled in Caine's mind, the wolf within him staking his claim.

Caine returned his attention to her and continued, "His bark is worse than his bite…well, mostly."

"Caine," Landon warned.

Kaitlyn laughed and smiled at Caine. "It was nice to meet you, too. You're more laid-back than—" she cut her eyes to Landon briefly "—your brother."

Jealousy fisted in Landon's gut that Caine seemed to have won Kaitlyn over.

Caine flashed him a winning smile, then glanced at Kaitlyn's shirt with a pointed look. "Nice T-shirt. I've never seen that one."

Landon gritted his teeth, resisting the urge to pick the were up by his pants and toss him out of his cabin on his ass. Instead, he growled low in his throat. To Kaitlyn it would sound like a grunt, but he knew Caine would recognize the sound for what it was—a command to get the hell out.

"Gotta go. See ya later, bro," Caine said before he strolled out of the kitchen.

Once the front door shut behind him, Kaitlyn turned to Landon. "Your younger brother's sweet…though his looks are different from yours—much darker. Do you favor your father or your mother?"

Landon grabbed a piece of bacon from the pan. Leaning back against the stove once more, he bit the crunchy meat and responded to her question automatically. "I don't have any parents."

Her interested expression turned regretful. "I'm sorry to hear that. You lost both your parents?" she asked as she scooped up a forkful of eggs.

The bacon lodged in his throat at her interpretation of his flippant comment. He felt so comfortable around Kaitlyn, he hadn't thought to censor his response to her question. Considering he'd come from a petri dish, he'd told her the truth. Landon choked the piece of food down and coughed to clear his throat. "Yes, both of them are gone."

A sad, faraway look crossed her face as she chewed on a piece of bacon. "I lost my dad when I was six. My mom is in the hospital, dying of cancer. I guess that'll make me an orphan, too."

Kaitlyn's innocent comments jammed the knife of guilt even deeper into his chest, reminding him what he'd forgotten while loving on her sweet body a couple hours ago—humans were so fragile.

"Even after they're gone, your parents will live on in your heart." He'd said that as if he knew what he was talking about. Jachin and Ariel would soon have a child—the first mixed-race Scions' descendant. He wanted to understand the parent-child bond he'd witnessed only in humans. He believed it must feel very much the way he felt for every single were in his Lupreda pack—strong love and even stronger responsibility for their well-being. But committing himself to Kaitlyn pretty much assured that would never happen. As much as he wanted to, he couldn't have sex with her. He didn't think he could hold his rougher side back while he drove inside her and felt her body convulse around his cock.

"Finish your food," he said in a gruff tone, then picked up another piece of bacon and walked out of the kitchen.

Chapter 8

Kaitlyn stared after Landon's retreating back. *What was that about?* she wondered. He'd said something very meaningful and profound about her parents and then bam—he'd turned cold on her and walked out of the room.

The smell of a newly built fire drew her out of the kitchen. Dawn was breaking the sky as she walked into the living room. Landon stood next to the fireplace, leaning against the mantel. He stared into the fire as if he were thinking deeply about something. Even though they'd been intimate a couple hours before, Kaitlyn didn't know what to say to Landon. He acted so distant now.

"I wanted to thank you for helping in the alley last night." When he didn't speak, she tilted her head and continued, "You never did say how you managed to get me out of there."

Landon met her gaze. "I took them by surprise."

She shook her head, trying to remember, but it was all so

fuzzy. "You took out two vampires? You had to have taken them completely unaware to have come out of that fight unscathed."

Landon picked up the poker and jabbed at the logs on the fire, moving them around to keep the flame going. His biceps flexed with his movements. "Sandra called and told me where you were and that you were trying to get in touch with me." He set the poker back in the stand. "What did you want to talk to me about?"

Kaitlyn rubbed her arms, glad for the fire's warmth in the cool room. With the vampires' attack, she'd forgotten about the reason she'd called Landon. She hoped he would finally tell her the truth now that they'd connected on a more intimate level.

"My mother never gave me many details about my father's death when I was a child, so I was at the library researching what had happened."

Landon's eyes snapped to hers. "What did you need from me?"

Tension knotted her stomach, but she plunged on. "My father was attacked and killed in Morningside Park."

"I know there's more coming." Landon crossed his arms and waited for her response.

She spread her arms wide. "Don't you see the connection? Maybe whatever was burned the other day in the park was the same creature who mauled my father. We both know the Tacomi case connects to the case in the park. You didn't want me pursuing it, saying it was too dangerous. I want to know what you're not telling me. Who or what was strong enough to overcome and burn that thing in the park the other night?"

His jaw flexed. "As of last night, we know not all vampires are extinct." He left the implication hanging between them.

Vampires were known for their strength and speed, but the

thing's aura she saw in the park hadn't been a vampire. It had hardly resembled the human form. "Whatever was burned, it wasn't a vampire. I want to know what it was."

"Isn't the fact you were almost killed by a couple of vampires enough?" he roared as he jammed his hand through his hair.

She could see she wasn't getting any answers from him. *So much for intimacy bringing us closer together,* she thought with a mental snort of anger. "Fine. You don't want to be straight with me and tell me what you know. I'm out of here."

"Kaitlyn."

She ignored him and started to head toward the stairs when she realized she didn't know where Landon's house was…only that it was in the mountains. Swiveling back to face him, she grumbled, "Where the hell am I, anyway?" The swift movement cost her. Her head began to spin and her vision blur.

Landon caught her before she hit the floor. "Easy, Kaitie," he said in a soft tone and he lifted her against his chest. "You were attacked by vampires." He carried her toward the couch. "You need more rest."

He smelled so damned good, her head swam. "My chest burned during the attack," she mumbled against his shoulder, her mind groggy. "I thought the wounds would be worse, but they're just pink scars."

"You still suffered trauma." He sat down on the couch and stretched out on his back, pulling her on top of him. The sensation of his hard chest behind her back and muscular arms around her waist felt good, like a strong, warm security blanket. Or was it his lips, brushing against her temple that relaxed her?

"Maybe I'll rest for a bit longer," she sighed. The fight went out of her when she turned her nose toward his throat and inhaled. She couldn't get enough of his masculine smell.

Landon's thumb rubbed back and forth along her ribs, setting a leisurely, comforting pace. While the fire crackled and popped in the background and his body heat cocooned her back in toasty warmth, Kaitlyn knew they still had issues to deal with, but she was too wiped to argue. For now, she burrowed closer, allowing herself to fully relax until her eyes drifted closed.

Kaitlyn awoke to the sound of Landon's heavy breathing in her ear. The fire had died down and the sun had changed direction across the room, telling her she'd slept for quite a while. Underneath her back, Landon's chest rose and fell at a harsh rate. He was dreaming. She turned her face into his throat, and his pulse beat a rapid staccato against her nose, making her own heart race. He held his cards so close to his chest, yet she still wanted to comfort him. She wished she understood the strange connection she felt with this man.

She pictured Landon loving on her, making her scream like he had earlier that day and excited chill bumps formed on her skin. Biting her lip, she pressed her thighs together to assuage the ache that centered within her. She wanted to feel the weight of his body on top of her, to inhale his arousing scent, feel his strength as his big hands touched her everywhere. She wanted to catch her breath and hold it as he slid inside her—hard and deep.

Running her fingers up Landon's muscular thigh, Kaitlyn squirmed closer while she curled her other hand around his warm neck.

Landon's breathing had leveled off. She smiled and slid her hand higher up the soft denim.

With each inch her fingers drew closer, she felt his erection harden and swell underneath her buttocks.

When her wandering hand had almost reached the edge of his erection, she realized Landon's chest was perfectly still…as if he were no longer breathing.

As soon as the tips of her fingers ran along the side of his rock-solid shaft, Kaitlyn heard a low rumbling growl a split second before she found herself on her hands and knees on the soft carpet beside the couch.

Landon's fingers encircled her wrists, while his muscular body covered hers; his chest to her back, his hips to her buttocks, his thighs surrounding hers.

Her pulse skyrocketed at the lightning change in their location; the sheer primal position. He'd moved so fast, her head spun.

She froze, unsure what to do. She'd never felt so exposed or so turned on in her life.

When Landon pushed his knee against her inner thigh, silently telling her to spread her legs, her heart slammed against her chest and her breathing changed to rapid pants.

As soon as she moved her thigh, his grip on her wrists tightened and he pushed her hands forward on the carpet several inches. Kaitlyn's sex throbbed and she dug her nails into the carpet as she waited for Landon's next move.

His fingers cinched tight around her wrists and he took a long, drawn-out inhaling breath as he ran his nose along her shoulder, then up her neck. His warm breath bathed the back of her ear and he whispered in a husky tone, "You have no idea how very breakable you are."

She pushed her hips back against him in wanton invitation. "I'm ready to find out."

Landon reacted, hitching his hips forward against her at the same time he let out a feral snarl and clamped his teeth on the soft spot between her neck and her shoulder.

He didn't bite down. He just held her in place, unmoving and dominant.

Kaitlyn found Landon far more earthy and primal than she'd expected. She couldn't believe how much this "still waters run deep" facet to his personality tripped her trigger. She didn't fear him. Instead, she hoped he'd release her soon so she could move against him.

When his breathing rushed through his nose in harsh gusts and a slight tremor skidded across his body above hers, she vaguely realized he was holding himself back, trying to calm down.

She didn't want him to be calm, dammit. She wanted—

Before she could finish the thought, Landon released her and stood.

Kaitlyn flipped her hair over her shoulder and sat down on her butt to face Landon. He stood by the window, staring out, his hands deep in his jean pockets.

"Your shirt and jacket are a total loss, but your jeans are clean," he said in a dull tone without looking at her.

"Landon—"

"You can keep the shirt. Get dressed and I'll take you home," he cut her off.

His rejection didn't sit well with her, but she'd be damned if she'd beg for a reason for his hot-and-cold behavior. Rolling to her feet, Kaitlyn stood. "If you drove me here in my car, then I'll drive myself home."

He finally met her gaze. "We're in the Shawangunk ridge, Kaitlyn. I don't relish walking back to town."

It was on the tip of her tongue to tell him that's exactly what he was going to do, but common decency prevailed over hurt feelings. He *had* saved her life. Chest aching, she turned and walked upstairs to change clothes.

* * *

Once Kaitlyn disappeared from view at the top of the stairs, Landon pulled his shaking hands out of his pants pockets and flexed and unflexed his fists to help regain control over his desire to go after her.

When he'd woken to her sexy body squirming all over him, while her hand slid up his leg and her arousal filled his senses, Landon had been dreaming of his fight with the vampires over Kaitlyn. He lost complete control.

Before he knew what he was doing, he had her in a Lupreda mating position. Her smell had been the final straw. He clamped his teeth on her skin, holding her still, while the desire to mark her roared through his thoughts.

At that moment, the wolf had taken over. His senses were keener. He heard her thudding heart, smelled her readiness for him. The arousing scent wreaked havoc with his human mind, making it difficult to think, to rationalize. She might not be Lupreda, but his reaction to her attraction, to her scent, was one-hundred percent wolf.

That thought was what knocked some sense into his brain, allowing him to unlock his hold on her body and walk away. His wolf had taken control, and if he followed his natural instincts, he couldn't guarantee he wouldn't hurt her.

He glanced through the window at the late afternoon sun shining through the trees and breathed a sigh of relief that it hadn't been evening when she'd touched him. The moon was nearing its full cycle and its lunar pull, calling to his inner wolf, might've been more than he could fight. He regretted losing the bullet and necklace in the alley during his fight with the vampires. Over the years, he'd gotten used to the forced restraint that kept him from shifting.

Kaitlyn was too important to him. He either needed to find or replace the damn necklace, or he'd have to distance himself from Kaitlyn for a few days until the moon receded.

An hour later, Kaitlyn turned her car off the highway onto a side road. Landon raised his eyebrows. "Taking the scenic route back to town?"

That was the first thing he'd said to her the whole trip. She tried not to let it bother her, but all she could think about the entire time they drove in silence was *why* Landon refused to trust her enough to tell her what he knew. And he *did* know something about the burning at Morningside Park. "Just killing two birds with one stone," Kaitlyn replied as she took an immediate left onto a dirt road.

"You drive these back roads often?" Landon asked as her car thumped over several potholes in the road.

"Only when I'm visiting an old family friend." Once Kaitlyn reached the gravel portion of Hank's driveway, she revved the engine and pulled into a spot beside Hank's beat-up truck. Putting her vehicle in park, she said, "You can wait in the car. I'm just picking something up."

As soon as she opened the door on her side, Landon did the same on his. She narrowed her gaze at him across the car's roof.

He shrugged. "I'm not good at sitting around."

"Typical man," she murmured and closed her car door.

"Kaitie, my girl," Hank called as he walked out of his cabin, the screen door slamming behind him.

Kaitlyn ran up the porch and hugged the stocky man with thinning gray hair. Hank gave her a bear hug and patted her back. "It's great to see you after so long." Glancing past her, he jerked his salt-and-pepper beard toward her car. "I take it you aren't staying for a bit. Who's your friend?" Hank squinted.

She cast her gaze over her shoulder. Landon leaned his tall frame against the side of her car, his arms crossed over his chest.

Returning her attention to Hank, she gave him a half smile. "That's Landon Rourke. You might've run across him at the station. He's a P.I. who has helped the police work cases in the past."

"Ah." Hank nodded, his brown eyes flitting to her over-sized T-shirt then back to Landon. "I knew he looked familiar." Rubbing his chin, he continued, "I take it you're here for your dad's stuff."

"I am. I was in the area so I thought I'd swing by and pick it up."

Hank's gaze narrowed. "Rourke live around here?"

She nodded. "About an hour away."

Hank started to pull the screen door open, then paused. "Don't you think your boyfriend should live closer to you? You know…in town?"

"Hank!" She hoped Landon hadn't heard Hank's question. "He's not—"

"He's a bit old for you, isn't he?"

She found the sixteen-year difference in their ages exciting. Landon came across as someone who'd "been there, done that." So many guys she'd dated were still immature boys in a lot of ways. Landon Rourke was *all* man. Kaitlyn straightened her spine. "Who I choose to date is up to me."

He nodded. "I know, I know, but with your dad gone, I can't help but ask these fatherly questions."

Kaitlyn smiled at him. "I'm fine, Hank, really. Landon's just a colleague."

Hank's gaze dropped to her T-shirt once more. "Uh-huh."

"Oh, for Pete's sake. It's a long story."

Hank smirked. "I'm retired. I've got all the time in the world."

Kaitlyn set her lips. She didn't need an interrogation about a man who set her blood on fire one moment only to distance himself from her the next. He ran so hot and cold, she wanted to scream in frustration. "The box, Hank."

"Right. Be back in a sec."

A couple minutes later, he returned with a two-feet-by-one-foot box. Setting it in her arms, he said, "This is all his stuff. I didn't rummage through it. Your dad liked his privacy."

Kaitlyn hefted the box closer to her chest. "Thanks. I'll make sure to put it with the rest of my dad's things."

As she neared her car, Landon approached and took the box out of her arms. "You want to put it in the back?"

Kaitlyn nodded. She didn't want to talk. Hank's probing questions made her realize just how much she wanted a relationship with Landon, which was insane, considering how little he seemed to trust her. She respected his intellect and his keen instincts, not to mention the man had just saved her life, but it bothered her that he kept so closely to himself. He certainly knew all *her* dark secrets.

As she watched Landon load the box into the back of her vehicle, she couldn't help but stare at the sun glinting off his short, light brown hair, appreciate his strength as his arm muscles flexed with his movements and admire how well his faded jeans fit his nice butt. She gave a sigh of frustration, then moved to the driver's side and climbed in her car.

During the drive to town, Landon stayed quiet, giving her plenty of time to think about them. They might have trust issues, but god she wanted this man with a level of fierceness that should've scared her. Instead, it only excited her. She knew her conclusion was irrational. When it came to Landon, she was quickly learning that her emotions weren't driven by logic, but instead, they sprang from an earthier, more fundamental source she couldn't explain.

Once Kaitlyn's car rolled to a stop in front of Landon's apartment complex, he got out and shut the door. Leaning into the window, a sexy smile tugged at his lips. "Thanks for driving your old-as-dirt boyfriend back to town."

Heat rushed her cheeks. Damn, he'd heard the entire conversation. She gripped the steering wheel while pent-up frustration fueled her response. "Boyfriend?" She shook her head. "You walked away and left me wanting. I thought older men knew better. Let me know when you decide to grow up."

Chapter 9

Kaitlyn's answering machine blinked as she carried her father's box of stuff into the office. She squatted and set the box down beside the couch, then winced when a hard, jabbing sensation pinched the top of her leg. Standing, she quickly dug her hand into her right jeans pocket to find the culprit and withdrew a silver chain with a mashed bullet slug dangling from it. She'd forgotten she'd stuffed Landon's chain in her pocket before she'd passed out.

Turning the bullet slug, she noted some etchings along the surface that looked like letters. She held the metal up to the light and squinted, trying to decipher them, but they were warped and distorted by the bullet's mangled shape.

With a sigh, she lifted the chain over her head and let it drop around her neck. She'd give the necklace back to Landon the next time she saw him.

Before she checked her messages, the headline in the

newspaper she'd brought in caught her eye: The Vampires Are Back! She quickly scanned the article. Amid the hype, it said that two vampires' burned bodies had been discovered in the alley next to the library and that the local police had contacted the government for help. *Where did the new Garotter regime fit in?* she wondered as she picked up the phone and dialed her cell phone provider. The last thing she needed was a five-hundred-dollar cell phone bill because some bozo had found her phone and gone crazy with it.

After she'd asked them to suspend her cell phone service until she could either retrieve her phone or let them know it was stolen, the answering machine's two blinking messages drew her over to the credenza. Kaitlyn pressed the play button.

"Hey, girl," Abby said in a chipper voice. "You've been quiet lately. I called your cell and didn't hear back, so I'm leaving you a message here, too. How'd your haunted house date with Mr. Hottie go? Hmm? Call me."

"Hot and cold," she mumbled and waited for the next message to play.

"I told you I'd keep you in the loop on the subject we discussed," Ron's voice came across the machine. "We're on tonight. Check your cell. I might be sending some images your way as a backup. More than likely we won't need them if tonight's the night and this bust goes down the way it should, but I grew up in Boy Scouts. What can I say...it's ingrained."

As the line went dead and the answering machine whirred to a stop, Kaitlyn was already on her telephone, dialing Ron's cell.

It rang but went straight to voice mail. "Ron, I got your message. Call me," she said, then hung up.

Kaitlyn nibbled her bottom lip and stared at the answering machine, wondering if Ron had sent anything to her cell phone. And she'd just suspended it! Not that any of that mattered if she didn't have the phone, anyway. She'd lost it when the vampire had tossed her across the alley. She had to find her cell phone.

After she quickly changed into a new set of clothes, Kaitlyn grabbed her keys and purse and then headed out the front door.

It was dark by the time Kaitlyn parked down the road from the alley near the library. She shivered and glanced out her window, half expecting more fanged vampires to jump out from behind another parked car.

Checking that her gun was securely snapped to her hip, she grabbed her flashlight and got out of her car. Her steps slowed as she neared the alley. Yellow crime scene tape that had cordoned off the area now hung limply at the sides of the buildings.

Trying not to dwell on the thought of what had happened to her the night before, she turned on her flashlight and swiftly moved the beam of light back and forth along the alley. Between the teenage punks, the homeless, the police and fire-fighters that went through this area yesterday, she'd be lucky if she found her phone. Still she had to try.

There were a few parked cars blocking her view of the roadside. Kaitlyn walked behind the first car and squatted, sweeping her flashlight under the car.

Nothing.

She crawled on her hands and knees to the next car and flashed her light underneath it. Someone yelled and Kaitlyn's heart jumped in her chest. Her free hand went to her gun, hovering on the snap that held it in place.

"I want my beer back, you prick," a teenaged kid snarled in anger somewhere down the road.

Kaitlyn let out a sigh of relief and returned to her search. Hamburger wrappers blocked her view and she used the end of the flashlight to move the paper.

Still nothing.

She was just about to get up from her hands and knees position and move to the next car, when someone peered around the car's front end. He was crouching on the same level with her.

Kaitlyn let out a small yelp. Glaring at Landon, she leaned on one hand and shone the light into his face with her other. "What are you doing here?"

Landon's green gaze locked on the bullet swinging back and forth around her neck. "I lost my necklace the other night. I hoped I'd be able to find it."

Feeling like an idiot, Kaitlyn quickly stood and lifted the necklace off her neck. "I crawled over it last night and recognized it as yours. I tucked it in my pocket before I passed out," she said as put the necklace in his hand.

When he clasped his fingers tightly around the chain, she asked, "Why *do* you wear a bullet around your neck?"

He took a step closer and slid his finger down the V of her sweater and along her cleavage. She gasped at his intimate touch and was taken by surprise when he lifted her necklace and dangled the silver wolf in front of her. "Why do you wear a howling wolf around yours?"

She pulled the necklace and charm off his finger. "It was a present from my father."

"Me, too," he said with an almost regretful look as he lowered his necklace over his head to lie against his khaki T-shirt.

His father had given him a spent bullet? How bizarre. Maybe they'd hunted together or something.

"Why are you here?" he asked.

"I'm looking for my cell phone. I lost it out here some-where when I was attacked."

Landon's jaw tensed. "I'll help you look for it. It's not a good idea for you to be hanging around dark alleys by yourself."

As they both circled around the third car and squatted to peer underneath it, Landon said, "I highly doubt your cell's still here. If the fire hoses and clean-up crew didn't sweep it up, then some locals might've taken it. I hope you've reported it stolen."

"I did, earlier." Crap. She hadn't thought about the deluge of water that had probably swamped the alley last night.

"Nope, not seeing anything," Landon said as he straight-ened to his full height.

Kaitlyn stood up and moved to the center of the alley. Sweeping the flashlight across the asphalt once more, she thought about Landon's earlier comment about the fire hoses.

Her flashlight followed the street's natural decline. When she saw the leaves and trash clogging the storm drain at the end, she ran over to the drain and began to push the gunk out of the way with the toe of her shoe.

Her light reflected off a splash of silver and Kaitlyn pushed more leaves and trash out of the way with her shoe until she saw the edge of her cell phone.

Bending, she quickly lifted the cell phone and cast Landon a triumphant smile. "Found it."

"For all the good it'll do you." Landon came to a halt next to her and chuckled as water dripped down the side of the phone.

"The leaves could've protected it. I might get lucky." She flipped open the phone and tried to turn it on. Nothing. It was deader than dead. Now what was she going to do?

"You can always buy another one."

"No. I need *this* phone," she said and snapped the phone shut.

"I get the feeling this is about more than a dead cell phone. What's wrong?"

Kaitlyn's gaze snapped to his. A concerned expression had settled on his face. How dare he act like he cared. She wanted to shake him for being the nice guy, for being there for everything but *them*.

He didn't trust her enough to tell her what he knew, yet he expected her to share with him? But the truth was, she had no one else to talk to. Landon had proven he could keep secrets. He already knew about her Tacomi case and he wasn't involved with the force, so she could trust he wasn't the mole. She rubbed her forehead, trying to decide what she should tell him. *Damn, how'd all this get so complicated?*

Landon's finger tilted her chin up. He'd moved closer, his tall frame and warmth invading her personal space. "What's wrong, Kaitie? I want to help if I can."

It was dim in the alley but she could still see the sincere look on his face. His earthy scent, mixed with the smell of his leather jacket, teased her senses. When he called her Kaitie…the intimate name made her skin prickle in response.

Kaitlyn started to speak but Landon's lips met hers, cutting off her words. His kiss was reverent and slow as if he wanted to savor the way she tasted. It was the kind of kiss, full of banked intensity, that made her knees threaten to give way.

When he ended their kiss, his smile was tender yet his eyes held an amused glint. Glancing down at her hands, she realized that in the throes of his mind-numbing kiss, she'd gripped his coat lapels with the flashlight and cell phone still in her hands and pulled him closer.

Her fingers quickly uncurled from his jacket and she

smoothed the crumpled leather. "Um, sorry. I don't know what came over me. I—"

Landon's knuckles brushed her cheek and he lifted a strand of her hair, slowly winding the wavy red lock around his finger. Admiration reflected in his eyes. "You have to admit…we make a great team."

She wasn't sure if he was referring to them on a professional level or a personal one, but she did know she trusted his honest offer to help.

Nodding, she stepped away to regain some control of her jumbled thoughts and emotions. Landon always threw them into chaos whenever he went all "hot" on her. She didn't want to get caught up in his heat again only to be on the receiving end of a rejection once more.

"I don't want to discuss it here. Follow me to my house and I'll fill you in."

By the time Kaitlyn reached her house, her hormones were calmer and she was able to think clearly. Landon drove up behind her and followed her inside.

When he started to speak, she held up her finger and indicated he should follow her to her home office. Kaitlyn pushed the replay button on her answering machine and backed away to lean against the desk while she waited for Ron's message to play, but Abby's message came up first.

Abby talked so fast, she was already at the part where she asked about Mr. Hottie. Kaitlyn choked back her yelp of embarrassment and rushed to pound on the stop button.

Landon raised his eyebrows and crossed his arms.

Refusing to acknowledge his low chuckle, Kaitlyn quickly pushed play once more.

When Ron's voice came across the line, Landon's amused

expression changed. He lowered his arms and listened intently until the message ended.

His gaze snapped to hers. "Have you heard from Sparks since he left this message?"

She shook her head. "I called and left a message on his cell phone but I haven't heard back. He left me this message last night."

Landon glanced at her ruined cell phone sitting on the desk. Shrugging out of his jacket, he tossed it onto the cushy reading couch underneath the large window and then pulled his cell phone from the clip on his hip.

"If the water didn't fry your card, we can still make this work," he said as he slid the back of his cell phone off and pulled out a white chip. Setting the card and his cell on the desk, he picked up her cell phone and slid the back cover off hers.

"What are you doing?" She moved to stand beside him.

He popped a similar slim white card out of her phone and held it up. "Your card was pretty tight in there. Hopefully, that kept the water out. This card holds all your cell phone information. Theoretically I should be able to just slide your card into my cell phone and it would act as if it was yours. If people dialed your cell phone number—" he held up his phone after he'd slid her chip into it and closed the back "—then this phone would ring."

Understanding dawned. She took his cell phone and turned it on. "You're saying I should be able to receive any unread messages or voice mails from this phone now, right?"

He nodded. "As long as my phone is 'unlocked,' yes, this phone would now act as if it were yours."

As his cell phone cycled through the start-up sequence, she slid him a sidelong look. "And you know all this because…"

He flashed a wicked smile. "I've needed information from a cell phone for a case here and there."

"You P.I.s bend all the rules, don't you?" She shook her head and laughed as she dialed her cell phone number then punched in her passcode to check her voice mails.

When she got an error message, she remembered she'd suspended her phone service earlier. Kaitlyn quickly made another call to her provider to tell them she'd found her cell phone. "They said it might be an hour or two before the re-activation takes effect," she told Landon as she hung up the telephone.

As Landon nodded his understanding, a thought occurred to her. "If Ron did send me attachments, how will I get to them?"

"Your phone's screen will be too small to really see anything. Once you're able to get to your messages, forward the attachments to your personal e-mail address. We should be able to view them from your computer."

She smiled, glad she'd asked for his help. "I knew I kept you around for a reason." Setting his cell phone down on the desk, she walked around to the other side to turn on her laptop.

Landon's chest tightened as he watched Kaitlyn bend over her keyboard. She'd left her hair down tonight. He could still feel the silky strands between his fingers from when he'd touched it earlier. Her taste lingered on his lips and her smell in his nose. Whenever he inhaled, his body tensed with the need to touch her again.

He looked away and the moon outside caught his attention, drawing him to the window. He stared at the near perfect roundness through the sheer curtains. It wouldn't be full for another night, but already he felt its beckoning pull like he had for the past eighteen years.

He glanced back at Kaitlyn. Her brow furrowed as she leaned over the keyboard. Beautiful, stubborn, oblivious to what he was, physically strong for a woman her size, but so very fragile compared to his werewolf strength.

Each time he was in her presence, his need for her grew stronger. It was as if—he turned and stared at the moon once more—the longer he went without shifting, the stronger the wolf inside him became, insisting he act on his Lupreda instincts with Kaitlyn.

She's yours. Claim her.

She's human. Closing his eyes, he set his jaw. The constant internal battle made his chest burn. He took a deep breath. He'd be fine as long as he kept his distance.

"Ron mentioned sending images. Come look at these programs. If he did send me something, can you suggest which application I should use to view them?"

Landon walked behind the desk and looked at the screen over her shoulder. "For the two most likely image file formats you'll see come through…" He leaned close and pointed to two icons. "One of these two programs should work."

While Kaitlyn clicked to open the first program, Landon couldn't make himself move away. Instead, he stayed close and inhaled her sweet smell. Her scent could take him to his knees. If he were in wolf form, he'd want to roll in it, cover himself with his…mate's scent.

Kaitlyn *was* his mate. He'd acknowledged the truth in the cabin, but he'd walked away to protect her. She'd been so ready and willing, so aroused it had taken all his will power *not* to act on what they'd both wanted. The thought of sliding inside her warmth exhilarated and scared him—he didn't want to hurt her. He was so much stronger.

But if he could keep the wolf at bay, he could be the kind

of lover a human woman would expect. If he stopped fighting himself, he should be able to keep the Musk form dormant. The necklace would guarantee he wouldn't start to shift.

He moved even closer and filled his lungs with her scent at the same time he set his hands on either side of the keys.

Kaitlyn's fingers paused over the keys when Landon placed his hands on the desk. "Are you telling me that you're all grown up now?"

Landon brushed her hair over her shoulder and pressed a kiss against her neck.

Goosebumps scattered across her skin and her breath hitched. "I don't think I can take it again. I need your answer." She gripped his wrist and started to move his arm as if she planned to put some distance between them.

He gave a low growl and pressed his hips against hers, holding her in place while the unmistakable pressure of his hard cock lay against her sweet rear.

He heard Kaitlyn's heart race and she turned her head and kissed his right biceps, letting him know she wanted more.

Landon's pulse pounded, thrumming a rhythmic Lupreda mating beat in his head. His fingertips tingled as his were-claws clamored for release. He fisted his hands on the desk, trying to understand why he couldn't control these reactions. It was as if his body had a mind of its own.

Or his wolf did.

Back off, he mentally snarled.

When Kaitlyn straightened and tried to turn to face him, he lightly caught her hips and held her in place. "Not yet," his words came out, gruff and harsh. He had to focus not to apply pressure to her hip bones.

His wolf retreated, leaving him feeling torn up and raw inside. Kaitlyn leaned her back against his chest and said in a sultry tone as she turned her nose into his neck, "Don't you want me to touch you?" One hand skated up his neck to tangle in his hair and the other slid down his waist. Her nails scraped his back before she gripped his buttock tightly and yanked him hard against her.

"Let me touch you, Kaitie," he said in a husky tone and slid his fingers under her sweater to touch her soft skin.

Kaitlyn released him and surprised him by swiftly removing her sweater. Tossing it to the floor, she turned to face him and pulled his T-shirt free of his jeans. "Your turn," she said and began to lift the end of his shirt.

Landon's cock throbbed painfully against his jeans. He gripped his shirt and helped her remove it, tossing the cloth to the floor.

He held her waist with the barest touch as her hands slid across his chest. She explored every dip and hollow, her movements tender until she reached his nipples. When she leaned forward and ran her tongue along his pectoral, teasing the puckered darker skin with tiny nibbles, he closed his eyes and kissed the top of her head. She was precious to him even when she was driving him insane.

Landon leaned forward and slid her bra strap down her arm, planting a kiss where the strap had been.

Kaitlyn gasped when his slid his kisses lower to the curve of her breast. She cupped his jaw and lifted his chin.

Landon captured her mouth in a dominant kiss, his hands sliding up her back as he pulled her near-naked body close. The warm skin-to-skin contact mixed with her aroused smell spiked his arousal. He couldn't get close enough.

Kaitlyn pressed her lips hard against his, then sucked on his tongue as she yanked at the buttons on his jeans, ripping the fly open in a quick, fast jerk.

The beast in Landon's head whispered, *She smells so good because she's yours. Let your spirited self go. She wants the primal you taking over, not this controlled half.*

No! he argued with his demanding wolf. He thought back to their lovemaking. *She smelled like Lupreda because I wished it so, then I wouldn't have to worry so much that I'd hurt her. I want to believe she can handle the real me, but she can't. Go the hell away.* Landon slid his lips down Kaitlyn's neck as he unsnapped her bra. They both pushed it aside so he could continue his path to her nipple.

The wolf gave a cynical laugh. *I'll always be here, torturing you. I'll never go away. Let her see a little of the real you.*

He gripped the back of her jeans and she let out a mewling gasp of pleasure when his hot mouth captured her nipple and sucked hard on the tip.

As her hand slid inside his boxers, his grip on her jeans tightened. The moment her fingers surrounded his aching cock, Landon's hold on her jeans cinched and hips jerked forward. Tearing fabric sounded alongside their harsh breathing.

Landon froze. He realized his claws had extended on their own, taking care of the barrier that separated them. Her jeans were ripped down the back from the waist all the way to the top of the pants legs.

Kaitlyn laughed and wrapped her arms tight around his neck, pressing kisses against his jaw. "Well, that's one way to get me out of my pants, He-man."

He trembled deep inside. He hadn't even felt his claws extend. What if that had been her flesh? It was foolish to think he could hold it together with Kaitlyn. She brought out his most primal instincts whenever they touched.

After his claws retracted, he placed his hands around her waist and started to set her away. "I'm sorry."

Kaitlyn's arms cinched tight around his neck. "Hell, no, you don't. You're finishing what you started, mister. I don't give a damn about my jeans."

It could've been you. Landon wrapped his arms around her slim frame and buried his nose against her neck. "I'm so afraid I'm going to hurt you. I would never forgive myself, Kaitie."

She ran her nails hard down his back, making his inner wolf jump in excitement. "How do you know I won't hurt *you?*" she whispered in his ear, then took a step back and shimmied out of her torn jeans, "I'm not a porcelain doll, Landon. I'm a tough cookie. If I'm ever in pain, trust me, I'll let you know."

Holding her torn pants up by her finger, she smirked. "Nice job, by the way. That's the fastest a man has ever gotten me out of my pants."

Landon's wolf snarled at the idea of another man trying to get into Kaitlyn's pants. He pushed her jeans off her finger and said in a low tone, "How about we don't let anyone else try to break my record."

Kaitlyn crooked her finger and backed away until she reached the couch. Flipping the wall light switch off, she lay down on the furniture and met his gaze with a challenging one. "Give me a reason not to let anyone else try."

She looked so beautiful with only the moonlight shining on her fair skin. Her cheeks were flushed, and her red hair made a striking complement to the soft, dark green cushions beneath her. Her arousal beckoned him with sweet, musky notes full of desire. Landon didn't think twice as he shed the rest of his clothes and walked over to the sofa.

Kaitlyn tried to keep her breathing even as Landon approached the couch. His imposing height and broad-shouldered, muscular frame should've intimidated her, especially considering he was worried he'd hurt her. Instead, she'd never been as caught up in another man in her life.

The way he moved, with a stealthy, powerful grace, his thigh muscles bunching and his abs flexing with each step he took toward her, only made her want him more. When he went down on one knee and the moon's light reflected on his intense expression, she held back a shiver of excitement and pressed her finger against the small indention in his chin.

"Have I told you how sexy this makes you, and that I have a hard time breathing when you're near?"

Landon placed one hand on her thigh and touched her temple with the other. Rubbing a strand of her hair between his fingers, he captured her finger in his mouth and slowly shook his head.

The sensation of his wet tongue and lips sucking on her finger made her gasp and arch her back.

His warm hand slid up her thigh, and he massaged the slim muscles, then tugged slightly to let her know he wanted her to spread her legs.

Sparks of anticipation built within her as he inched his fingers closer. She was so wet and ready for his touch, she squirmed and moved to the edge of the couch. Anything to be closer to him.

Landon's smile was rakish as he started to let go of her finger. But Kaitlyn turned her finger upward and used her hold to draw him close. Her heart threatened to beat a hole in her chest when she withdrew her finger from his lips.

Even though his face was just an inch away from hers, Landon didn't kiss her. Instead he searched her gaze as he touched her entrance, then slid a finger deep inside her channel. A carnal smile tilted his mouth and he withdrew his finger and pushed back inside. "You're so wet and warm." His lips formed a thin line. "And so small."

Rocking her hips to his slow, thrusting movement, she slid her fingers down his abs until she reached his erection. "And ready," she finished at the same time she wrapped her fingers around the hard flesh.

Landon shuddered and closed his eyes for a second. When he opened them once more, his eyes were a much lighter green. "Your eyes—"

His lips claimed hers at the same time he added another finger, stroking her body to new highs. Landon's fierce kiss seduced her, while his alluring earthy scent and masterful hands claimed her body. The erotic combination sent her emotions into a frenzied tailspin.

Kaitlyn kissed him back and bucked against his hand…all while her grip moved along his length. She wanted to feel him taking her body the way his fingers played; just as slow, just as deep and so hard she screamed in pleasure.

Before she could react, Landon dipped his head and his mouth joined the symphony his fingers played on her body.

Kaitlyn's hand slid off his cock as her entire body centered on his tongue laving at her sex, the press of his mouth, aggressive and hard, while his fingers turned and stroked her desires to a new tune—higher in pitch, faster in tempo.

Digging her nails into his shoulder, she moaned and bowed her back, loving his talented mouth. As her orgasm began to surge within her, she desperately wanted to let go, but she didn't want to come without him this time.

She loved his strength and his honor, even his selflessness as a lover, but deep inside she knew tonight was about dominance and control…and establishing roles. Landon had such a powerful presence; she wanted him to know he wasn't always going to call the shots between them.

Clenching her teeth to resist the building desire spiraling inside her, she lifted his chin away from her body. She didn't give him a chance to refuse. Instead she slid off the couch onto her knees and pulled his mouth to hers.

Landon set his other knee down on the floor and gripped her waist tight. Yanking her body flush with his, he kissed her with a primal fierceness that sent pleasurable heat shooting to all the right places.

He tasted like her and smelled like him; earthy and so damned sexy she couldn't get close enough. She inhaled deeply as their tongues swept against each other.

Landon's musky scent smelled stronger, making her head swim and her nerves jangle in response. Kaitlyn gripped his hard shoulders and broke their kiss so she could press her lips against the pulse beating at his neck.

He threaded his hands through her hair and planted a kiss on her forehead, murmuring her name.

Sliding her hand down his hard stomach, Kaitlyn met his gaze and watched his eyes when her fingers wrapped around his erection in a firm hold.

His hips jerked forward and a low growl rumbled in his chest. Right before he closed his eyes, she saw the color shift again, turning even brighter. His jaw tensed and his hand went around her wrist, stopping her arousing strokes.

"Let me set the pace. It's better this way," he gritted out through clenched teeth.

She arched her eyebrow, then lowered her head and laved at the moisture on the tip of his engorged erection, enjoying the harsh groan he made. He was so tense and rock-hard, his entire body felt like a statue. *My very own, beautifully carved god to pleasure,* she thought as she slid her lips fully down his cock, taking him deep into her mouth.

Landon's grip on her wrist loosened. His fingers found their way into her hair to cup the back of her head, while his other hand slid down her back to the curve of her buttock.

The room suddenly spun and Kaitlyn found herself on her knees, facing the back of the couch and leaning across the seat. Landon's chest was pressed against her back, his erection along her buttocks while his hands locked hers in place, spread-eagled against the cushions. His lips brushed against her ear and he gave a warning growl. "You don't know what you're messing with, Kaitie."

She turned her cheek against the cushions and pushed back against him, panting out, "I want what you walked away from earlier today. I want this…I want you out of control."

Landon's grunt sounded almost angry as he let go of her hands and lifted his chest off her back. His hips still held her pinned to the couch and she lay perfectly still, waiting. She was afraid to move or breathe, afraid he'd walk away again.

When his hands spread across her upper back, then slid down to the curve of her waist in an aggressive caress, she closed her eyes and let out an unsteady breath. "You'd better have condoms," she said, though she dared not move an inch.

Landon leaned across her back once more. As he reached for his jacket, he kissed her temple. "Be careful what you ask. You might get more than you bargained for, my demanding little cop."

She smiled as he retrieved a condom from his pocket and tossed his jacket aside. "I'm counting on it, my dominant P.I.," she shot back.

A couple seconds later, he captured her hands again, knotting his fingers with hers. "You like that I call all the shots."

Kaitlyn gave a low laugh and pushed her hips back against his once more. "I like to let you *think* you call all the shots."

Landon used his hold to quickly lift her to an upright position against his chest. Wrapping his arms around her waist, he held her in place with a vise hold. He kissed her neck and spoke in a voice she'd never heard him use before, harsh and authoritative. "You *will* let me set the pace. This is for your own good. Understand?"

Her heart raced at the change in his tone. He wasn't asking. When she nodded, the tension in his arms lessened and his hands uncurled from hers to slide up her sides, touching every curve along her body.

"Are you sure you don't want to turn around?" he said in a husky voice as his lips created a heated path along her neck.

She shook her head and grabbed his hands, moving them to her breasts. Her entire body was on fire. "I want what you wouldn't give me before." She began to pant when his palms slid across her nipples in a slow, purposeful drag.

"Have you ever had sex in this position before?" he asked, his voice rough.

She felt his heart pounding against her back and smiled. Her own heart was running a 10-K marathon. He wasn't as calm as he let on.

Turning her head, she kissed his jaw and ran her nails up the sides of his taut buttocks. "Once. It was okay."

As soon as she'd said the word *once,* his hands cupped her breasts in a possessive hold and his gaze locked with hers. "There is no more past. Only now."

"Is that a promise that I'll like it?" she asked in a breathless voice.

His expression turned dark and his fingers rolled her nipples. "You tell me when you're done screaming."

"Cocky ma—" she started to say, but he pinched her nipples, cutting off her words in a gasp of pleasure and pain. Liquid heat flooded her sex and she put her hands on the couch for support when her legs began to tremble.

Landon pressed his chest along her back and continued to tease her nipple while his other hand flattened down her stomach and then slid into the red curls between her legs.

When his fingers dove between her legs and slid into her heat, she cried out as a bit of satisfaction slammed through her. He thrust deep and his palm chafed her sensitive nub. Her hips instinctively pressed his hand against the couch. She began to move against him, moaning in sheer ecstasy.

"You feel so good." He rasped against the side of her throat, his broad shoulders surrounding her. Heat emanated off him as if he were raging with fever.

"Then do something about it…for both of us," she babbled, unable to think coherent thoughts any longer. His musky scent enveloped her, making her head woozy as if she were having an erotic dream she never wanted to wake from.

Landon's breathing came in choppy gusts. He withdrew his hand from her body and gripped her hips.

Lifting her as if she weighed nothing, he held her suspended a few inches off the floor. His thighs aligned with the back of hers and the teasing tip of his cock brushed her entrance. His grip was so tight, she knew she'd have bruises, but she didn't care. Kaitlyn crushed the cushions under her hands as her body vibrated with need. "Now, Landon!" she screamed.

He thrust upward at the same time he pushed her hips down. Kaitlyn gasped at his snug fit and the deep fullness that stretched her walls further than she thought possible.

Lowering her knees to the floor, Landon's voice was tight. "Are you in pain?"

"No," she sobbed. Tears tracked down her cheeks as her emotions vaulted. "Just don't stop. Please, don't stop."

"I couldn't go back now if I wanted to." He withdrew and slid back inside her channel. "You're stuck with me in every respect."

Kaitlyn pushed back against each of his aggressive thrusts, taking him as deep as she could. Her entire body tensed as her orgasm built to body-shaking levels.

Breathing in heavy gasps, she begged, "Make me scream."

Landon gripped her hands and pressed them onto the cushions once more. His hips slammed into hers hard as he aligned his chest with her back.

His deep penetration sent tremors echoing through her sex, and a keening cry rushing past her lips.

"Tell me you want this, Kaitie," he grated out, his tone like gravel.

She was speechless with need and he began to move his hips in a small circle touching every part of her.

"Ah-h," she moaned from the new sensations clamoring inside her. They were so raw and deep, she felt them all the way to her belly. Her breath caught and she moaned. "Yes! I want this!"

He pulled almost completely out, making her want to whimper. But this time when he sank to the hilt, his teeth clamped on the tender spot between her shoulder and her neck.

Landon only meant to hold her with his teeth. He couldn't believe his canines were erupting. He knew what they meant, but he didn't expect them to appear while he wore the necklace.

His wolf was mating with Kaitlyn, preparing to mark her, despite the silver binding him.

No! Landon mentally roared, trying to rescind his canines. He slightly loosened his hold on her skin as his four canines continued to elongate. Disbelief rushed through him when his cock began to tingle with additional heat. It didn't matter that he wore a condom, his body was reacting to hers. Wanting to mate.

Kaitlyn moaned and arched her back, spreading her legs to allow him better access. "You feel harder." She clenched her walls around his cock and gave a low groan. "Feels so good, like we're on fire."

It's what she wants.

Landon shuddered and tried to regain control. *She doesn't know what she's asking for.*

His wolf snorted. *She's asking for you. That's all that matters.*

"End this torture, Landon," Kaitlyn's voice shook. "Bite me and make me come."

The vampires had told the Lupreda that if they ever bit a human in their wolf form then they would never be able to shift back to human form. Did that mean he wouldn't be able to shift to a wolf if he bit Kaitlyn while in human form?

He didn't know what rules applied. All he knew was that Kaitlyn completed him, made him feel like he belonged, at least with her.

Moving his palm down her stomach, he slowly ran his finger along the center of her wet folds.

Kaitlyn grabbed his hand and pressed his fingers hard against her. Whimpering, she began to rock against him, showing him what she wanted.

Landon had never been more jacked up. Her aroused scent turned sweeter and he knew she was on the very edge. His jaw ached with the need to clamp down.

"So hot," she mumbled and a sheen of sweat began to coat her skin. The salty flavor sent Landon over the edge.

Mine! he mentally roared and his canines sank into her soft skin. She screamed at the same time her sex clamped hard on his cock in gripping convulsions. As her orgasm rushed through her, the tight sensations sent a deep shudder through his body. He released his hold on her shoulder and laved at the bite before he began to move within her. Each time he slid back inside her sweet body, he pressed her hips hard against the couch with dominant, feral thrusts.

Kaitlyn met his aggressive nature with her own. She didn't just take what he dished out, she pushed back against him, spiking his desire. As her second orgasm rippled through her, his own climax exploded in a shower of pulses that shot from his spine to his groin and back in jaw-grinding, erotic succession until he was fully spent.

Breathing heavily, Kaitlyn hung her head toward the couch. Landon's heart thumped hard as he reverently kissed his mark on her shoulder. When she flopped down on the couch in sheer exhaustion, he pressed his lips against her temple then laid his chest across her back, squeezing her hands under his.

He'd never felt so out of control, so primal and vulnerable at the same time. Kaitlyn stripped him bare. He'd never love another as much as he cherished this woman.

When their breathing finally evened out, she said, "So are you going to tell me about the biting thing?"

Landon's heart skipped several beats. His chest ached as he withdrew from her and stood up from the couch. While he disposed of the condom, he felt Kaitlyn's gaze on him. If he told her what he was and she didn't accept him, he'd be exposing the whole pack.

He walked back over to her side and scooped her up. Lying down on the couch, he spooned her, but she rolled over onto her back and regarded him with a steady gaze.

Landon ran his finger across the two red spots that remained on her skin. He knew identical marks would grace her back as well, branding her as taken. The marks would never fade and they would forever carry his scent, letting the other Lupreda know whom she belonged to. The sight was both exhilarating and bittersweet. In the Lupreda world, she was his, but in her human world he had no true claim on her if she didn't wish it.

His eyes collided with her blue-brown ones. Lacing his fingers with hers, he kissed her knuckles and answered her question. "I won't bite you again unless you ask me to."

Her fingers tightened around his. "That's not what I asked you, Landon. I asked why."

He told her as much of the truth as he could. "You bring out a primal side in me no other woman has. I can honestly say I couldn't control myself."

She glanced at the red marks on her shoulder and shrugged. "It's okay. They're already fading. They'll be gone tomorrow."

No, they won't, my little mate. "Would it bother you if they didn't go away completely?"

She gave a sheepish smile and her cheeks flushed. She was gorgeous with her red hair in wild disarray against his arm. "It'd be like a hickey on display."

Everyone would know you are mine. He ran his finger across the tip of her nose. "They would only know if you showed them." His knuckles traced her cheekbone. "Did you like it?"

She captured his finger between her teeth, then ran her tongue around the tip. Sliding her lips around his flesh, she sucked hard as if she were enjoying a lollypop. His groin instantly responded to each sucking pull she made until his erection pulsed against her thigh.

Nipping the tip of his finger hard, she pulled it from her

mouth and gave him a sexy smile. "Does that answer your question?"

Landon dipped his head and kissed her long and hard. When she started to run her hand down his stomach, he chuckled and gripped her wrist. Sliding onto his back he pulled her body on top of him. "Let's rest for a bit."

Kaitlyn gave a heavy sigh, but she laid her cheek on his chest, tucked her arm around his waist and entwined her legs with his, snuggling close. "For a minute or two."

Landon stroked her hair until her breathing turned even in sleep. He lay there with the moonlight shining down on them, thinking. If all he could have was this human life with Kaitlyn, he'd miss interacting with his pack, but he'd have her. Finding one's true other half didn't always happen. He would cherish her with every fiber of his being.

Chapter 10

Kaitlyn woke to the warmth of Landon's arm slung over her waist as she lay beside him on the couch. He was sleeping quietly. A five o'clock shadow covered his strong jaw, making him sexy as sin. It was still dark outside, but the moon's light lit up the room in a soft blue glow. She wondered how much time had passed. Had it been at least two hours?

Lifting Landon's arm, she gingerly slid off the couch. Behind the desk, she picked up her jeans and sighed at the broad rip from the waistband all the way to the crotch. Dropping her jeans, she scooped up Landon's T-shirt. She slipped into the soft cotton material that fell to the top of her thighs. His heady scent permeated the shirt as if he'd enveloped her completely. Kaitlyn inhaled the smell from the collar of the shirt and walked back to the couch to stare at Landon.

She couldn't believe how powerfully electric their lovemaking was. She'd had a feeling they'd be good together, but holy cow, she had had no idea how good.

"You grew up to be a very bad boy," she whispered with a pleased grin.

Deciding to let Landon sleep until she could confirm her cell phone was back in service, she started to walk away when her gaze landed on the box she'd brought home from Hank's place.

Landon's jacket had slid off the couch, catching the box lid and opening the top of the box.

Turning on the small banker's lamp on the desk, she knelt beside the box. Stacks of papers and folders were on one side, and a small tackle box, full of fishing wire and lures, was on the other. A palm-sized wooden container with a howling wolf engraving covered a four-by-six photo in the third corner. She smiled and lifted the box and the photo. Her breath caught when she pulled the picture close. It was a snapshot of Landon crossing a street. He appeared to be unaware someone had taken the shot.

Turning the photo over, she read the date the picture was printed, and her heart lurched. It was dated over eighteen years ago.

She stared at the photo once more, frowning in confusion. Why had her father had a picture of Landon? And how could an eighteen-year-old photo of Landon pass as if it had been taken yesterday? Had he always looked very mature, even in his twenties?

Setting the picture down, Kaitlyn lifted the tiny wood box and slid the carved cover open. A handful of bullets spilled into her palm, startling her. She'd expected something sweet, like a trinket for her or her mother perhaps, not bullets.

The bullets' color surprised her. They were all silver, not dull, but shiny and uniform in color. Most of the bullets she'd worked with were either copper in color or a mixture of lead and copper.

Picking up one of the bullets, she turned it to read the lightly etched initials on the side near the tip. J. M.

Kaitlyn's hand shook as she realized where'd she seen similar etchings, though they were twisted and marred.

She grabbed the photo and walked on wobbly legs over to the couch. Sitting down beside Landon, she lifted the bullet slug on his necklace and compared it to the bullet in her hand. They were the same—her father's. She bit back a sob and closed her eyes.

Landon's warm fingers surrounded hers, still holding the slug on his chain.

"Kaitlyn? What's wrong?"

She opened her eyes and tears streaked down her cheeks. Something had been nagging in her mind, something about Landon, but she just couldn't pin it down. The picture told her he had a connection to her father. She put her father's bullet and the picture in his hand. "Tell me why my father had a picture of you in his belongings and why you're wearing his bullet around your neck."

Her questions tore at Landon's heart. He didn't want his mate to hate him...and she would when she found out the truth. The picture of him surprised the hell out of him. When had James McKinney taken that shot? And why?

He sat up and frowned. Shaking his head, he handed her the picture. "I'm just as surprised as you that your father had a picture of me."

Her lips trembled and her eyes shimmered with more unshed tears. "But you do know why you wear his bullet around your neck."

Landon would do anything to take away the look of dread on her face. But she was his mate, the woman he'd fallen in love with three years ago. He owed her the truth, even at the expense of exposing his very existence. He put the bullet in her hand.

"That night in the park. He was shooting into the woods after—I was trying to protect someone. It all happened so fast. I didn't mean to kill your father, Kaitlyn." He tried to touch her, but she jerked away and stepped back from him as he finished, "You've got to believe me."

"My father was mauled, Landon." Her voice held a tremor. She gasped and shook her head as if remembering something. Her eyes went wide. "That was you in the alley, fighting the vampires. You were huge."

Landon was up and by her side in a split second. He caught her arms before she hit the floor. "Easy, Kaitie," he said as he steadied her shoulders.

"Don't touch me!" Kaitlyn shoved at his hands and backed away until the desk blocked her retreat "Dear God, what are you?" She glanced away, her mind racing as she thought out loud, "That…that burned body in the park, the aura I saw…" Her gaze snapped back to his. "He was a werewolf, wasn't he?"

"Technically he was called a zerker, but for all intents and purposes, yes, he was a werewolf."

When he finished speaking, her hand was on her chest. She was breathing so heavily he thought she might hyperventilate. Landon felt helpless in his inability to calm her. "You need to take deep, easy breaths or you're going to pass out," he warned.

She waved her arms and yelled, "How else am I supposed to react? I've just discovered that the man I had sex with less than an hour ago not only killed my father, but he's a freaking werewolf."

Landon's chest ached at the betrayal in her gaze and the shock in her voice. "Kaitlyn, I—"

Rounding the desk, she grabbed his pants and tossed them to him. "Get out!" she said and pointed to the door.

The silence between them was deafening as Landon stepped into his boxers and jeans. He was in the process of buttoning his pants when his cell phone rang.

Their gazes collided across the desk.

She reached for his phone and glanced at the caller I.D. "It's Ron." Flipping open the phone, she pressed it to her ear. "Ron, I got your message."

Landon's keen hearing picked up the other side of the conversation. His fists clenched when he heard a voice he'd learned to loathe over two years ago.

"I'm glad to hear it, Kaitlyn. Now I want you to listen to *my* message."

"Remy? Where's Ron?" Her confused gaze locked with Landon's, and she tilted the phone away from her ear and mouthed, "Can you hear this?"

He crossed his arms over his chest and gave a curt nod.

"Let's just say…he won't be needing his cell phone any longer. But before he checked out of this life, I believe he sent a message to your cell."

Landon heard Kaitlyn's heart ramp up. "What have you done to Ron? God, Remy! Are you psychotic?"

"Hardly. I just believe in a cause."

"To the point you'd kill people?"

"You have until two to bring your cell to the High Line, the abandoned train yard in Chelsea on Twenty-fifth Street. If I don't get it by then, we've got someone standing by to make sure your mother will meet her maker a lot sooner than nature plans."

"Bastard!" she spat, her entire body tensing in anger. "If anyone goes after my mom, I'll take you all down."

Remy didn't respond to her threat. Instead his tone was dead calm. "You will meet me, and don't even consider getting your cop buddies involved. I'll know if you do and I'll make the call. Not only will your mother die, but you'll be too busy trying to explain to the police why you murdered Ron to mourn her sudden tragic death."

Her phone hand trembled and she glanced Landon's way. He immediately moved behind her and put his hands on her shoulders for support.

Letting his wolf half take over, Landon was able to speak in her mind. *Get him to tell you how he set you up. He's a cocky bastard, too smug in his own brilliance.*

Her surprised gaze jerked to his. He knew she was shocked to hear his voice in her head. Squeezing her shoulders gently, he nodded toward the phone.

She kept her eyes locked with his as she egged the Garotter on. "You don't have the brains to pull that shit off, Remy."

"Everyone heard your argument at the precinct the other day," he snarled.

"I haven't spoken to Ron since earlier this week."

He *tsked.* "How soon you forget. Phone records will show that you called Ron's cell earlier today, and you were so helpful by answering his call just now."

"I have a feeling Ron died last night. This phone call took place after his death."

"Don't you realize we're smarter than you? We've made sure it'll be hard to determine his exact time of death, but when they find Ron's body, evidence will prove you murdered him. All it takes is an anonymous call to the station about a suspicious smell and you're toast, Kaitlyn." He gave a heavy sigh. "I've grown tired of this battle of wits bullshit. You always were too stubborn for your own good. Be smart this time. Be here at two sharp with that damned phone."

She closed the cell phone and her entire body began to shake. Landon didn't think twice. He pulled her into his arms and held her close. For a few seconds, she leaned into his chest, then immediately stiffened and pushed out of his arms.

Landon let his hands fall to his sides even as his Alpha tone kicked in. "Don't let the issues between us keep you from accepting my help. You need someone to protect your mother as well as someone to back you up when you meet with Remy."

Her lips thinned into a stubborn line and his gaze narrowed. "You can't possibly be in two places at once. Let me help you, Kaitie."

As soon as she nodded, he picked up the telephone and dialed Caine's number.

While Landon filled Caine in on their situation, Kaitlyn's insides quaked. Moving on autopilot, she shrugged out of his shirt and laid it on the desk, then gathered her clothes and walked upstairs to find warmer clothes to wear for her meeting with Remy. Heavy coats weren't conducive to being able to move fast when the need arose.

After she'd dressed in another pair of jeans, a red T-shirt and a black zip-up sweat jacket, Kaitlyn stood in front of her bureau and pulled her hair back in a low ponytail.

Her face looked pale and her eyes stared vacantly at her. She knew she was in some kind of trancelike shock. She was entirely too calm right now considering everything she'd just learned about the man she'd grown very attached to in a short amount of time. Damn, she'd really started to care deeply for him.

Grinding her teeth, she berated herself for being such a fool...she'd known something about him was different.

Right now her mother's life hung in the balance. She couldn't screw this up.

Turning away from the mirror, she walked over to the closet and opened the doors. Standing on her toes, she slid her hand along the top shelf that ran the length of the closet above the hanging clothes bar. Her fingers brushed the rim of her baseball cap, pushing it further back on the shelf.

Her entire body tensed when Landon reached over her and pulled down the black cap. "This what you're looking for?" he said as he handed the hat to her.

"Thanks." She took the cap and glanced up at him, but Landon wasn't looking at her. His gaze was locked on the wolf painted on the wall next to the door. She'd painted over the pink walls years ago, but she'd never had the heart to cover the wolf. His deep-brown coat and the silver markings along his ears, the tip of his muzzle and around his shoulders made him appear majestic and proud as he sat on his haunches in the tall grass. Like a sentinel, his steady gaze never wavered from her, no matter her position in the room.

Remembering her dream of the wolf shifting in the air, she set her jaw. She jammed the hat on her head and pulled her ponytail through the back, then gestured to the wolf and said, "A furry friend for you," before she turned to walk away.

Landon caught her arm and held her in place, his voice tight. "Did your father paint that wolf for you?"

She pulled out of his hold, both frustrated and guilty that his touch still affected her. "My father commissioned an artist to paint it to his specifications." Before Landon could reply, she walked out of the room and back downstairs to the office.

When Landon followed her into the office, she was so frustrated she wanted to scream. She had a little over two hours before she had to be at the place Remy had designated.

Heaven forbid anything went wrong—her mother's life was at stake. Grabbing up her keys, she turned to leave.

Landon blocked her path in the doorway. "Where are you going?"

She tried to brush past him, but he put his hands on her shoulders and held her in place. Her gaze met his and her insides trembled in fear for her mother. "I want to see my mom. Visiting hours might be over, but I'll sneak in if I have to."

"If you go anywhere near your mother, they'll think you're trying to interfere. You know they're watching her."

Her shoulders sagged. She knew he was right.

Landon's thumbs slowly slid back and forth across her collarbone. "I'm sorry, Kaitlyn...for the past. I wish to hell I could undo it."

She didn't want to talk about his role in her father's death. The wound was just too raw. Straightening her spine, she shrugged out of his hold and walked over to pick up Landon's phone. Since she'd received a phone call on Landon's cell, that meant it was in full service again.

She scrolled through the messages and found one from Ron. Forwarding it to her e-mail account, she walked around the desk and tapped on her keyboard, waiting for the message to show up. A news flash popped up on her browser screen.

Tacomi truck in accident. Driver killed. Guns missing.

"The Tacomi accident is in the news now," she said. Heart racing, she refreshed her e-mail inbox. Two photos popped up when her e-mail finally arrived. She opened them in the program Landon suggested and wasn't at all surprised that Remy starred in one. It was a picture of him holding a gun. In the background, the Tacomi truck was on its side as if it had been in an accident. The other picture was a bit blurry, but she blinked when she saw a shadowy outline near the Tacomi vehicle she hadn't expected. Clicking on both photos, she hit the print button and waited for the color printer on the credenza to start printing.

Landon glanced at the printer when it whirred to life. "He did send photos?"

She nodded and swiped the first picture from the tray, then walked it over to him. "No wonder Remy's desperate for my phone. This places him at the scene of the crime."

Landon skimmed the photo and glanced at the quiet printer. "And the other one?"

Kaitlyn retrieved it and set it in his hands. Walking away, she leaned against the desk and crossed her arms. "That second one definitely makes me scratch my head. It almost looks like a black panther. What do you think?"

Landon's jaw flexed and his gaze narrowed. He set the pictures on the waist-high bookshelf near the doorway. "Your eyes aren't playing tricks. That's what it looks like to me, too."

"That's just bizarre," she said. When the tense silence between them drew out for five long, agonizing minutes, she finally spoke, "I'm assuming you want to discuss the meeting with Remy once Caine gets here. While we're waiting for him, why don't you tell me where werewolves came from. You fought those vampires like you'd tangled with them before."

Landon leaned back against the doorjamb and crossed his arms. "I have. Werewolves exist because the vampires created the Lupreda to have a worthy adversary to hunt."

She winced at his word *hunt*. "That's so barbaric." Then again, she had to remind herself, Landon wasn't human. He'd defeated two vampires with his bare hands. The man, er…Lupreda could take care of himself.

Landon shrugged. "It all changed when the vampires

started dying twenty-five years ago. They withdrew from their stronghold and we had our freedom."

"Do you know where the vampires came from? Why they were so vicious to humans?"

He nodded. "The original vampires were humans who volunteered for the government's secret Scions project. The project's goal was to use genetic manipulation to create the ultimate superhuman who could resist potential future threats from enemies, not unlike the biological terrorism against our paper monetary system decades ago."

"But why did the vampires attack the humans?"

"Because the scientists treated them like lab rats with cruel tests and no life outside the research facility. Eventually, they revolted."

"And then they went on a rampage of attacking humans for food and creating werewolves to hunt, is that what you're saying?"

He rubbed the back of his neck. "In a nutshell."

She frowned. "How is it that we knew about the vampires' existence, but not werewolves'?"

He smirked. "Because werewolves weren't attacking humans. The vampires engineered us such that if we bit a human while in our wolf form, we'd stay in that form permanently. It was a great incentive to behave."

She grabbed her shoulder. "You bit me. Is the reverse true? Am I going to turn into a werewolf?"

He straightened and dropped his hands to his sides, his expression insulted. "That wasn't a wolf bite."

"It sure felt like one to me," she shot back in annoyance.

Before she could blink, he was standing an inch from her. Staring down at her with challenging eyes, he said in a husky tone, "You didn't seem to mind."

Heat spread through her cheeks. She moved away from his penetrating stare to scan the titles of her father's wolf and werewolf lore books on the wall behind the desk. Glancing Landon's way, she asked, "Do you think my father knew what you were and that's why he had a photo of you?"

Landon didn't speak for several seconds, then he shook his head. "I don't think he knew until that night in Morningside Park."

She shrugged off any deep, heart-wrenching thoughts about her father and Landon on that fateful night. She couldn't fall apart right now.

What she needed were answers. Landon's mention of Morningside Park spurred another question. "Did a vampire burn your zerker?"

"No."

His stoic, one-word response wasn't cutting it. She narrowed her gaze. "But you know who did, don't you?"

Landon debated whether or not to tell her the truth…or at least his theory. Even he wasn't sure, but the Velius was the only conclusion he could come to, especially since one had shown up near a Tacomi truck.

He sighed and adopted her earlier position, leaning against the desk. "Once the vampires had created us, they abandoned their lab. There were those among my pack who wanted to experience the thrill of the hunt instead of being hunted. Unknown to the vampires, some Lupreda began to secretly experiment, creating a prey simply called Velius."

He paused as a portion of the prophecy flitted through his mind. *The hunted becomes the hunter, no longer the prey.*

"So you weren't in cages, let out only to hunt?" she asked.

He shook his head. "No, the silver collars the vampires forced us to wear not only kept us from shifting but bound us to an area as well."

Widening her stance, she folded her hands behind her back. "Go on. I'm listening."

His jaw tightened when he thought of that hateful lab. "Only a few Lupreda knew about the new prey. There were those of us who didn't agree with the entire project."

"You mean *you,* correct?"

He nodded. "And a couple others, but I acted. I couldn't believe the Lupreda would subject another race to the same fate, either by us or by the vampires when they discovered their existence. I destroyed the lab and set the few subjects free."

"Bet you weren't very popular among your kind."

"Nope," he said with a shrug. It was ironic that he'd come so far since then, earning the pack's grudging respect.

"What prey *had* the Lupreda created?"

He met her gaze. "Shape shifters, specifically humans who could shift to panthers…at our discretion, of course."

"Of course," she said with a frown, then began to pace in front of him. Kaitlyn looked much younger than her twenty-four years in her jeans and baseball cap, but still just as beautiful to him.

"You think these panthers have survived and are seeking some kind of vengeance?" she asked.

Her question brought a segment of the prophecy back to his mind.

The hunted becomes the hunter, no longer the prey.
An enemy in your midst is less dark and more gray.
Examine your failures and there you will find
the answer to all your questions in time.

The panthers were the only answer that made sense. Ironically, an insurrection of a different kind. Someone had tried to pit the werewolves against the vampires. The Lupreda had definitely failed with the Velius. But what did the "An enemy in your midst is less dark and more gray" part mean? Burning three zerkers and trying to start a war between the weres and the vampires was pretty damned dark in his book. And how the hell were the panthers skulking around without leaving a smell behind? They'd definitely had a distinctive scent in the past.

"Hel-l-l-lo-o-o-o." She snapped her fingers in front of his face. "Human to werewolf, come in."

Landon loved her spunk. He wished her father's death didn't hang between them, but at least she was still talking to him. "I was just thinking how so much of what has happened fits in with a prophecy I've been told by a vampire."

Her eyes widened. "A vampire? It seems to me you guys wouldn't be on speaking terms."

"It's a long story."

Her lips formed a stubborn line. "I've got the time."

Landon relayed the story about the prophecy and Ariel's book attracting Jachin's attention. He went on to explain how he'd forged a truce with the vampire leader, who eventually took over the leadership of his vampire clan and fell in love and became a mate to the human woman he'd kidnapped.

When he finished, Kaitlyn had a stunned look on her face. "Wow! That's like a movie or something, it's so unbelievable."

"According to humans, so are werewolves and vampires, yet we exist."

"And now, so do the panthers."

He shook his head. "I didn't know for sure until I saw that photo. Now it all makes more sense."

"But you've smelled them at the park, right? Don't you werewolves have a supersonic sense of smell? And what about the handprints?"

Landon scowled. She'd hit a nerve. "I didn't smell anything and neither did Jachin. They're somehow masking their scent. None of the weres mentioned sparkles when the zerkers were taken." He gave her a fierce look. "But now we know the panthers are connected to the Mafia and the Garotters."

Understanding dawned on her face as all his past warnings started clicking into place. "Yeesh! That's not good."

Landon stood and stepped close, cupping the back of her neck. "You're not just dealing with human bad guys anymore, Kaitie. That's why I called Caine and some others in for help."

She gripped his wrist, her eyes wide. "Others? How many werewolves are in your pack?"

He slid his thumb along her cheek. "One hundred and fifty."

A knock on the door interrupted them. The weres were close enough for him to detect their scents. Landon met her questioning gaze. "It's Caine, Laird and Roman."

When Landon's younger brother, Caine, and two other tall men walked into her office, crowding the room with their broad-shouldered, muscular builds, Kaitlyn could only stare at them. Even in their human forms, they were an intimidating group. Knowing they were *all* werewolves made her move a little closer to Landon.

"This is Laird." Landon nodded to the auburn-haired man about her age with piercing blue eyes.

Just as tall, but a bit slimmer in build than Landon, Laird

inclined his head. "Nice to meet you, Kaitlyn. I understand you're a cop."

His steady gaze and open smile instantly set her at ease. Kaitlyn nodded. "Thanks for offering to help."

"You mean we had a choice?" A blond-haired man with an affable smile peered around Laird's shoulder. He tucked his shoulder length, windblown hair behind his ear, looking more like a laid-back surfer than a man who could shift into a powerful beast.

"Zip it." Caine frowned at the blond were, then smiled at her. "It's nice to see you again, Kaitlyn, though I wish it were under better circumstances. You'll have to ignore Roman. He always says whatever pops into his head. Some people don't get his twisted sense of humor."

Landon put his hands on Kaitlyn's shoulders. Pulling her back against his chest, he addressed the weres. "There are a few details I want to relay."

When Landon spoke, all the roguish smiles and relaxed poses vanished. Tension instantly filled the air and their respectful gazes locked on the man standing behind her. The command Landon carried over the other men with just a few words was amazing to watch and admire.

"We were able to retrieve the information Ron sent Kaitlyn. There's proof that at least one Garotter was involved in the recent Tacomi truck accident. I need you to be on your highest alert. The Velius are involved. There is also a connection between the panthers and our zerkers. I believe they may have been behind the zerkers' kidnappings and subsequent murders."

"You found all the zerkers?" Laird asked, confusion flitting across his handsome face.

Landon nodded.

"The panthers are real?" Roman asked. "Man, I thought all that was just an urban legend told by the older pack members."

"Why haven't we smelled them?" Caine followed up.

"That's one question I wish I knew the answer to." Landon released Kaitlyn's shoulders and retrieved the photo she'd printed out. He handed it to Caine. "Do you see the shape in the background?"

Roman and Laird crowded around Caine to see the picture.

Caine glanced up and snarled, "Son of a bitch!"

Landon's expression didn't change. It held the same down-to-business look. "Let's talk about how this meeting with the Garotter is going to play out."

"You think the panthers might be there, too?" Caine asked.

Landon's tone hardened. "Be ready for anything. I want you, Laird and Roman to follow Kaitlyn to the train yard. Park a few blocks away and arrive on foot. I don't want the man Kaitlyn's meeting to know you're there. He might have men watching, so keep your eyes open as you approach. Take him alive. We need someone to roll over on this whole operation."

Kaitlyn's chest squeezed in concern. "That's risky. What if there are other men there, these Velius? None of you can track their smell."

Landon glanced at the weres. "We weren't able to detect a scent after the fact, but I can guarantee these guys will be able to hear the panthers' hearts beating if they're in the vicinity."

He met Kaitlyn's gaze and finished, "I'm going to the hospital to make sure your mother stays safe."

Caine pulled his cell phone off the clip on his jeans pocket and handed it to Landon. "Take my cell. We'll call you after we've taken care of these bastards. It's on vibrate mode."

Landon nodded and tucked the slim cell phone away in his pocket. Turning to Kaitlyn, he said, "Do you have an ankle gun?"

When she nodded, he put his hands on her shoulders, and his intense green eyes seemed to stare right into her soul. "I'll protect your mom. Promise me you'll stay safe."

Chapter 11

Kaitlyn's stomach felt as if an army of bugs were crawling around inside. By the time she parked her car down the road from the area she was supposed to meet Remy, she was a bundle of tightly wound nerves. Other than her car, the only other vehicle she saw was Remy's black BMW. One lone streetlight illuminated the street but left the area she was supposed to meet Remy eerily dark.

She strapped her gun around her ankle then pulled her jeans down to cover her weapon. Grabbing Landon's cell phone off the seat, she erased the mail she'd sent herself from the memory log, then put the phone and her keys into her jacket's front pocket. Retrieving her flashlight, she got out of the car.

As she walked up the road she surreptitiously glanced around the abandoned area, looking for men who might be hiding up on the abandoned track or around a thick steel railroad support. Night shadows loomed everywhere, but the place appeared completely desolate. Only a lone figure stood underneath the tracks, silhouetted against the moonlight.

Stomach tensing, Kaitlyn curled her fingers tight around the flashlight and drew comfort from the indentions Landon had left behind on the hard metal. Even though he wasn't there, the knowledge he'd made sure she was protected kept her focused and strangely calm. Out of the corner of her eye, she saw Caine peer around the corner of the brick building. She didn't react or acknowledge him in any way as she stepped onto the crumbling sidewalk and then approached the area where Remy waited.

Turning the flashlight on, she walked into the pitch-dark under the tracks.

"Show me that you have the phone," Remy demanded as her phone began to ring.

She pushed her keys out of the way and pulled the cell phone out of her pocket, shining the flashlight on it to let him know she'd brought it. She checked the caller I.D. and saw it was Ron's cell.

"I can't believe it. For once, you listened," Remy said, when she came to a stop ten feet away from him.

"You didn't give me any choice." She flashed the light his way to make sure he wasn't holding a weapon. His arms lay casually by his side, as he snapped a cell phone shut and her cell stopped ringing. The cell phone in his hand was weapon enough for her. She did *not* want him making any calls about her mother. Her jaw tensed.

Remy basically looked the same: medium height, short blond hair, except he'd been working out. She could tell his shoulders and chest appeared wider under his coat. But the calculating look in his brown eyes was very different. "I can't believe that you killed Ron and you've threatened my mother's life. You've changed a lot in two years."

His eyes narrowed. "Much as I would like to take credit, I didn't kill Ron and the other cop…Wayne, was it? Kent did. As far as I'm concerned, I *haven't* changed. I was always the same. You were just too busy building your career to see the 'real' me."

She really had been obsessed with work. Somehow his comment made her feel a little better about her misjudgment of him. She'd been right about Ron and Landon. And apparently her initial sense about Kent had been right on, if Remy was referring to her partner Kent as the man who killed Ron and Wayne.

Kaitlyn tried to stay focused and keep him talking so Caine and his guys could canvas the place for other men. "Then it's a good thing I was oblivious or I'd have dumped your ass long before then. You're so wrapped up in these Garotters. They have you stealing guns from Tacomi, issuing murder threats and now blackmail. They've warped your mind."

"The cops' deaths were a small price to pay for protection. The guns were needed. You'd have to be dead not to have heard the news. Two burned vampires were found in an alley. The vampires are back, Kaitlyn!" Before she could respond, he took a breath as if to calm himself. "Enough of this. Hand over the cell phone," he snarled. "If I don't call my man in—" he glanced at his watch "—seven minutes, your mother is gone."

Kaitlyn's heart rate ramped. She stalked toward him, stopping a couple feet away. "You lying son of a bitch! That wasn't our deal."

He held out his hand for the phone and gave a deadly smile. "Let's just call it a little insurance."

Kaitlyn started to put the phone in his hand when a heavy thump sounded over their heads. A pulsar gun rattled to the cement from the tracks above them, quickly followed by sounds of men fighting and grunts of pain.

"You bitch!" Remy grabbed the cell phone out of her hand and swung his fist toward her face.

Kaitlyn ducked and swiveled, jamming the end of the flashlight into Remy's side as he spun out of control.

The cell phones scattered across the cement. He howled in pain and charged her, throwing her against the brick wall.

As air whooshed from her lungs and pain splinted up her spine, Remy grabbed her neck and squeezed hard.

Panicking, she dropped the flashlight and tried to pull his hands off her neck, digging her nails into his skin. Her vision blurred, but she managed to knee him in the groin.

Remy flinched and his hold slipped a little, allowing her to take a breath. She was about to knee him once more when he was suddenly ripped away from her and thrown across the street, where his body collided with the other brick building.

Roman and Laird were in her face, their expressions full of concern. "Are you okay? Can you breathe?"

She saw Remy try to take a swing at Caine from his hands and knees position, but Caine slammed his fist into his face, sending him to the ground.

Kaitlyn knew how strong and deadly the weres could be. She managed to croak, "Don't let Caine kill him."

Laird shot across the thirty-foot distance, capturing Caine's fist before it came back down on Remy, who was struggling to get up. "Easy, bud. She wants him alive."

Kaitlyn approached Remy and stood over him. Blood trickled from his busted lip. He blinked several times, trying to stay conscious as he leaned up on his elbow. A triumphant smile tilted his swelling lip. "Your mom's time is up."

Rage consumed her, turning her stomach. "You're going to call off your man!" Kaitlyn growled and reached for Remy's jacket. He jerked away from her grasp and fell back onto the pavement. "Too late." He laughed before his eyes rolled back in his head and he passed out.

Kaitlyn immediately ran back across the street to retrieve Landon's cell phone from the cement. Her throat constricted as she flipped open the phone. Locking gazes with Caine, she called out in a curt voice, "Your number."

While Caine rattled off his cell number, she quickly dialed. When the phone finally started to ring, she sent a silent prayer that Landon had reached her mother in time.

The phone rang and rang and rang until the voice mail picked up.

Caine walked up beside her and she shut the phone. "He's not answering."

He turned and barked orders to Laird and Roman. "Get the two men we took down, as well as this prick." He gestured to Remy's unconscious body. "There's some rope in the back of the truck. Tie them up and keep them quiet until we return."

Nodding to Kaitlyn, his expression hardened to grim lines. "Let's get to the hospital."

Kaitlyn let Caine drive her car so she could continue to try Caine's cell number as they drove to the hospital. She quickly discovered werewolves' fast reflexes came in handy. Caine flew down the roads so fast, she didn't dare look at the speedometer, let alone the objects zooming past in a blur of dark shadows; buildings, cars and streetlights.

Something Landon had said about being created by the vampires came back to her when she glanced Caine's way. "You're not really Landon's little brother, are you?"

He smiled and shook his head. "No, but it was the best way at the time to explain me breaking his door down. I thought he was hurt. He'd let out this wailing howl—" Caine stopped speaking and cleared his throat. "Well, anyway. Landon might not be my flesh-and-blood brother, but he's been a wonderful mentor. I would follow his lead any day over that idiot Nathan."

His comment surprised her. "Landon's not your leader?"

Caine shook his head as he parked in front of the hospital. "No, he's not Alpha, but he should be."

Kaitlyn's thoughts shifted back to her mom as she jumped out of the car and ran toward the hospital. Caine zipped past and held the hospital's glass entrance door, waiting for her to catch up.

She reached the door and said, "Mom's on the fourth floor. Room four-twenty. I'll be there as soon as I can. Go!"

Caine was gone in an instant, so fast he was just a dark blur speeding down the hall. Only the door to the stairs slowly closing told her where he'd gone.

As Kaitlyn took the cement stairs two at a time, she considered alerting hospital security, but she didn't know what they'd encounter up there in her mother's room; human or panther bad guys. She didn't want to endanger any more people than necessary, not to mention exposing Landon and Caine if their werewolf half was called on to protect her mother.

When she reached the fourth floor, Kaitlyn pulled her gun from the holster around her ankle, then quietly opened the stairwell an inch.

A strong antiseptic smell wafted her way, making her nose itch. She peered through the crack. Early morning quiet and fluorescent lights shone down the deserted hall. The nurses' station was empty.

Tucking her hand and the small gun inside her sweat jacket's front pocket, Kaitlyn opened the door. She walked briskly down the hall and was going to zip past the desk when she saw the nurse's rolling chair overturned next to a lateral filing cabinet. Paperwork was everywhere.

Heart pounding, Kaitlyn ran up to the desk and peered over the edge. A nurse with short blond hair was lying on her back. Blood pooled on the carpet from a wound on the side of her head.

Rushing around the desk, Kaitlyn knelt next to the young woman and felt for a pulse on her neck. She had one, but it was sluggish.

Kaitlyn stood and quickly grabbed the phone. Dialing zero she waited for the man at the front desk to answer.

"Front desk."

"This is Kaitlyn McKinney. A nurse on the fourth floor has been injured. She's lying on the floor behind the nurse's station. Tell them to hurry. She's lost a lot of blood."

"Sweet mercy. I'm on it!"

After he hung up, Kaitlyn dialed 9-1-1. Once she'd called the incident in, she rounded the nurse's station and ran down the hall to her mother's room. One person poked his head outside his room door, then quickly shut it as she zoomed past.

Kaitlyn's throat seized as she entered the room. It was in total shambles. The tray table was bent in half and the chair that usually resided beside her mother's bed was across the room, broken apart in two pieces. Marbles were scattered everywhere and the glass vase was broken on the floor at the foot of the bed.

Caine stood, fist in the air, over a dark-haired man who was either passed out cold or dead. Her gaze quickly locked on her mother, who lay quietly with her eyes shut.

Dear God, please let her be alive. Pushing marbles to the side with her shoes, Kaitlyn rushed to her mother's side and lifted her limp hand. Her mother's face was in deep-sleep repose. Kaitlyn pressed her thumb to her mother's wrist and waited to feel a pulse.

A steady thump rushed under her thumb as Caine said in a soft voice beside her, "Landon got here in time. They were in her room but didn't get a chance to touch her. I'm amazed she slept through all the ruckus."

"It's the meds she's on for the pain. They make her sleep deeply." She touched her mother's salt-and-pepper hair and her heart ached. Turning her attention to Caine, she frowned. "Where's Landon?"

Caine's expression hardened and he jerked his chin toward the window. "He went after the panther."

Kaitlyn followed his direction. The room's window had been completely shattered. She'd been so caught up in making sure her mom was okay she hadn't noticed the cooler night air flowing into the room, or Landon's torn, blood-stained T-shirt on the floor below the window.

Her stomach tensed. "You think he'll be okay?"

"He'll be fine." Caine grinned. "He'd howl if he needed me."

Shaking her head, Kaitlyn pulled the extra blanket at the bottom of the bed up over her mother's legs and upper body and tried to not worry too much about Landon.

She glanced at the man still lying on the floor. "Tell me he's still breathing."

Caine snorted in disgust, then nodded.

Relieved, Kaitlyn swept the room, looking for the notepad that usually resided on her mother's tray stand. When she saw it underneath her mother's bed, she retrieved the pad and found the pen on the floor next to the mangled tray stand. That's when her gaze landed on the automatic handgun under her mother's bed.

"It was his," Caine sneered, jerking his gaze to the man on the floor.

Kaitlyn kicked the gun across the room, then began to scribble a note on the paper. "I had to call the police. A nurse was attacked down the hall. You need to go. Get back to Laird and Roman." She tore off the paper and put the note in his hand. "Deliver Remy and his men to the front door of the precinct, along with this note. Then take off. Don't stick around."

Caine crumpled the note slightly and glared at the guy on the floor. "I should stay with you."

Her eyebrow rose. "He's human, isn't he?"

"Much to my disappointment." He sounded annoyed. "Landon was fighting them both, trying to keep the men away from your mom when I came in. Once the Velius saw he was outnumbered by two weres, he jumped through the window."

Loud voices and radio squawks echoed outside in the hall. The police had arrived. Kaitlyn's pulse raced. She shooed Caine toward the door. "Go!"

He shoved the note in his pocket and shot past her.

Turning, she called out, "Not that way…" but he was already diving out the window. She ran to the window and barely caught a glimpse of him as he zigzagged around several cars, a shadowy blur in the dark night.

"Show-off," she muttered.

The sound of a man groaning drew her attention. Kaitlyn turned at the same time the dark-haired man on the floor rolled over, holding his jaw.

Fists clenched, she moved close when she realized who he was. The partner Ron had assigned her. Ron had trusted Kent with his life; had believed him to be an honorable man.

"My jaw," Kent moaned and curled onto his side, holding his face. "I think it's broken."

"I doubt it. Though if it is, it's no less than you deserve, you murdering bastard."

He growled and swiped for her ankles. She jumped into the air, avoiding his hand. As her feet landed, she brought her fist straight down on his cheekbone, knocking him out once more. "That's for trying to kill my mom!" she gritted out and shook her hand to dissipate the pain splintering through it. Damn, his face was hard.

After she'd tossed the broken chair out the window to explain the window's condition, she restrapped her small gun in her ankle holder, then balled up Landon's torn shirt and tucked it next to her keys in the front pocket of her sweat jacket.

Grabbing Kent's shirt collar, her muscles strained as she dragged him to the door, opened it, then dropped his unconscious body across the threshold.

"Officer. Down here. This man tried to attack my mother," Kaitlyn called out to the police officer standing in front of the nurse's station.

Kaitlyn sat in a boardroom the hospital staff had allowed the police to borrow so she could fill out her official statement report. The report was already written. She read over it once more while an officer sat across from her.

In her report, she told the story from the beginning of her original assigned Tacomi case to Remy and the Garotters blackmailing her into giving them evidence Ron had sent her before they killed him in exchange for her mother's life. She also reported that they had supposedly planted evidence on Ron's body to frame her. She'd left Landon, Caine and the other weres out of it, just stating there were bystanders she didn't know who had come to her aid, then disappeared.

Once she'd finished scanning her statement, she signed it, then slid the paperwork across the table to the police officer, John Roberts.

He read over the document, while an appreciative half smile tilted his lips. "Man, you sure know how to make a splash, McKinney." Glancing up, his expression turned serious. "Some of this didn't happen by the book, though. Once the lawyers get a hold of it, you know as well as I do there's no guarantee how much will stick."

She rubbed her temples, completely exhausted and brain-dead at that point. "I didn't have time. My mother's life was at stake." Placing her hands on the table, she leaned forward, her stomach suddenly a tense knot. "Tell me you all have Remy and his two men in custody."

He nodded, then thrummed his fingers on the table. His brow furrowed as he stared at the report. "You know we're going to need more proof. If we can't get these guys to roll on each other, a lot of this is just your word against theirs."

She withdrew Landon's cell phone from her pocket and opened it. Scanning to the attachment Ron had sent her, she slid the open phone across the desk to John. He picked up the phone and glanced at the display. "You mentioned this in your report. It still doesn't prove who murdered Ron and Wayne. And that's *if* the men tell us where we can find the bodies so we can prove they're dead."

Kaitlyn pulled her keychain out of her pocket. "You can use this to get them to talk." Taking the voice recorder that Abby had given her off her keychain, she set in on the table and pushed the replay button.

John listened to the entire conversation she'd had with Remy as it replayed on the tiny voice machine. The voice recorder stopped, cutting off right before Remy had attacked her.

He smiled and slid the recorder into the evidence bag. "You've done a helluva job, Kaitlyn. I hope they nail the bastards to the wall for Ron and Wayne's deaths, the attempt on your mother's life as well as the gunrunning."

She sat back in her chair with a tired sigh. "Me, too."

Fortunately, Kaitlyn's mom didn't wake up until after they'd moved her to a new room.

The sun was just beginning to peak over the horizon when her mother opened her eyes. Her gasp drew Kaitlyn's attention. She jumped up from her catatonic half-awake state in her chair and rushed to grab her mother's hand. "Mom? Are you okay? Are you in any pain?"

Her mother smiled. "I guess today's going to be an okay day. I was just surprised to see you. What are you doing here so early? You look exhausted, sweetie."

Kaitlyn leaned over and kissed her mother's cheek. "I love you, Mom. They mentioned they were going to move you due to renovations, so I wanted to be here when you woke up."

Her mother's soft gaze tracked the room. "I've been moved?"

Kaitlyn nodded. She didn't like lying to her mother, but she didn't want to upset her with the whole sordid truth. She knew her mom would worry about her. Pointing to the window, she said, "You'll get a lot less hot afternoon sun in this room. You're on the seventh floor now."

Her mother's eyes drifted closed. "That'll be nice."

She sounded so detached, like she was fading away. Kaitlyn blinked back her tears. When her mom didn't open her eyes right away, her heart jerked. She squeezed her mother's fragile hand. "Mom?"

Her mom's eyes fluttered open once more. "I'm still waking up, I guess. You usually come at night."

Breathing an inward sigh of relief, Kaitlyn kissed her

mom's forehead and stepped back. "I'll let you rest, but can I come back tonight?"

Her mom slowly nodded. "Of course you can. I'll see you tonight."

Kaitlyn pulled her car keys out of her pocket and walked outside her mother's room. Closing her eyes, she leaned against the wall in the hall. She felt as if someone had put her in a washing machine on "soiled" and then used the extra-long spin cycle. She'd never been more physically and emotionally drained in her life.

Landon's alluring, magnetic scent entered her mind and she almost doubled over at how real and very comforting the smell was. She gripped her stomach and waited for the memory to fade, but it didn't.

Resigning herself to carrying around his wonderful scent in her mind all day, she sighed and opened her eyes. She gave a small gasp of surprise to see Landon sitting on the bench across the hall from her mother's room. "How long have you been sitting there?"

"Long enough." He looked so serious as he stood and approached her.

He wore a long-sleeved navy-blue checkered button-down shirt hanging open over a heather-gray T-shirt. Faded jeans and a pair of scuffed boots rounded out his rugged look. Only, this wasn't an affected look. The faint stains on his jeans told of hard work. And she couldn't forget his wolf half. Landon was as outdoorsy as a man could be.

He stopped in front of her, his light brown hair slightly damp and wavy, as if he'd run his hands through it several times. Even the soap he'd used mixed with his own musky scent to create a new, tempting aroma.

He looked so devastatingly handsome and virile, her

stomach felt as if it were being twisted inside out. She curled her fingers into a fist to keep from reaching for him, to lean into his strength and feel his arms around her again. She couldn't forget how much everything had changed.

When she saw the red scar running along the side of his neck, her first instinct was to touch it and to comfort him. Her gaze jerked to his. "Are you okay?"

"I'm fine." He reached for her hand and uncurled her fingers. Taking her keys, he said, "I came to take you home, Kaitie. You look dead on your feet."

"Thanks for the compliment," she mumbled, trying to grab back her keys. "I can drive myself home."

"If you want to get home, you'll have to meet me at your car."

Before she could blink, he was gone. Just like that.

She would never get used to these weres' speed. Clamping her teeth together, she set off after him.

Landon was leaning against her car as she walked up.

When she was three feet away, he stood beside the passenger door, holding it open.

Shrugging off her annoyance, she climbed into the passenger side. Though she'd never admit it to him, Landon was right to offer to drive her. She was so tired she wasn't in any condition to drive.

As Landon backed out of the parking spot, Kaitlyn closed her eyes and laid her head back against the headrest.

Kaitlyn awoke and her head was stuffy and groggy as Landon lifted her out of her car.

"Wha— Mmm." Squinting against the sunlight in her eyes she tried to focus, but her vision blurred. She wrapped her arms around his neck and hid her eyes from the bright light.

"We're at your house," Landon said, holding her close.

"Mmm'kay," she mumbled, completely incoherent. She felt like she was floating on velvet-coated steel. Landon held her securely as he carried her inside and then turned to walk her up the stairs. His boots made light thumping sounds on the hardwood stairs.

Her hat magically came off, and she kicked out of her shoes right before glorious softness surrounded her back. She realized he'd laid her on her bed.

Fingers lightly touched her throat. "Son of a bitch!" Landon whispered. She realized he must be looking at the bruises Remy must've left behind when he'd tried to choke her.

"'S'kay," she whispered. He started to pull away and her heart lurched. Cinching her arms tight around his neck, she yanked him close and begged, "No, please."

When the mattress dipped and he lay down beside her, pressing her head to his chest, her body relaxed. There was a slight tug on her hair and the rubber band disappeared, replaced by Landon's fingers slowly combing through her hair.

Emotions welled, strong and fierce within her, making her chest tighten and her eyes sting. When Landon wrapped his arms around her, the tears finally fell.

Kaitlyn cried for her father. She cried for all the lost years. She sobbed for her mother, for the near panic she'd felt when she'd thought she might lose her tonight and the knowledge that even though they'd caught the bad guys, her mother's fate hadn't changed. Every day she wondered if that was the day the cancer would finally take her mom away from her.

She trembled at the thought of being alone, of having no one to turn to, no one to love and cherish. Her thoughts naturally turned to Landon, and her heart ached.

Burying her nose against Landon's hard chest, Kaitlyn felt

as if she were falling deeper and deeper into a bottomless abyss. She wrapped her arm tight around his waist and felt him kiss the top of her head. Snuggling close to his warmth, she held on for dear life so she wouldn't be sucked into complete darkness and lose herself forever.

Chapter 12

Kaitlyn rolled over in bed and tucked her hand under her pillow. A few seconds later, reality set in, dispelling the blissful sleepiness from her mind. She opened her eyes and stared at the sun shining through her bedroom window. The sunlight appeared softer, less glaring, and the angle was in line with late afternoon. Had she truly slept the day away?

Her head throbbed slightly and she remembered how she'd fallen asleep—bawling her eyes out like a baby…on Landon, no less. She tensed. How utterly embarrassing. She was supposed to be so tough. Knowing she'd have to face him eventually, she took a deep breath and rolled over…to an empty bed.

Instinctively, she knew Landon wasn't in the house anymore. Kaitlyn ran her hand along the feather pillow that still held an indention from his head and whispered, "Thank you."

What time was it? Glancing at her watch, she sat up

quickly. Four-thirty. She needed to take a shower and eat before she headed back to the hospital.

While the shower's warm water sluiced over her, Kaitlyn leaned against the shower wall and thought about Landon's role in her father's death. Her stomach knotted as she pictured Morningside Park in her mind's eye, her father bleeding and Landon…how had he felt? She'd been avoiding thinking about that fateful night, but she needed to acknowledge the truth and make peace with how she felt, so she could move on.

It was a gift from my father, she'd said to Landon about her wolf charm.

Me, too, he'd said, but it was the look in his eyes and the tone of his voice that stuck with her. He'd appeared tense and regretful.

Did he wear it as a reminder of some kind? Past mistakes, maybe? "Oh, Landon." She squeezed her eyes shut and hot tears welled. She knew he regretted taking her father's life, but how could she be expected to forgive that?

He saved yours and your mother's life, didn't he?

He did and she hadn't really thanked him for that. But could she consider never seeing Landon again? Not having him in her life at all?

No! her mind screamed. *He's a good person. He challenges me, respects my opinion and is the most primal yet tender man I've ever been with. He recognizes and responds to my moods and he lets me be myself.* Landon was everything she'd wanted.

God help her, she loved him with a fierceness that tore her up inside. Her stomach churned and her chest felt tight as the realization sunk in. She turned and let the water pound her face. Hundreds of tiny wet punches for her traitorous thoughts. *He killed your father.*

Steam filled the room, and its thickness, combined with her guilt, nearly closed her throat.

Kaitlyn shut off the faucet. She stood in the quiet shower, letting the cold air that seeped past the curtain bombard her wet skin. When her teeth began to chatter, she pulled a towel down from the hook on the wall and began to dry herself off.

With a heavy heart, she climbed out of the shower and got dressed.

After she'd eaten, Kaitlyn walked into the office to shut down her computer. She realized she'd left it on overnight. As she was clicking through the shut-down sequence, her thoughts turned to her mother and what she'd bring her tonight. Kaitlyn always brought a small gift of some kind to brighten her mother's day.

Her gaze landed on the small wooden box with the carved wolf on top. She'd left it sitting on the carpet next to the couch. Her mother would love that. Walking around the desk, she sat down next to the cardboard box and emptied the bullets out of the wooden keepsake.

She pushed the cardboard box's lid off and gently laid the bullets in the corner where the wooden box had resided. The stack of papers piled inside the folder on the other side of the box drew her attention. Lifting the folder, she laid it in her lap and opened it. Her heart jerked when she realized the stack of handwritten letters inside were from her father to her mother.

Kaitlyn felt as if she were intruding by reading the letters and poems, but her heart swelled at the wonderful gift she could give her mother tonight. When she finished reading them all, her cheeks were wet again, but she sniffed at the legacy of love her father had left behind.

Setting her favorite letter on top, she stood and collected her purse and keys from the table in the hall.

* * *

As Kaitlyn passed the nurse's station on the seventh floor, the gray-haired nurse called out to her, "Miss McKinney."

Kaitlyn stopped and looked her way. "Yes?"

The older woman gave her a sympathetic smile. "I just wanted to let you know your mother had a rough day earlier. She's awake now, but she may not be up for a long visit."

Kaitlyn clutched the folder and wooden box against her chest, disappointment setting in. "Do you think I should come back tomorrow?"

The nurse shook her head and shooed her on. "Of course not, dear. Go visit your mom. She really looks forward to your visits."

Kaitlyn thanked her for the update before heading down the hall to her mother's room.

"Ah, my second visitor of the day," Sharon said with a pleased yet tired sigh as Kaitlyn walked in.

Kaitlyn tried not to notice the deep circles under her mother's eyes or the drawn look on her face as she approached the bed. Kissing her mother on the cheek, she pulled back and teased, "Technically, you're getting the same visitor, but one who has a lot more rest, a bath and some food under her belt."

Her mother gave a soft laugh as Kaitlyn pulled the chair closer to the bed and sat down. "While I agree you do look much better, Kaitie, I was referring to the nice man who paid me a visit earlier today."

Kaitlyn jerked her gaze to her mother's, worry gripping her chest. Thoughts of demanding twenty-four-hour security for her mother flashed through her mind. "What man?"

"A friend of yours and very handsome I might add." Her mother gave her a knowing smile and raised her eyebrow expectantly.

Kaitlyn leaned forward, crushing the folder in her hands. "Who, Mom?"

"He said his name was Landon Rourke and he worked with you on a case recently." Her mother frowned. "Why didn't you tell me you'd been promoted to detective? Your father would be so proud, sweetie."

Kaitlyn didn't know how she felt about Landon visiting her mother. She hoped he hadn't told her mom about the case and that's why her day hadn't gone so well. "What did he say?"

"He just said you helped crack a case and that I should be very proud of you."

Relief rushed through Kaitlyn, relaxing her tense shoulders. "Is that all he said?"

Sharon nodded. "In so many words, but..." her mother stared at the wall, her expression far away as she finished, "...the way he talked about you, the pride in his voice and the look on his face. It reminded me of the way your father used to look when he talked about me." Her mother's pleased tone faded and her eyes closed. "Well, many moons ago, back in the early days. I'm suddenly feeling very tired."

Kaitlyn reached for her mom's hand. "Mom, don't talk such nonsense. Dad has always loved you. Wanna know how much?"

Her mother's eyes fluttered open. "What do you mean?"

Kaitlyn pushed the wooden box into her mother's other hand, then flipped open the folder. "I found that keepsake in Dad's stuff I brought back from Hank's the other day."

Her mother sighed as she stared at the box. "Hank's place was where your dad took off to when he needed time alone. I swear he spent more time there than Hank did."

"Hank lives in the mountains full-time now."

Her mother closed her eyes again. "Thank you for the box, Kaitie."

Kaitlyn felt her mother's interest waning. "No, Mom, that wasn't the main thing I brought." Squeezing her mother's hand, she picked up a letter and said, "Just listen."

My dearest Sharon,
Have I told you how much I love you? How much I cherish the moment you said, "I do"? From the day you walked into my life, I finally felt like a whole person, like the other half of me was complete. I know we went through some rough times in the past. Trying for a child for years and years without success took a toll on both of us. And then Kaitie came into our lives and brightened our days and nights with her constant chatter and childlike view of the world. Her evanescence was infectious, renewing the vigor in our family, but you know…as much as I love our Kaitie and couldn't imagine life without her, if we hadn't had her, my love for you would still be as strong as it is today. I know I don't say it often enough. I guess I've kept things to myself a lot. It's just my nature. But I do love you with every fiber of my being, Sharon. I love the way your eyes sparkle when you're teasing and the way you laugh. I always find myself smiling, too. And your sweet touch, aaah, my love, nothing compares. You're everything to me and always will be.
Your loving husband,
James

She glanced up at her mother to see her eyes were still closed, but tears were streaking down her temples. Her mother sniffled, then whispered, "That's the best present I've ever received."

Emotions clogged Kaitlyn's throat and she squeezed her

mother's hand. Finally, she found the words. "There are tons of letters and poems from Dad in this folder. Would you like me to read more?"

Her mother slowly nodded but kept her eyes closed. "Yes, please. That would be wonderful."

Kaitlyn read through every single letter and poem. When she finished, she looked up. Her mother's eyes were lightly shut and she had the most peaceful expression on her face.

"Mom?" Instinctively, Kaitlyn felt for the pulse on her wrist. There wasn't even a tiny flutter.

The letters and folder scattered across the floor as she jumped up and pressed her ear to her mother's chest. Sharon McKinney's heartbeat was peacefully silent.

Kaitlyn hugged her mother and sobbed until her head hurt. Sitting up, she touched her mother's soft cheek. "I love you, and I'll miss you, Mom. At least now you're not in any more pain. Tell Dad I love him."

A couple hours later, Kaitlyn drove up to her house, feeling achy and exhausted, as if she hadn't slept or eaten in days. She parked beside Abby's car, wondering how she was going to tell her friend she wasn't in the mood to chat.

Abby got out of her car and met Kaitlyn as she got out of hers.

Kaitlyn eyed the brown paper bag in Abby's arms, then squinted at Ab's face in the darkness. "What's in the bag?"

Abby lifted the top of a bottle of wine out of the bag.

Kaitlyn shook her head. "I'm not in the mood to celebrate anything, Ab. I'm sorry."

Abby pulled the bottle all the way out of the bag, a somber look on her face. "It's merlot. A wine for chilling and talking. I brought some cheese and crackers, too."

Kaitlyn realized her friend was a lot more subdued than normal. "You know about my mom, don't you?"

Slipping the bottle of wine back into the bag, Abby wrapped her arm around Kaitlyn's shoulders and steered her toward the front door. "Landon called me."

Kaitlyn stiffened and halted. "Landon?"

Abby nodded, tears glittering in her eyes. "He called me an hour ago and said I should probably come see you tonight. That you would need a friend to talk to." She squeezed Kaitlyn's shoulders. "I'm so sorry about your mom."

Landon's thoughtfulness tore at her heart. "Thanks, Ab. I could use a few glasses of wine and a friend's shoulder."

Abby leaned over and kissed her on the cheek. "My shoulder's right here, girl."

"I've got so much to do over the next few days, with arrangements and such." Kaitlyn sniffled. "I don't want to disappoint the 'Hall' kids. You and those teens are all I've got now, Ab."

"Don't worry about Handleburg. I've got you covered until you're ready. Come on, let's get inside. It's chilly out here."

Abby turned out to be a lifesaver. That night she got Kaitlyn to tell her what she wanted, and then she took care of all the funeral arrangements.

Two days later, the day after she'd attended Ron and Wayne's funerals, Kaitlyn returned from her mother's early morning funeral, feeling numb all over. On that crisp fall morning, with the sun shining brightly, her mother had been lain to rest beside her father. The funeral had been crowded with the entire precinct as well as several retired cops who'd worked with her father. The overwhelming turnout was heartwarming, even during such a sad event.

Kaitlyn had given the eulogy. She'd talked about finding her father's letters to her mother and then had read one of her father's poems. She'd ended by saying, "My father loved my mother deeply and I'm happy she died knowing just how much. True love *will* endure the obstacles life throws at you. When you go home, give your loved ones a hug and tell them how much they mean to you."

The congregation had given a standing ovation when she'd finished. Kaitlyn had thanked them on behalf of her father and her mother and let them know how much she appreciated their support.

Standing in front of her house now, she picked up the bouquet of flowers that were sitting on her front porch and read the card.

Know that my thoughts are with you, Kaitie.
Yours,
Landon

That afternoon, while Kaitlyn was cleaning the house to ward away thoughts of being alone, the doorbell rang. She answered it still wearing her bright yellow rubber gloves.

Caine glanced at her ratty red tank top and a pair of holey gray sweat pants. "Nice outfit."

Was something wrong with Landon? Even as her stomach tensed, she adopted a nonchalant pose and blew a piece of her hair, that had fallen from her clip, out of her eyes. "What can I do for you, Caine?"

"Can I come in?" he asked at the same time he stepped past her into the foyer.

Kaitlyn mumbled, "Be my guest," as she shut the door behind him. Chilly air rushed in, cooling down her sweaty body.

Caine shoved his hands in his jeans pockets and rocked back on his heels. "I just wanted to say how sorry I am about your mom. Landon and I attended the funeral."

"You did? I didn't see you."

He nodded. "Landon thought it best if we stayed back. He didn't want to upset you."

"Why would you two attending my mom's funeral upset me?"

Caine's dark eyebrows rose over his hazel eyes. "Well, because of your dad."

Kaitlyn stiffened at his comment. Bending, she picked up the bucket of cleaning supplies she'd set in the hall to answer the door. "It's done and over with. Let it go."

"That's kind of what I wanted to discuss with you."

She arched her eyebrow, then turned and started to walk up the stairs. "If you want to talk, you'll have to follow me while I clean. I'm on a mission this afternoon."

"I see that," he mumbled from directly behind her as she turned into her bedroom.

Kaitlyn flipped on the bathroom light, then squirted bathroom cleaner in the sink and across the countertop. While she waited for the liquid to do its job, she picked up a sponge. "What's on your mind?"

Caine leaned his back casually against the doorjamb for a second. Then he stood upright as if he'd seen a ghost. He stared at something in her bedroom.

"What's wrong?"

He nodded toward the wall near her door. "Who painted the wolf on your wall?"

She sighed and shook her head. "You Lupreda all think alike. Like I told Landon, my father had a local artist paint it to his specifications."

"Ah." He nodded and resumed his relaxed pose against the doorway. "I'm here to ask for forgiveness for Landon."

Her lips tightened. "Shouldn't he be asking for that himself?"

Caine shook his head. "He'd kill me if he knew I came here. He believes he deserves your anger."

"Well, that makes two of us. He killed my father, Caine. He might've saved my mother's life, but that doesn't change the fact he took my father's."

"He has regretted what happened ever since. Did you know that all these years he's watched over you?"

Her eyes widened. "What do you mean?"

"Landon has always been there in the background, making sure you were okay. He even set up the college fund so you could go to the college of your choice."

She frowned, shaking her head. "My scholarship was for children of police officers who'd been killed."

Caine raised his eyebrow. "Set up by an anonymous donor."

She nodded slowly as the realization sank in.

"Landon tried his best to make up for taking your father from you. He did what he could to compensate for that."

Why didn't Landon tell me all this? Then again, it would be like him not to, she thought with a mental snort. *Stubborn man.* While she was processing Landon's sheer dedication, she started to scrub the sink in slow swirling movements.

Caine continued, "I'm not asking you to forgive what happened, just to place the blame on the right party."

Glancing up, she paused. "What are you talking about? Landon was the one who mauled my father."

Caine lifted his hands in the air. "He was only acting to protect me."

Kaitlyn just stared at him, her heart thudding in her chest. "Tell me exactly what happened."

After Caine relayed the whole story of what happened in Morningside Park, she felt a little sick to her stomach. The details were more than she'd bargained for…on all counts.

"Landon was acting as he always does—as Alpha to protect a pack mate from attack. My guess is that your father saw our female Lupreda running through the woods screaming and me in Musk form chasing after her and came to the wrong conclusion."

"My father would've done what any cop worth his mettle would do. Protect the innocent," she whispered as some of the puzzle pieces clicked together in her mind.

Caine moved to stand next to her, his voice going softer. "If you want to hate someone, then hate me, Kaitlyn. Landon is the true Alpha of our pack. I believe one of the reasons he hasn't fought for the official role is because of what he did to your father eighteen years ago. He blames himself and wears that bullet slug to keep him from shifting."

She frowned in confusion. "How does the bullet keep him from shifting?"

"The silver in your father's bullets almost killed me. If it weren't for Landon, I never would've survived. The bullet is just a reminder, but the silver chain he chooses to wear around his neck is what keeps him from shifting to either his Musk form or a full wolf form during the full moon's cycle. It's a carryover from the silver collars the vampires made our kind wear to keep us from shifting until they wanted us to."

That's why he took off the chain in the alley, she realized.

Water dripped from the sponge into the sink. Its quiet plunks against the porcelain were the only sounds in the room as her mind turned over everything Caine had told her.

She began to scrub the sink furiously. "You mentioned my father's death as one reason. Why wasn't Landon already Alpha?"

Caine crossed his arms and leaned against the sink's

cabinet. "Because his sense of smell isn't as sharp as all the other weres. It never has been."

She met his gaze with surprise. "A werewolf who can't smell?"

Caine shook his head. "No. His sense of smell is still far greater than a human's. It's just not as sharp as the other weres'."

The injustice made her chest tight with fury. Straightening, she pointed her sponge hand toward him in a quick jerk. "Are you saying that silly reason is the only thing keeping him from being Alpha?"

He flicked the soapy water off his jaw with a frown and nodded. "The Omega have disqualified him from being able to participate in the annual Alpha run because his scenting skills aren't one hundred percent on par with the other weres." Caine straightened, standing to his full height. "Anyway, I want you to think about forgiving Landon and accepting him as your Lupreda mate."

She blinked a couple times, then swirled the sponge around the faucet until it shone. "I thought we were talking about forgiveness. I'm not Landon's Lupreda mate."

Caine's fingers brushed across her shoulder in the spot where Landon had bitten her. "This says differently."

Chapter 13

Caine's statement made her cheeks flush. When she'd accused Landon of giving her a wolf bite, his response had been so serious and intense. *That wasn't a wolf bite.*

"You're wrong," she whispered and glanced at her shoulder. Both shocked and strangely excited by the concept Landon had branded her, she scrubbed harder.

His voice turned to steel. "Lupredas only mark when they find their true mate. It's a lifetime commitment and not taken lightly among our kind. Think about what I said," Caine advised, turning to leave.

As soon as she heard the front door shut behind him, Kaitlyn lifted her gaze to the mirror. Two red spots graced the area between her neck and her shoulder. A matching pair were on the back side.

Landon's mark for all to see. A mate's mark, Caine had called it.

It had been a couple days since Landon had bitten her, yet the red marks hadn't lessened in intensity. She'd been so distracted with everything going on, she hadn't paid attention to herself as she got dressed the past couple days.

Landon's mate. Her spirits soared and she instantly felt remorseful for the involuntary elation. But Caine's story made her think long and hard. She knew in her heart that Landon truly regretted what had happened, and yet even though he didn't know if she would ever return his feelings, he had committed himself to her.

Is it so wrong for me to care for him? she asked herself.

She wished she could talk to Abby about Landon, but his world was unknown to humans. She didn't want to expose the Lupreda any more than necessary, even to a trusted friend. Knowing Abby, her friend would tell her she was being an idiot, that the past had happened eighteen years ago and Landon had done his best to make amends ever since.

Once she finished up the bathrooms, she took another shower and walked downstairs. The house seemed so very quiet to her now. Even though her mother had been at the hospital for a couple months and she'd been living there on her own, there was something very final about the silence in the house she'd grown up in with her parents.

She'd saved cleaning the office for last. Her father's folder with all his letters to her mother sat on the desk, waiting to be put away. With a sigh, she restacked the letters and put them neatly in the folder. Sliding the cardboard box toward her, she started to set the folder back on the books, but they'd tipped over when she jerked the box. She set down the folder and sat beside the box to straighten the books.

When she lifted them, her gaze landed on a thin, gold-leafed book that had a rubber band around it. Curious, she set the other books down and removed the rubber band.

The book fell open to the middle page. It was a journal her father had kept. She flipped back to the beginning and looked at the date of the first entry. It was dated almost twenty-five years ago.

The strangeness started a month after that enormous dog bit me in the park. He was black with a torn left ear and one blue and one brown eye. I'll never forget his sharp teeth clamping down on me.

Her gaze widened and she continued reading. She discovered her father was never the same after that incident, even though he put up a good front for her mother.

Sharon would never understand this need to run through the woods, the way I crave raw meat every now and then. Something has changed.

She flipped forward, skimming more pages.

Hank lets me borrow his cabin when it gets too rough for me in the city. He understands my need to be with nature. He doesn't know it's because I've changed.

The pages flew by.

I paused when I passed by a stranger in the street today. Something about him seemed familiar, yet I'd never met him before. I followed him, staying way back. I watched him go into the woods in Morningside Park.

He was gone for hours and when he came back, he looked rejuvenated…like I always feel when I walk around in the woods for hours on end.

Was her father talking about Landon? She skimmed even further.

Wolves!!! I just can't stop thinking about them. Bought more books about them and even a werewolf lore book. It has become an obsession I can't seem to shake.

"Oh, Dad, I had no idea," she whispered as she continued to turn pages, her pace frantic in her need to understand his obsession.

I saw a wolf in the woods today! He was a majestic beast. Bigger than I thought wolves normally grew to be.

Later in the journal, her dad's entries seemed more disjointed, as if he was going through some kind of breakdown or deep depression.

I think I'm going crazy. I have these primal urges when the moon is full. I come to the cabin then. To get away. I walk through the woods, enjoying all the earthy smells around me. Sometimes I run as fast as my legs will carry me…and then I wake up on the forest floor naked. I don't remember how I got there.

I feel so alone sometimes. Like no one understands me. Thank God Sharon still loves me, though she doesn't know how I feel. I'm going to Morningside

Park tonight. Maybe I'll see that man again and can talk to him about his long walks in the woods.

He had to be talking about Landon. The picture of Landon in the box made more sense now. She flipped to the last page of his book. It was dated a couple of days before her father's death.

I waited for him three different times now. Maybe he doesn't go to that park anymore. I feel so alone. I've made special bullets. Even etched my initials in them. One should do it, but it might take more than one. I'm going back to where it all started. I'll miss my family deeply, but they're better off without me. I'm not the same person I was seven years ago. I always feel so...out of control. I don't think I'll ever be the same again.

Kaitlyn let the journal slip from her fingers onto the floor. Her father had known something about Landon was different. He'd sensed it, but he hadn't known why he was drawn to him. Landon was a natural Alpha. He exuded a confident bearing that demanded respect. Her chest squeezed as she considered the fear her father must've experienced and the knowledge he'd gone to the park to end his own life. Had he been bitten by a werewolf in his wolf form? There was one way to find out.

Picking up the telephone from the desk, she dialed Caine's number.

Two rings later, Caine answered. "Hello?"

"Caine, it's Kaitlyn."

"I knew you'd come around—"

"Hush and just listen. Do you have a black wolf in your pack with a torn left ear and one blue and one brown eye?"

Caine didn't answer for a second. "Yes, we did. His name was Andre. He committed suicide twenty-four years ago."

Her stomach tensed. "Why did he commit suicide?"

"Because he didn't shift back to human form when daylight arrived. Time passed, and he remained a wolf. There were rumors he must've bitten a huma— Why are you asking me about Andre? And how do you know about him?"

Kaitlyn released a heavy sigh. "Because he bit my father almost twenty-five years ago. I just found my father's journal. I—I think the wolf's bite changed my dad. He became obsessed with wolves and started spending a lot of time in the woods, feeling a stronger pull to nature when the moon was full. He'd seen Landon on the street and was drawn to follow him. Then he saw Landon enter the woods in Morningside Park and not return for hours. Caine, the reason he was at the park that night…he was planning to kill himself. He'd never felt the same since he'd been bitten."

"And then he saw us in our Musk form," Caine replied with a sad tone. "I'm so sorry, Kaitlyn. I didn't think this was possible, but it sounds like your father was going through a wolf-like change, and Andre's bite had made him one of us in thoughts and urges. That's why he would've been drawn to Landon. The instinct is strong to be with the pack— Holy shit! Now it all makes sense."

Her heart thumped and she pressed the phone closer to her ear. "What are you talking about?"

"Wolves are by nature pack animals. Landon lives alone as a lone wolf, but that's not what he really wants. He wants to be with his pack. I didn't realize what he was doing until now."

Kaitlyn shook her head. "What are you blathering on about?"

"Remember all the wolf things in Landon's house? The

wolf picture on the wall, the wolf on the end table and the wolf carved from a tree trunk near his kitchen?"

She nodded. "Yes."

"When I was at your house, I noticed all your dad's wolf stuff. Don't you see what your father and Landon were doing? Even though they were lone wolves, they still surrounded themselves with wolf images, like they were creating their own surrogate pack." He sounded so excited. "I've always had these frustrating questions in my mind, but now I know for sure, Landon does want his pack." Caine's excitement calmed. "Have you come to any conclusions about Landon yet? Did reading your father's journal help?"

"Don't push it."

"You two are made for each other. Landon's the closest thing to a brother I'll ever have. He deserves happiness."

Kaitlyn sighed. "The truth is, I care very much for Landon. I know he's a good man with a strong sense of leadership. He was responsible for my father's death, but now that I know the circumstances, I realize his protective instincts would've kicked in to defend his pack. I understand the motivation. I'm just so sad it had to happen like it did."

All this talk about her father being changed made Kaitlyn realize that she was connected to the Lupreda, too. As James's offspring, she might have some of the wolf traits. That could explain why she was so drawn to Landon's smell and why she had the "seeing" power that she did. Come to think of it, all her life, no matter the scrape, she'd always healed very quickly, and she'd never been sick a day in her life. The signs were all there, but not enough for her to notice if she didn't know to look for them.

"I'm sorry, too." Caine sounded truly regretful. "Well, I guess I'll let you go then."

"Wait, Caine! I think I might know of a way for Landon to be allowed to participate in your Alpha run."

"I'm listening."

"I need you to take me to your Omega."

"That's impossible. You aren't Lupreda."

She smiled. "I'm pretty sure I can prove otherwise."

"That's not enough, Kaitlyn. I can't bring a human into the pack. It'll break all our rules. Our home is hidden for a reason."

"You're going to have to trust your gut instead of your sense of smell this time," she insisted.

He gave a heavy sigh. "I've seen you in action. You're a smart, determined woman. If you say you have a plan you think will work, I have to let you try. Plus, the pack needs to know about your dad." Caine's tone was suddenly dead serious. "But I can't come get you until tomorrow."

Frustration tensed her shoulders. Her hand tightened on the phone. "Why not?"

"Because it'll be dark soon and it's a full moon. During the full moon, Lupredas naturally shift to wolf form. We don't have control over that. Once daylight arrives, I'll be able to shift back to my human form. The only control we do have is shifting to our Musk form."

"And Landon?" she asked, guilt bunching her spine. "Has he worn that necklace all this time?"

"He doesn't shift at all. I know he misses it."

His regretful tone made her stomach knot. "We all wish we could change the past, Caine. All we can do now is set the present on the right path."

"Right. I'll call you tomorrow, Kaitlyn."

When he hung up, she did the same and stared at the wall of wolf books. *I'm part Lupreda.*

* * *

"We'll walk from here." Caine pulled his silver truck into the woods off the side road he'd taken deep into the Shawangunk mountains. Shutting off the engine, he then flipped open his cell phone.

"Laird. We'll be there soon." He paused and listened. "I don't care. Use whatever excuse you can to get the Omega together."

As he shut the phone and slid it in his back pocket, Kaitlyn climbed out of the truck and took in their surroundings. Trees, sporting leaves in various shades of orange, yellows, reds and browns, blew with the crisp wind. They were literally in the middle of nowhere.

Caine got out and came around to her side. He held up a rolled-up handkerchief. "To protect my pack's location, I'm going to have to blindfold you."

She frowned. "But I'm Lupreda, too."

"Not until the Omega deems you to be."

A determined expression settled on his face, and she realized she wasn't changing his mind. *This is for Landon,* she told herself and turned around.

Caine tied the bandanna around her eyes and grabbed her hand. Pulling her along, he said, "Think of it as an adventure."

Kaitlyn held her other hand out in front of her. She took a couple of steps and immediately tripped over a rock or something. She didn't like this kind of adventure.

Caine gripped her elbow, righting her. "Follow my lead instead of trying to step off on your own.

Relaxing, she put herself in Caine's care. It wasn't easy, but she did it by focusing on other things. Since her sight wasn't an option, she used her other senses. Birds chirped and leaves crinkled as they walked. The musky smell of decaying leaves and rich earth stirred around them with each step they took. She smiled at the small things she might not have noticed if she hadn't been blindfolded.

A half hour into their hike, she noticed they were definitely traveling uphill. The thought of the impending meeting with other Lupreda started to knot her stomach. As Caine maneuvered her over a stump or a big rock, she asked, "Tell me about the Omega."

"What do you want to know?" He tugged on her arm to let her know they were turning left.

She followed, glad she'd worn boots today. "You said that the Omega would have to decide if I'm Lupreda or not, but didn't you tell me your pack had an Alpha? I'm assuming that means your leader. Who rules the roost? Or maybe I should say, what's the pecking order so I don't blunder while presenting my case?"

Caine chuckled, addressing her choice of words. "Just so you know, there's not a fowl among us. We're pretty fearless."

"Bock, bock," she taunted. "You haven't answered my question yet."

"Yes, you're right. There is an Alpha named Nathan. He's an insecure, jealous SOB who has no business leading our pack. Landon tangled with Nathan a few months ago, pretty much challenging Nathan in front of the whole pack...over the vampires."

She stumbled and came to a halt. "The vampires? Oh, wait, Landon told me how he'd forged a truce with the leader of the Sanguinas. He just didn't mention the details behind it."

Caine squeezed her hand and tugged to let her know he was starting to walk again. "Nathan banned Landon from the pack for his inference and has been gunning for him ever since. Normally the Alpha would decide your status, but because your audience with the Omega about Landon hinges on you being accepted in our pack as a member, I'm taking you to the Omega for both."

She nodded her understanding. "Who are the Omega?"

"The Omega are past Alphas who were challenged during the run and lost. Because they have strong leadership skills and the respect of the pack, they move on to be the equalizing factor behind the current Alpha's decisions if he is ever challenged by a pack member."

"Are you saying that they overrule the Alpha?"

"No, they don't usually. It's rare for them to get involved. In the case of the annual Alpha run, obviously the Alpha can't be the one deciding on the rules or who wins if there's a tie. An unbiased party, one who's 'been there, done that' oversees this area."

"Ah, now I see where the Omega come in." Sticks snapped under her shoes' hard soles at the same time as a bird flew past. She instinctively ducked but kept moving. "If your pack does this run every year, don't you have a lot of members in the Omega?"

Caine laughed. "The run is more than just a race of physical endurance. It's proof of leadership skills and combat strategy as well as how the were uses calculated tactics to beat his opponents. Alphas rule until they can't keep up with the challengers, which is usually a long time considering we don't age like humans do. Therefore, we only have a few Omega."

Werewolves aged how much slower than humans? she wondered. The eighteen-year-old picture of Landon in her father's belongings popped into her mind. Landon hadn't aged at all in almost two decades. The idea that he would still look the same while she turned into a shriveled prune over time just wasn't right. Damn, she hoped she'd inherited that youth gene from her dad. "As far as the Omega are concerned, is there any one member that seems to rule?"

"Address them all with equal respect, but I can pretty much guarantee Garius is going to be the one asking you all the questions. He's the oldest Alpha of our pack. They follow his lead. Damn, this is going to be one helluva talk. The Omega will be shocked to learn that a wolf's bite can turn a human. I bet if we had known about your father, we could've helped him accept his wolf."

Caine's comment jabbed right to her heart. She gasped and stumbled. He caught her before she hit the ground. "Sorry, Kaitlyn. That came out wrong. It was my way of saying, I wish we could've helped your dad."

Kaitlyn nodded her understanding. "I know what you meant."

"Good. Now, I hope you don't mind…" he said holding on to her hands.

When he paused, Kaitlyn started to say, "About what—"

But she found herself thrown face down over Caine's shoulder. He gripped her hips. "This walking is going too slow. We'll be there soon— What the hell do you have in your pocket?" he said as he adjusted her on his shoulder.

"My father's journal."

"Got it. Ready to fly?" Caine asked. "Close your eyes."

"Very funny," she mumbled behind the blindfold and locked her arms around his waist.

The breeze picked up and whirred past her ears. Caine was in full werewolf speed now. She was thankful for the blindfold, because she wasn't able to open her eyes to see just how fast they were going. She would've been tempted and sure enough, motion sickness would've been the immediate result. Instead, she took easy breaths and tried not to think about Caine's superhuman speed.

A few minutes later, Caine set her on her feet and pulled off the blindfold. Kaitlyn blinked until her vision adjusted to the daylight.

Turning her around, he pointed and whispered in her ear, "Welcome home, Kaitlyn."

Kaitlyn stared at the beautiful brick mansion with black shutters and thick carved columns supporting a porch that wrapped around the sides of the house. Deep green ivy grew along the sides, bracketing the home like those tiny picture corners in scrapbooks. The massive house was definitely picture-worthy in every respect.

Dense trees surrounded the house, the branches arching over the roof as if trying to hide its existence from the outside world. Trees created a natural camouflage barrier, while allowing dappled sunlight to filter through the leaves. By any standards, the Lupredas' home was impressive.

"I'm speechless," she said.

Caine laughed. "Takes your breath away, doesn't it?" He started toward the house, beckoning her. "Come on. They're waiting on us."

Before she followed, Kaitlyn quickly moved her gun from her ankle holster to her jacket's front pocket. She had no idea if she'd be accepted or not. It was ingrained in her to think like a cop. She always came prepared.

Once she followed his lead up the porch stairs and through the huge front door, her stomach tensed. What kind of reception would she receive, she wondered.

They didn't even get a chance to shut the front door behind them before she found out.

"What the hell have you done, Caine?" A man with long blond hair sat up from his lounging position on the sofa in the main room and stared at them.

Caine instantly moved in front of Kaitlyn. "This is none of your concern, Brian. Go back to doing what you do best."

Kaitlyn couldn't miss the sarcasm in Caine's tone. No love lost there.

In an instant, the other were was a few feet away from Caine, snarling. "You know the rules. No humans. Ever."

The tension between the men hung thick in the air. Other people, both male and female, even a few kids, walked over to observe. Some leaned against the thick columns, separating the entryway from the living area. Others surrounded Caine and Kaitlyn in a large semi-circle.

"You'd like that, wouldn't you?" Caine growled. "For Nathan to have a reason to kick me out."

The speculative stares of the strangers around them unnerved Kaitlyn. Some frowned while others just shook their heads. Murmurs abounded. Her first instinct was to move closer to Caine, but the louder the general buzz hitched, the need for order drove her forward between the men.

She met the angry were's gaze and kept her expression neutral. "I'm here because I'm Landon's mate."

A shock wave of gasps rippled over the crowd.

"You dare to address me?" Brian's thin face grew mottled and he narrowed his gaze.

"She smells like Landon," someone said.

"I don't care," Brian snarled. "Landon's not a member of this pack. *You* don't belong here, bitch."

The people behind Brian began to back up. *Not a good sign. Were they expecting a brawl?* Kaitlyn set her teeth and wrapped her fingers around the gun in her pocket. She gave him a cold smile. "Thank you for the compliment. Now back off, hound!"

Brian gave a menacing growl. Claws extended from his fingers right before he lunged for her.

One second the furious man was leaping through the air toward her, and the next he was skidding across the floor, on his side.

"That was a warning. Go near her again and I'll kill you," Landon said in a deadly tone.

Kaitlyn turned to stare at Landon in surprise. "What are you doing here?"

His green gaze narrowed on Caine and then slid to her. "I could ask you the same thing."

Kaitlyn met Landon's stern stare. Her heart leapt. He looked so rugged with several days growth of stubble on his jaw. His chest muscles pressed against his light blue T-shirt and his biceps flexed as he fisted his hands. She knew he was pissed that she had come into his territory, but she wasn't sure what to tell him.

Caine intervened. "Landon. I'm glad you could make it—"

At that moment, a man with short blond hair jumped over the railing from the top floor and landed beside Landon. The floor shook with his hard landing. He immediately stood and bellowed at Landon, "I told you to stay away. You've signed your death warrant by returning."

Landon smirked. "Any time you want another good ass-kicking, I'm ready, Nathan."

The blond man stuck his barrel chest out even farther. He looked like a cock, puffing up for a fight. Kaitlyn waited for him to start scratching at the floor. *No chickens. Ha! Caine was wrong.*

"Landon and the young woman are here at my request."

Everyone in the room turned to stare at a tall, imposing, dark-haired man with gray along his temples. "Garius," Caine whispered in her ear.

Hoping to defuse the fight about to erupt between Landon

and the Alpha, Kaitlyn stepped toward the retired Alpha. The crowd parted, allowing her through. She stopped a couple feet away from the Omega leader. Meeting the gazes of the small group of men behind Garius, whom she believed were the other Omega, she nodded to acknowledge them all. "Thank you for your invitation."

Garius bowed his head slightly, his blue eyes boring into hers as he spoke in her mind. *Laird and Roman spoke very highly of you, Kaitlyn McKinney. I don't believe you would come here lightly.*

She bowed her head in respect, then met his steady gaze. "I humbly seek admittance to the Lupreda pack as a member with full rights and privileges."

A roar erupted behind her and Nathan was instantly beside Garius. His chest heaved and he glared at her. "How dare you insult my position by asking the Omega." He pounded his fist on his chest. "I'm the Alpha of the Lupreda. I banished your—" he sneered at Landon, who'd stepped beside her "—mate months ago, which leaves you no right to ask for admittance. None!"

Garius stroked his chin for a second, then frowned slightly. "He's right."

Kaitlyn's gaze traveled over Nathan's bunched fists to his curled upper lip, twitching in canine hostility. He was full of self-important arrogance. Dismissing him, she met Garius's steady stare. "Then it's a good thing I'm not asking for admittance as Landon's mate. I'm asking admittance to the pack as a blood Lupreda, well and true."

Chapter 14

Pandemonium swept the entire room. Weres growled in fury, shouting obscenities.

As shocked as Landon was by Kaitlyn's announcement, he wouldn't allow his mate to be insulted. "Enough," he roared, and the entire pack quieted down.

"Address me with your question." Nathan reached out to grab Kaitlyn by the arm.

Landon locked his hand on Nathan's wrist, stopping him dead. Shoving the man back, he growled. "Unless you want to pull back a nub, don't attempt to touch her again."

Nathan snarled and stepped toward Landon when Garius put up his hand between them. "Put your canines away for the moment. This issue needs to be addressed first."

Turning to Kaitlyn, Garius gave a formal bow and swept his arm behind him. "Why don't we move into the living room where we can all be more comfortable as we discuss this—" he glared at Landon and Nathan "—like civilized human beings."

A couple of snickers sounded in the background, and Landon couldn't help but smirk at Garius's choice of words. He knew it was intentional.

Kaitlyn took Garius's proffered arm and he led her into the living room. As they walked into the huge living area, they stood in one of the two separate seating sections. Currently the huge foyer and hall was occupied by all hundred and fifty curious weres, waiting for the saga or, even better, a fight to unfold.

Kaitlyn, what are you doing? Landon wanted to ask. When his gaze caught Caine's, he narrowed his, telling Caine with one look, *You're dead meat.* But he stayed quiet, waiting to hear what the hell Kaitlyn was cooking up in that beautiful head of hers. Damn, he'd missed her these past few days.

He'd come to the Lupreda house because Laird had called, telling him the Omega wanted to see him. He knew he needed to fill them in on what he'd learned about the panthers' existence, but he'd stayed close to his cabin these past few days, staring at the moon and wishing he were on the hunt with his fellow weres at night. Each night the necklace felt heavy around his neck, binding him to his human form.

When Garius offered Kaitlyn a seat, she shook her head. "I prefer to stand."

Garius's gaze challenged Nathan. "She has requested admittance to this pack on the authority that she is indeed blood Lupreda. You are the Alpha. If she proves she is of our blood, you are bound by the ruling and must accept her into the pack. If you cannot fairly judge or don't feel you can be impartial— as a good leader should be—then the Omega will take over the proceedings."

Nathan pushed his shoulders back and stepped up to

Kaitlyn. He leaned close to sniff her and Landon tensed, ready to spring to Kaitlyn's defense.

Garius put a staying hand on Landon's chest and slowly shook his head.

With steady breaths, Landon was able to calm his protective wolf…just barely.

Nathan straightened and backed away, a smug smile on his face. "If she can prove she's blood Lupreda, then I'll admit her with full rights and privileges."

Kaitlyn met Garius's gaze. "Who do I address? You or him?" she finished, glancing at Nathan.

"You'll address Nathan with your request. He's the Alpha and will pass a fair judgment."

Nodding, Kaitlyn turned to Nathan. "Is there a black wolf in your pack with a torn left ear and one blue and one brown eye?"

Landon tensed. *Where was she going with this?*

Nathan shook his head and replied in a pleased tone. "No. There isn't."

Kaitlyn's lips thinned. "Let me rephrase the question. Did there used to be a black wolf in your pack with a torn left ear and one blue and one brown eye."

Nathan clamped his lips together, then gave her a curt nod. "Yes. He is dead now."

"How did he die?" she asked, tilting her head to the side.

Landon had a feeling Kaitlyn already knew all the answers. He cut his gaze to Caine, who lifted his shoulders in an innocent manner. *Yeah, right.*

"He committed suicide," Nathan said, through gritted teeth. "For whatever reason, Andre didn't shift back to human form at the end of the moon's cycle. He remained in wolf form."

Kaitlyn pulled a thin, gold-leafed book out from the deep pockets in her jacket. As she looked down at the pages, slowly flipping through them, she asked, "What is the rule that the Sanguinas made for the Lupreda about biting humans?"

A collective gasp rose among the pack and murmurs started anew.

Nathan's gaze narrowed. "How do you know so much about our pack?" He glared at Landon. "He shouldn't have divulged our pack history."

"Answer the damned question, Nathan." Landon was so on edge he wanted to snap the man's neck.

The Alpha addressed Kaitlyn. "We were told that if we bit a human while we were in our wolf form, we wouldn't be able to shift back to human form."

Kaitlyn walked over to Garius and handed him the opened book. "This is my father's journal that dates back almost twenty-five years ago. Please read the pages that it's open to."

When Garius finished reading the first two pages of the journal out loud, Landon looked at Kaitlyn and realization sank in. She was indeed part of his pack and always had been.

Kaitlyn met his surprised gaze and gave him a small smile.

Elation filled his heart, making it beat hard against his chest.

"Lies!" Nathan pointed at the book in Garius's hands. "She made up the whole thing, fabricated this silly journal, but our senses speak the truth. She's one-hundred-percent human."

Kaitlyn pulled something out of her pocket. As she unfolded it, Landon realized it was a hunting knife. When she turned the knife to her palm, he understood her intent. She cut a slice in her hand before he could reach her.

Landon was by her side, pulling off his shirt as red blood flowed freely along her palm.

Taking the knife, he set it on the coffee table and tried to grab her hand so he could use his shirt to stanch the blood flow, but she pulled her hand away and lifted it high, calling out in a loud voice to the general pack. "Werewolves, what do you smell?"

"Lu-preda!" They all howled in unison, their collective voice deep with conviction.

Landon grabbed her hand and pushed his shirt against it to wipe away the blood. "Crazy woman," he said with a smile, right before he swept his tongue over her wound to help it heal.

"I love you, too," she said, cupping his jaw and turning his eyes to hers.

Her loving gaze sent warmth straight to his heart. Landon's fingers tightened around her wrist and for a few seconds, all the sounds around them faded into the background until it was just them.

"There's a lot I have to tell you," she whispered, then continued in a normal voice, "Being accepted into the pack isn't the main reason I came today."

Surprised, Landon watched her turn and address Nathan. "I think it's unanimous that I'm blood Lupreda. Do you disagree?"

Landon relished how she didn't really ask, but instead, stated a fact while thoroughly putting Nathan in his place. Damn, he loved this woman.

"You are Lupreda," he said through gritted teeth, fury emanating off him.

"Now that we have that settled…" She paused and addressed Garius and the other Omega standing behind the couch. "I have something I would like to discuss with the Omega."

"You will ask me!" Nathan roared.

Did he just see the man stomp his foot? Landon chuckled inwardly even as his mate continued to confound him.

She glanced at Nathan. "You would *not* be impartial when it comes to Landon, so, yes, I have every right to take my case about *my* mate to the Omega for their judgment."

"She's correct, Nathan," Garius said in a calm tone. He looked at Kaitlyn. "State your case."

"I want my mate to be able to participate in the annual Alpha run."

Nathan choked, then growled low in his throat.

As much as Landon appreciated Kaitlyn's putting Nathan in his place, he didn't want her to speak on his behalf. He didn't need to be reminded he was lacking in the pack's eyes.

Garius shook his head. "I'm sorry, but Landon's muted sense of smell keeps him from qualifying. We've ruled on this a long time ago."

Landon gritted his teeth. "I want this to stop now."

Kaitlyn frowned at him, her hazel-blue eyes narrowing. "Why? You deserve the chance like every other were."

"Yeah, Landon, why don't you just go ahead and let her wear your pants, too, since she seems to be fighting your battles for you." Nathan sneered.

Landon fisted his hands and glared at Nathan. "I could wipe the floor with you. You know it and I know it. That's all that matters as far as I'm concerned."

"What about your pack, Landon?" Kaitlyn asked. "Don't they deserve the best Alpha they can have?" Before he could reply, she turned back to Garius. "Do you have a room in this big honking house where we can make it completely dark?"

Garius raised a dark eyebrow and the corner of his lip quirked upward. "Now you've got me completely intrigued. Come along to the library. I believe it's big enough for the entire pack."

Landon tried to reach for Kaitlyn, but she quickly side-stepped him and was swallowed up in the crowd, who followed the Omega and her to the library.

Nathan was the only one left in the room. He snarled at

Landon. "When this silly charade is over, I'm going to finally eliminate you once and for all."

Landon chose to ignore him, mainly because he was curious as hell what his mate was up to. He started to walk away when Nathan continued, "And when you're dead and gone, I think I'll take Kaitlyn as my mate. She needs to be broken. Maybe then she'd make a good bitch—"

Landon slammed his entire body into Nathan, sending him flying into the living room. When the Alpha landed on top of the coffee table, he fell into it, shattering the glass underneath him.

"Stay away from me and mine, or die," Landon ground out before he walked away.

By the time he got to the room, all the heavy curtains had been drawn, closing out the daylight. The overhead chandelier sent a golden glow down on Kaitlyn's gorgeous red hair as she stood before the entire pack with Garius and the other Omega flanking her right side.

Landon shouldered his way through the crowd until he stood just outside the group of people closest to Kaitlyn. He crossed his arms and frowned.

When Kaitlyn reached into her pocket, Roman called out, "First a book, then a knife. Hell, I'm expecting the kitchen sink next."

The entire group of weres laughed uproariously. Landon would've laughed, too, if he wasn't currently being laid out like an animal about to be dissected and found lacking.

Again. Landon's jaw tensed with his displeasure.

When they began to quiet down, Kaitlyn had a serious look on her face as she pulled out the bloody shirt Landon had left behind at the hospital and held it up in the air. "Will this do?" Digging her empty hand into her other pocket, she then held up something small and black, and continued in the same vein, "Or would this be better?"

Sudden quiet swept over the room as everyone realized she held a gun. Even as Landon tensed, he respected how effectively she'd captured their attention.

After they sat there in edgy silence for several seconds, a slow smile spread across her face. She tucked the gun back into her coat pocket and said, "Oh, come on. Roman's not the only one with a sense of humor, people."

The entire group laughed uproariously once more, but when she held up her hand, they instantly silenced and gave her their undivided and respectful attention.

Bravo, Kaitie, he silently praised her as his chest filled with pride.

Holding Landon's shirt up for everyone to see, she asked, "What do you see?"

"Tears."

"Blood stains."

She peered into the crowd. "What do you smell?"

"Landon's blood."

"Anything else?" she asked as she raised an eyebrow.

A few of the younger male weres walked up and touched the shirt, then leaned in to smell it. "We smell Landon," they all agreed.

She held the shirt toward the Omega. "And you?"

All the men nodded and Garius answered. "We see and smell what the other pack members do."

Kaitlyn waved toward the crowd. "Will someone please turn off the lights?"

When the room went completely dark, Landon jumped to attention, his mind racing. Was she doing what he thought she was doing?

"Now what do you see?"

"We can see in the dark, Kaitlyn," Laird called out. "We see and smell the same."

"And you, Garius? Is it the same for you and the other Omega?"

"Yes, Kaitlyn. Nothing has changed."

She turned to Landon and held up his shirt. "Landon. What do you see?"

"I see iridescent sparkles all around the tears in the shirt and on the shoulders," he replied in a casual tone.

Facing the group of weres, Kaitlyn said, "It's pitch-dark in this room to my human eyes, but I see more than Landon. I see actual handprints where the man who attacked him must've pushed on his shoulders before he swiped his claws down Landon's chest."

"Claws?" someone asked.

"Yes, claws," she agreed. "But these claws were from a panther."

Angry snarls erupted in the crowd.

"Turn the lights on," Garius said in a hard voice.

When the lights flipped on and the room quieted, Garius glanced from Kaitlyn to Landon. "Why can you two see this and we don't?"

Kaitlyn shrugged. "I've always had a kind of sight that allows me to see auras around dead bodies. I think my ability to 'see' what I do comes from my werewolf half trying to compensate for my human limitations."

Gesturing to Landon, she continued, "Just like Landon's 'sight' probably stems from his body compensating for his muted sense of smell."

Holding up the shirt, she addressed the entire pack. "Today I've proven to you that Landon has a skill none of you possess.

Should you all be kept from the hunt because you couldn't go out there today and help us find where these panthers are hiding? They *are* leaving behind this trail. It's just one only Landon and I can see."

When the weres sat there in stunned silence, Landon moved to stand beside her. "Maybe it would matter more to you if I told you the panthers were responsible for the zerkers' murders, not the Sanguinas. Yes, all three zerkers have been killed."

Yells of outrage echoed in the room.

Garius held his hands up to silence them. When the weres settled down, he nodded to Kaitlyn. "Well done, proving your point. I agree with you, but let me discuss it with the other Omega—"

Landon turned back to the crowd to see Nathan hurtling through the air. He slammed against Landon, knocking him to the floor. Nathan tried to jam Kaitlyn's knife into his jugular, but Landon turned at the last second, taking the knife's blade deep in his shoulder.

Pain splintered through his body, and Landon roared his anger, shoving Nathan off him and into the crowd of weres.

When Landon pulled out the knife and jumped up to go after Nathan, Kaitlyn called his name. Landon paused, his entire body bunching, ready to fight. He fisted his hands as she approached him.

Kaitlyn lifted his necklace over his head. Stepping to the side, she placed the chain around her neck. "Go kick his dirty-fighting ass."

As Landon leapt across the room, he already felt his change to Musk form rippling through his body; his jaw began to elongate, his knees snap and bend and his spine crack as his height elevated another foot and a half.

His clothes shredded as his body grew. Muscles popped

and tendons stretched in milliseconds. When he landed on his feet in front of Nathan, a light coating of fur covered his body from head to foot.

Landon vibrated with fury and the need for vengeance, but he waited for Nathan to fully shift to his Musk form. No one would claim this fight wasn't a fair one.

Kaitlyn watched Landon shift to his Musk form midair. When he landed with a heavy thud in front of Nathan, she could only stare in awe at the intimidating picture he made.

He'd grown well over a foot taller, and his shoulders and back had bulked up with thicker muscles and fur. But it was the snarl twitching on his muzzle and deadly sharp teeth that made her insides tense. He was scary as hell in this form. She wasn't afraid of him, but damn, she almost felt sorry for Nathan as the Alpha finally shifted to his own Musk form. Almost.

Covered in blond fur, Nathan might have a thicker chest, but he stood several inches shorter than Landon. All she knew was, Nathan couldn't compete with Landon's massive size.

"Take it outside!" Garius roared above the men's snarls.

Growling, Nathan took a swipe at Landon's chest with his deadly claws, leaving bloody gashes in his wake before he immediately leaped over the crowd to head outside.

Slimy coward, Kaitlyn thought as Landon took a powerful leap, clearing the crowd to land in the hall.

Most of the weres and the other Omega immediately followed, yelling their encouragement. Only a few weres lagged behind, arguing.

"Landon will tear him to shreds," Caine smirked.

"Nathan's a cunning-as-shit fighter, though," a shorter brown-haired man said.

"Nathan will win," Brian said with confidence.

"Wanna make a bet?" Caine challenged the blond man.

Brian got right in Caine's face. "You're on. If Nathan loses, I'll sit out of this year's Alpha run."

Caine chuckled. "It doesn't matter if you sit it out or not. Landon will dominate you and send you home with your tail tucked."

"Come on, you're missing the action," Laird yelled from down the hall.

All the weres ran out of the room, dropping their argument in lieu of witnessing a good Musk brawl in progress.

Kaitlyn started to follow, when she realized Garius had pulled the curtains wide open and had settled comfortably in a chair near the window—with her father's journal already open in his hand.

She considered the violation of her father's privacy, but thought maybe one of the Omega *should* know the whole story. Walking over to stand beside him, she asked, "Are you going to watch them?"

Garius gave a casual glance outside then returned his attention to the journal. "I know what the outcome will be," he said and slowly flipped the pages.

Worry knotted her stomach. She glanced out the window to see Nathan and Landon's arms locked together, teeth snapping. Their growls of fury sent a chill down her spine. She knew Nathan was as underhanded as they came. He would pull every dirty trick to defeat Landon. She frowned at Garius. "Don't you think you should be there to make sure it's a fair fight?"

He didn't look up from the book. "Such is life, Kaitlyn. There will be unfairness in fights. It's up to the wolf to anticipate such things, to be prepared for everything. Only the fittest, in *every* respect, will survive."

Kaitlyn's gaze shot to the window. Nathan took off into the

woods and Landon quickly followed, along with all the male and female weres cheering them on. "It just seems so brutal."

Garius's blue eyes narrowed as he met her gaze. "We are a primal race, Kaitlyn. If you don't think you can handle that, then Landon is not the man for you. He will rule this pack with fairness, but there will be times he must prove his dominance in order to keep their respect. They've needed a strong Alpha to lead them."

Her eyes widened. "Are you saying he'll be the new Alpha if he defeats Nathan?"

Garius continued skimming the pages in the journal. "He'll be the new Alpha until the run happens, at which time the Omega will allow him to participate. I have no doubt he will be victorious."

Nodding her understanding, Kaitlyn's chest tightened with concern for Landon, but she realized she needed to show strength and confidence in her mate when it came to this pack. She moved to sit in the chair next to Garius and waited for him to finish her father's journal.

A few minutes ticked past before he closed the book with a snap and handed it back to her. "This explains a lot." He appeared contemplative as he stared at the bullet slug around her neck. "Landon was the man your father had seen in the park, wasn't he?"

Kaitlyn slid the journal in her pocket and nodded. "Yes. Landon hasn't read this journal yet, so he doesn't know my father planned to commit suicide that night. I believe once Landon learns the whole truth, he'll be able to forgive himself."

"The question is…" Garius's penetrating stare made her want to squirm. "Have *you* forgiven him?"

Her own words from her mother's eulogy came back to her. *True love* will *endure the obstacles life throws at you.* She nodded. "Now that I know the circumstances and Landon's strong Alpha tendencies, I understand his motivations. My father is gone, but I know it was an accident. Landon has paid for it for eighteen years. I think it's time to let the guilt go."

Garius smiled and reached over to clasp her hand. "Agreed. Welcome to the pack, Kaitlyn McKinney. You have proven you are an Alpha's mate through and through."

When Kaitlyn squeezed his hand in return, Garius's smile widened into a smug grin. "Come on, let's go congratulate the winner."

She glanced out the window. No one was about. "But—"

"I just heard a victory howl."

Kaitlyn frowned. "I don't hear any—" She paused when the collective din of wolf howls finally reached her ears, echoing through the woods and penetrating the house's walls. One howl elevated above them all, sending a shiver of excitement down her spine.

Landon was the new Alpha.

Chapter 15

Why can't I stay? Kaitlyn mentally yelled at the injustice of being shuffled off to Landon's cabin right after the fight was over. She'd stayed quiet the entire time Caine had walked her through the woods at a brisk pace, because she'd spent the whole time fuming that Landon had sent Caine to take her to his home.

When Landon's house came into view, Kaitlyn put out her hand. She didn't bother with niceties. "I'll take the key and you can be done with your babysitting duties."

Caine shoved his hands in his front pockets and frowned. "That's pretty harsh."

She dropped her hand to her side. "It was meant to be. I don't know why I have to be carted away like some dirty little backwoods mutt who showed up at the door and no one wants."

Caine stopped walking and stared at her in surprise. "You think that we don't want you around? That Landon's embarrassed?"

Kaitlyn faced him and lifted her hands up in the air. "What else am I supposed to think? Why else shuttle me out of there as fast as you could?"

Running his hand through his black hair, Caine murmured something about stubborn females, then sighed. "Landon asked me to take you home so he could clean up. He didn't want you to see him like that."

"Like what?" she challenged. "I saw him shift to his Musk form. Now I can honestly say, 'you ain't got nothing I haven't already seen' with a straight face."

Caine chuckled as he started to walk toward the cabin.

Kaitlyn trailed after him. "Hey, what's so funny?"

His amused gaze cut her way. "The fact that you're going to constantly challenge Landon."

When she frowned, he laughed. "That's a good thing. Landon has spent too much time to himself."

Guilt crept into her chest, slowly pushing down its heavy weight.

Once they walked up the porch stairs, Caine pulled the cabin key out of his pocket. He handed it to her and leaned against the porch's railing, sobering. "I wasn't referring to you not seeing him in Musk form, Kaitlyn. I was referring to Landon not wanting you to see him all bloody and wounded from the battle with Nathan." He snarled when he said the man's name.

"What happened?" Kaitlyn asked.

"Landon had Nathan down and was going let him live when Nathan picked up dirt and threw it in Landon's eyes. The idiot went after Landon, trying his best to take him out while he was blinded by the dirt." He shook his head. "Nathan gave Landon no other choice. It was kill or be killed."

She blew out a frustrated breath at these Lupreda men trying to save her "sensibilities." "Caine, seeing Landon all bloody would've made me worried for him, instead of horrified at what he'd done to Nathan. I could tell Nathan was the kind who would take the fight all the way to the final end…for one of them."

Caine smirked. "Did you have any doubt Landon would win?"

"No, she didn't," Landon said as he came around the side of the cabin.

Kaitlyn drank in the sight of her mate fresh from battle. He had a gash on one cheek and a few scratches on his neck. A long tear was already healing along his left arm. He'd shaven and his hair was still wet, but damn he looked sexy as hell in a dark green T-shirt and jeans, staring up at her as if he wanted to devour her.

Landon nodded to Caine. "Thanks for watching over my mate." He glanced at the sun sinking low in the sky. "It'll be dark soon. Go and enjoy your last run for the month."

Caine whooped and jumped over the porch rail. He landed with the gracefulness of a cat, and took off running as soon as his feet hit the ground.

Kaitlyn turned to speak to Landon and bumped into his chest. She took a step back and frowned. "I don't think I'll ever get used to your speed. Over there one second, in my face the next."

Landon stepped right up to her. He ran his finger along her cheek, then down her shirt's V neckline. Deep green eyes locked with hers and his seductive smile sent molten heat throughout her body, setting her nerve endings on fire. "I got the impression you liked me up close and in your face."

She opened her mouth to speak, but the words wouldn't come. Now that they were alone, and after everything that had happened to them, suddenly she didn't know what to say, let alone where to start.

Landon lifted his chain from around her neck and then slid it over his head. Once the bullet settled into place against his chest, he said, "Let's go inside. It'll be dark soon."

Kaitlyn wanted to rip the chain off his neck and tell him to stop torturing himself, but she knew that for Landon to remove the necklace for good, he'd have to forgive himself first.

She allowed him to escort her inside and help her remove her coat. As he hung her jacket on the coat rack near the door, she pulled her father's journal from the front pocket and held it out to him. "I want you to read this."

Landon set his jaw and shook his head. "These are your father's personal writings. They weren't meant to be read by others."

Kaitlyn lifted his hand and placed the slim book in his palm. "That's where you're wrong. He would've wanted you, of all people, to read this and understand him."

Before Landon could say a word, she walked out of the room and into the kitchen.

Her hand shook as she opened the fridge. She decided she'd prepare something for dinner while Landon read her father's journal. Staying busy would keep her from wondering what he was thinking as he turned the pages.

When she didn't find anything in the crisper drawer, she murmured, "Does the man not eat *any* vegetables?" No fruit existed, either. She'd bet her last dollar the freezer was packed. She looked. Yep, full to the hilt. *I'm going to have to talk to that man about his diet. Or lack thereof.*

With a sigh, she raided the cabinets, looking for some wine. Water wasn't going to cut it. She smiled when she found a good cabernet in the pantry.

It had grown dark outside by the time she'd found the corkscrew and poured them a glass. Landon had to be almost done reading. Taking a couple sips of hers, she picked up their glasses and walked into the living room.

The lamp's soft light glowed against the couch, shining down on her father's journal. Landon stood by the big window, staring out in the darkness. When she approached, he turned and took the glass of wine she offered.

She looked at the book on the couch, then met his gaze. "Did you read it?"

Landon drank the glass of wine in one huge gulp.

She raised her eyebrow and took the empty glass from him. Setting the two glasses on the end table, she faced him. "I take it that means 'yes.'"

A couple of wolf howls echoed off in the woods somewhere and her gaze jerked to Landon's. Sheer torture and deep longing reflected in his gaze before he turned from staring out the window.

Lacing his fingers with hers, he said, "How did you figure out you were blood Lupreda? Just because your dad was bitten didn't mean you carried our blood."

"After I read my dad's journal, something Caine said struck me. He asked me why the vampires didn't instantly kill me like they had other humans."

Landon squeezed her hand and his face set in hard lines. "I don't want to think about what might've happened to you if I hadn't gotten to that alley when I did."

She smiled and kissed his knuckles. "When I walked into the library that night, I cut my finger on the door handle. A man was walking out at the same time I walked in. He immediately jerked his head my way and followed me back inside. That man was one of the vampires who attacked me."

"He smelled blood," Landon interjected. "Vampires are obviously drawn to it. Maybe you didn't smell poisoned to him.

Jachin said the poisoned blood is apparently being bred out of the younger humans."

She shook her head. "You told me the vampires bred the werewolves to hunt. Don't you see? When that vampire attacked me, he didn't bite my neck. Instead, he swiped his hand down my chest and ripped it open, then sneered, 'Wanna play, bitch?' Then the other vampire said, 'Giving us a good run, little red?' At the time I thought they were just throwing out insulting slurs, but once I read my father's journal I realized I carry his blood—they were calling me a wolf!"

"That was a helluva gamble you took." Landon shook his head in amazement. Leaning close to her neck, he inhaled, then ran his fingers in a tender caress along her jawline. "Why don't you smell like us?"

She leaned into his touch. "I guess because I'm the offspring of a changed human and a fully human mother." Tugging on his hand, she said, "Come on. Let's talk."

Landon followed her to the couch and sat down beside her. He wouldn't let go of her hand when she tried to turn and face him. Kaitlyn sighed and adjusted herself along his side while he ran his fingers over the book's cover. "Tell me what you're thinking," she asked.

He spoke in a low tone. "I think we could've had a great member of this pack. I wish to hell I'd known about your dad."

Cupping her hand on his jaw, she turned his face toward her. "Don't do this! I didn't share my father's journal with you to make you feel even more guilt."

Pain and regret filled his expression. "If I had just paid more attention. I don't understand how I didn't smell his blood. I know why I smelled the Lupreda in your blood, but not why I didn't notice it in him."

She was curious what he meant about her, but right now

they needed to remove the wedge between them. "Caine told me everything that happened in the park that night as well as the things you've done to make up for it ever since."

Landon flexed his jaw. "Caine has a big mouth."

"He wants you to be happy. He knows how much you love me."

Landon squeezed her hand. "I do love you, Kaitie, very much. I've always felt connected to you and I couldn't explain it. That's why I stopped working with the police. You grew up before my eyes and these past few years…my feelings were changing from protector to wanting you fiercely."

She smiled. "The feeling is very mutual. And that's why this…this between us has been so hard. I know my father's death will always be a tragic, sad part of our past. It will always be a part of 'us,' but I don't want it to be *between* us."

When Landon didn't speak, she continued, "Caine said that it was raining hard that night in the park. Doesn't the rain affect your ability to smell as keenly as you might've otherwise?"

Landon stared at their locked hands and ran his thumb rhythmically along the bend of her thumb. "It's true that the rain does hinder our ability to track, but I was right over him, Kaitie—"

"And you were covered in Caine's and your own blood."

His green gaze narrowed. "You're not going to let me hate myself, are you?"

She touched the dent in his chin, then kissed the same spot. "I think you've done enough of that for the both of us these past eighteen years. My heart mourns for my father and for all that you put yourself through for me. It makes me love you even more for it."

Landon brushed his lips against hers lightly, then gave a half smile. "I've never been more proud of you than I was today. You commanded the Lupreda and had them eating out of your hand like an Alpha's mate should."

"Quite literally," she chuckled and held up her wounded hand.

Landon ran his fingers across the faint pink scar that remained, then pulled her palm to his lips. Kissing the scar gently, he said, "You're everything I've ever wanted in a mate, Kaitlyn McKinney. Everything."

She touched his face and made him look at her. "Does that mean you promise not to hold back on me anymore?"

Landon frowned. "I don't know what you mean."

She snorted. "I know you touch me lightly, Landon. I've felt the difference when we made love. Your grip was harder, more fierce. I want you to be yourself with me. I don't want you to treat me like I'm some kind of China doll. Just like I expect you to understand that I still have a life in the city, that the kids at Handleburg still need me and my job—"

He held up his hand. "I got it." Then his expression sobered. "I know you've been out of the loop with your mom's funeral, but the government reestablished the Garotters. The other self-funded Garotter organization will go down, just like Remy, Kent and his men did, but their Mafia ties seem to have faded into the woodwork."

She shook her head, disappointment settling in her stomach. "I should've known it wouldn't be that clean."

Landon touched her cheek. "As far as the whole cop thing is concerned, we made a great team. I was hoping you'd consider partnering with me at my agency. I enjoyed working with the police on cases, so I plan to reinstate myself there."

She was surprised and a bit excited by his suggestion. The thought of sharing ideas with Landon while working closely with all the police officers she literally grew up with really appealed to her. She'd have the best of both worlds. "And when are you going to have time to work in the city while you're being Alpha here?"

He raised an eyebrow. "I killed that one panther from the hospital, but there are still other Velius out there. Garius and the other Omega made it very clear that as Alpha I'm responsible for resolving this panther issue before any more attacks happen. When we're not helping the police with cases, we'll use our contacts to help us find the Velius pride. We *will* find them."

Kaitlyn nodded her agreement, then scooted away from him on the couch. "Now about this whole touching thing," she began with a smile as she swept off her shirt and tossed it to the floor.

Landon's nostrils flared when her musky arousal and violet scent filled the room in a wave of erotic temptation. "I set the pace to keep you safe, Kaitlyn," he said in a stern tone.

"Safe from you?" She unsnapped the front of her bra and slid the straps down her shoulders. Tossing the scrap of lingerie to the floor, she said in a husky tone, "Not tonight, you don't."

When Landon reached for her, she quickly stood and backed up just out of his reach. "Ah, ah. Promise first," she said, unsnapping her jeans and stepping out of her boots.

Landon's gaze skimmed her beautiful body and his groin instantly hardened. He loved how her red hair swept her shoulders, an alluring contrast against her alabaster skin. From that sexy, confident smile on her face, to the slope of her shoulders, to her rounded breasts and her tiny waist inside unbuttoned jeans, his gaze devoured her perfection. At that moment, he realized that when his mate taunted him, her ethereal beauty literally radiated from her. She was so beautiful, he couldn't stop staring at her.

"If you need more encouragement…"

Before he could say, "No, I want to do it," her jeans and underwear were on the floor.

"Kaitlyn, you need to stop," he gritted out while his wolf roared in his head. *Take her. Her arousal is musky-sweet and ripe. That's a mating call.*

Kicking her pants away, she opened her arms wide. "I'm feeling a bit underdressed. Want to join me?"

She can handle you. Trust me. I will keep her safe, his wolf demanded. Landon clenched his teeth. *Shut up,* he yelled at his wolf.

"Maybe I'll just go climb into the nice comfy bed upstairs and think of all the naughty things I want to do to you," she said in a wistful tone.

Kaitlyn had just started to turn toward the stairs when everything blurred and cool air stirred around her. The next thing she knew she was on her back on Landon's bed. He hovered over her, his hands beside her on the bed. The intense look on his face made her shiver deep inside. "You really shouldn't push me, Kaitlyn." Running his finger down her cheek, he continued, "Lupreda blood might flow through your veins, but you're not as tough as a female werewolf."

Anger welled, making her stomach twist. Kaitlyn shoved at his chest, taking him by surprise. While she had the advantage, she pushed him over onto his back and straddled his stomach. Her gaze narrowed. "Watch who you're calling weak, werewolf."

Landon tugged on a strand of her hair, then gently cupped the side of her face.

"I know you're tough as nails here." His thumb slid across her temple, then his other hand moved up her rib cage to stop below her left breast, where her heart thumped a heavy beat. "And here."

The look of love in his eyes dissipated some of her indignation.

Sliding both his hands to her waist, he finished, "But if I truly let myself touch you the way I would a female werewolf, I could crush you, Kaitlyn. You're too precious to me."

Tears filled her eyes and she pounded her fist on his chest. "But I don't want you to have to be careful. I want your primal self totally involved, not some shadow of a lover."

Landon swiftly sat up until his face was an inch from hers. "Is that what you think? That I'm not giving you my all when we make love?" His warm hands slid up her back and he pulled her fully against his chest. "You're wrong, my little mate. I'm very aware of every breath, every scent, every damned sweet sensation until I can't think straight."

She tugged off his shirt and tossed it on the floor, then met his hungry gaze. Placing her hands on his shoulders, she trailed her fingers down his hard biceps and across his chest. When he tensed beneath her touch, she leaned close and whispered next to his ear, "I want to hear you breathing hard and know you're as into this as I am. Don't think, Landon. Just feel. Making love should be free and unnerving." Kissing his jaw, she rubbed his hard nipples with her thumbs.

A deep growl rumbled in his chest before Landon captured her lips with his. Kaitlyn was surprised by his ferocity, but she wrapped her arms around his neck and welcomed his warm mouth pressing against hers.

Landon's hands slid around her back and his thumbs pressed against the sides of her breasts. As he melded her body to his, he delved his tongue between her lips. The moment their tongues touched, an electric spark ignited between them. Her head swam with his scent and a sensual euphoria flooded her body. *How can he hold back?* she wondered, wanting nothing more than to melt into him and absorb his wonderful, masculine scent. To wallow in it.

An idea suddenly occurred to her—how she could guarantee he wouldn't be able to hold his wolf completely back from her. Pulling away, she slipped from his embrace and lay down against the pillows in a relaxed pose. Lifting her arms above her head in complete surrender, she said, "I'll let you set the pace only if you'll fulfill one request."

While Landon stood and shrugged out of his jeans, his gaze swept her body. The look of possessive heat in his dark green eyes made her skin prickle. He sat on the bed beside her and slowly traced his fingers down her stomach and along the indentation at her waist. "What's your request?"

His magnetic gaze held a sexual prowess that demanded a response. When she looked down her body where his fingers lingered, she was shocked to see that her legs had spread wantonly without her knowledge. Setting her jaw, she crossed her legs and met his gaze that now held amused male satisfaction. "I want you to speak in my mind while we make love."

Landon's eyes snapped to hers. His jaw flexed and his fist clenched over her stomach. "No."

She let out a heavy sigh and trailed her fingers down her own chest, tracing them over her sensitive nipple. "I suppose we're at a stalemate, then." His ravenous gaze devoured each brush of her fingers against the hard pink tip. She could've sworn she heard him swallow several times. Just to make sure, she pinched her nipple and closed her eyes, moaning at the arousal she experienced with him watching her.

Landon brushed her fingers away and his warm palm cupped her breast in a firm hold as if he were claiming ownership. She waited a couple of seconds, but she only heard her own wants and desires in her head. Sighing sadly, she met his gaze as she skimmed her fingers down her stomach. Nervous butterflies fluttered inside. She was trying to establish a give-and-take rhythm between them, which wasn't going to be easy with a dominant Alpha like Landon.

Her eyes stayed locked with his as her fingers reached her sex.

Landon grabbed her hand, his expression hard as granite. *This is dangerous. For me to speak in your mind, I have to let my wolf share my conscious thoughts.*

She smiled and turned her hand in his. "I know." Moving his hand back to her breast, she said, "Every time you touch me, I want to hear you say something to me mentally. Quit fighting him and let your wolf have free rein."

Landon's fingers involuntarily squeezed her breast. She heard his shallow breaths and raised an eyebrow.

This is blackmail, he growled, sounding very put out.

She laughed and skimmed her fingers across his thigh. "But what a glorious way for you to share yourself with me. Hearing your voice in my head while you're kissing me *everywhere* would only arouse me more. Think how explicit you could be," she said with a chuckle.

Landon moved over her on his hands and knees, his expression intense. Placing his knee between her thighs, he set his hands on the bed, bracketing her in.

"I don't hear anything," she sing-songed, enjoying this sensual dance with her mate.

"I'm not touching you," he shot back in a gravelly voice.

Kaitlyn lifted her leg and slid her thigh alongside his. "Now you are." She enjoyed the different textures of her soft skin against the hair on his muscular thigh.

When her knee touched his sac, Landon's deep green gaze lit with sparks of light green. He gritted his teeth and narrowed his gaze. *You said when I touch you.*

"Don't you want to?" she breathed out and lowered her hand toward his chest.

He caught her hand before she connected and pinned it to the bed. She started to move her other hand and he gave it the same treatment. *Dammit to hell, woman. I can't keep doing this.* His voice sounded rougher now. It was music to her ears.

She raised an eyebrow. "What's your issue? You've got me pinned to the bed, at your mercy. You can set the pace however you wish."

Landon growled low in his throat then dipped his head and captured her nipple in his mouth in a rough, yet pleasurable squeeze. She moaned and arched closer to him. "More."

The tension between them made her heart thunder in her chest. "Tell me what you're thinking," she gasped when he began to suck and nip at the sensitive skin.

That I want to feel your body clasping me tight with nothing between us. He wants this even more than me.

Kaitlyn moaned when he moved his mouth to her other nipple and licked teasing circles around the tip. "Wh—why does he want it more?"

His gaze collided with hers and she gasped at the color. It was a brilliant light green. She'd never seen it so bright before.

Landon's smile was downright feral. *He hasn't been allowed free rein. He's vibrating with the need to slam into your body, to make you fully his.*

Her pulse ramped to an even faster pace. Using her knee, she pushed his thigh and sent him off balance. When he fell on top of her, she wrapped her legs around his hips and said in a voice full of need, "Then what's stopping him?"

* * *

Landon literally shook to the core, he was holding so much back. He wasn't lying to her about his wolf. The beast was ramming his head against Landon's chest in fast, powerful thumps to the same rhythm of his rampant heart. The tips of his fingers tingled and worry for Kaitlyn rippled through him.

He opened his hands and slid them off hers to the top of the bed. Grabbing hold of the rough-hewn wood slats, he kissed her throat. "My wolf is primal in his desires. I—"

She put her hands on his face and lifted his jaw so he had to meet her gaze. "I love you. You must trust your wolf to care for my well-being as much as you do. You've watched over me all my life and kept me safe. Your wolf was a part of that journey. He loves me, too."

Wrapping her arms around his neck, she pulled him close and whispered in his ear. "Do you feel this wild heart hammering against your chest? It beats for you *and* your wolf, loving both equally. Let him go."

When she pressed her lips against his neck and undulated under him, Landon's hands cinched tighter around the rails. Kaitlyn's acceptance of him—hell, even her encouragement of his wolf—turned him on like no woman ever had. Her slick heat slid along his cock and she arched until the tip of his erection pressed against her sex.

He kissed her with every pent-up desire he'd ever held back. She moaned and met his tongue's aggressive thrusts with her own pent-up need. Her sweet-scented arousal permeated his wolf's senses, wrapping around him in provocative primal notes.

Pressing his nose against her neck, Landon inhaled her floral aroma and closed his eyes, tensing his entire frame. With powerful restraint, he slid the tip of his erection just inside her channel. Her ragged breaths made his wolf snarl his displeasure from being held back. Landon was so primed, he thought he might snap any second. Sweat coated his back as he fought his wolf. No matter what she said, he refused to trust the beast with his mate's life.

Kaitlyn's soft hands slid down his back, her calm, gentle touch a stark contrast to the battle waging inside him. *I will keep her safe.* His wolf's vow was low and edgy. He pawed his impatience inside Landon's chest, ready to pounce. Landon snarled at the wolf to keep him at bay.

"Let him have me," Kaitlyn panted in desperation and dug her nails into his back, pulling him further inside her.

Her primal response spiked Landon's. He growled and thrust deeply into her sweet warmth, groaning when she gasped in pleasure and tilted her hips, encouraging him.

"Harder, Landon. So-o-o-o-o good."

The wolf roared his satisfaction and his claws speared deeply into the bedposts. Landon held perfectly still and growled at the wolf. The beast snarled back and the combined untamed sounds rumbled in his chest.

"Landon," Kaitlyn panted. Sweat coated her skin and she trembled all over, waiting for him to move.

Kaitlyn put her trust in him, fully and completely. Landon knew he needed to make peace with himself. He took a deep breath and quit fighting his wolf. A splitting pain shot though his head. He grunted at the sharpness, even as he accepted his wolf. The fierce dual feelings melded into one, allowing him to retract his claws. As Landon fully absorbed his wolf, he slid his hands in Kaitlyn's damp hair and kissed her forehead. "I love you, Kaitie." His voice sounded ragged and raw as if he'd yelled for hours.

Tears shimmered in her eyes as she ran her fingers along

his temples. "Your eyes are shot with streaks of light green. I told you."

He smiled. "This wolf will always cherish and protect you."

She sobbed and hugged him close. "I love you, too."

Landon's feelings for Kaitlyn had grown even deeper with this unique experience. He never thought he would find a woman who could shred his heart and then mend it so thoroughly with something as simple as her complete trust.

When she began to squirm underneath him, he held her face. "My instincts are very base and primal. I can't guarantee I'll always been a gentle lover."

"Good. I'm glad to know you don't have total control." She gave him a broad smile and pushed him on his side and then onto his back. Straddling him, she grasped his erection and took him deep within her, moaning her pleasure.

Her eyes glittered with desire in the moonlight as she lifted up and then sank back down on his hard cock. Sweat glistened on her skin and she keened, throwing her head back. Her red hair fell down her back as her beautiful, lithe body clasped him, stroking them both to new pleasurable heights.

Landon grasped her slim waist and waited for her to repeat the erotic movement. When she did, he thrust upward and deep, making her cry out and beg for more. Every nerve in his body roared with heat as if he were ready to burst into flames. It wasn't just where their bodies met. He burned everywhere.

And then his cock began to tingle with sparks of molten heat. He wanted to roll her over and take her deep and hard, but Landon held back, waiting, hoping she wanted the same.

Kaitlyn gasped and sank down on him. Rubbing her body against him, her sultry gaze locked with his and she ran her nails down his chest. "Rough would feel really good right about now."

* * *

Kaitlyn's excitement vaulted to new heights when Landon reversed their position. Grasping her hands beside her head against the bed, he slowly sank inside her and said, "Is this what you want?"

She lifted her legs around his waist and bit her bottom lip. "Don't hold back."

Landon growled and pushed her deeper into the mattress with his forceful, downward thrust. Splinters of pleasure, spiked with heat, shot though her core, making her breath hitch. She squeezed her fingers tight around his. "Harder," she demanded.

Landon withdrew and gave a grunt of male pleasure as he filled her full once more. This time harder and deeper. He felt so hot and touched every part of her so completely she couldn't speak, but whimpered in total bliss.

When he didn't move and his hips stayed flush, cradled in hers, she just stared at him in disbelief. Her entire body was shaking with the need for release. She tried to move and he growled at her, his expression fiercely primal.

Kaitlyn felt as if he had grown harder and was stretching her even more. The heat inside her was almost unbearable. Her body began to shake. "Landon," she started to beg. She felt light-headed, ready to faint at the hot intensity.

Landon's jaw flexed, and as he groaned and ground his body against hers, she felt it; strong pulses hard and deep inside her. The vibrations sent Kaitlyn's own body spiraling over the edge.

As Landon withdrew and took her hard, she surged against him and screamed so loudly her throat burned. Her body convulsed and wave after wave of euphoria rocked through her core with her orgasm. Sheer ecstasy ricocheted throughout her sensitized nerves, shattering every idea she'd ever thought she knew about her own body and what it really meant to make love to another.

As Landon collapsed on top of her, breathing heavily, she took her own deep breaths and stroked his back in tender caresses. She was blown away by the realization that what they shared, this whole mind and body loving experience, was beautiful and precious. She'd truly found her perfect mate in every respect.

Landon rolled onto his side and pulled her against him. Kaitlyn started to lay her cheek on his chest, but his necklace was in the way. She moved to lift it over his head, but his mouth formed a hard line and he shook his head. Pushing the bullet to the other side of his chest, he then pressed her close. When she sighed and lay down, he kissed the top of her head and ran his hand down her back to the curve of her hip and then back up in languid strokes. She snuggled close to his hard, warm body and inhaled his intoxicating, musky scent.

The gentle brush of his fingertips against her skin made her feel so safe and comforted. As her mind and body began to relax, she thought about the chain and bullet around his neck and wished she could think of a way to convince him to remove it.

Chapter 16

A series of loud howls jerked Kaitlyn from her slumber. Landon wasn't in bed. He stood naked in the pool of moonlight staring out the window. She glanced at the clock and realized the sun would be up in an hour.

Heart thumping, she climbed out of bed and walked over to stand beside him. Landon pulled her in front of him and wrapped his arms around her waist as she stared out the window. Wolves littered the back lawn all the way to the trees. "One hundred and fifty," he whispered in her ear as the majestic animals in various shades from black to brown to gray and every shade in between continued their baying.

The howls were soulful and long, and her heart twisted when she realized they were paying homage to Landon as their new Alpha. He should be out there with them, enjoying the last bit of moonlight.

As the animals' song died down and they bounded off into

the woods, Kaitlyn turned in Landon's arms and touched the chain on his neck. "You should be out there with your pack. I want you to remove it."

Landon lifted her fingers to his lips. He kissed her palm and met her gaze, his own full of sorrow and regret. "I can't ever forget what I did, Kaitie."

She shook her head. "I'm not asking you to forget, just to forgive yourself." Lifting the wolf charm on her thin silver chain, she held it up. "My father gave this to me and told me the wolf would keep me safe. Ever since that day, I've worn this necklace."

When she started to lift the chain off her neck he frowned and held her hand in place. "What are you doing?"

She gave him a confident smile and removed her necklace. She felt strange and oddly freed as soon as her neck was bare. "I don't need it any more. I have my very own wolf to watch over me now." Placing her hand on his chest, she continued, "But he can only protect me and those he loves if he's not restricted in any way. Don't you see? The chain slows you down and keeps you from protecting us as an Alpha should. James McKinney wouldn't want that, either as a cop or as my father."

Landon clasped her hand and his hard expression shifted from understanding to acceptance. "If I remove this chain, I'll instantly shift to my wolf form."

The tension in her shoulders relaxed. Blinking back tears of relief, she said, "I want to see how beautiful you are. Let me do it."

When he nodded, she lifted the chain from around his neck. By the time she'd lowered the chain to her side, Landon had already shifted.

A huge brown wolf with silver markings along his ears and around his muzzle and shoulders stared intently at her.

Kaitlyn cupped her hand over her mouth and tears blurred her vision as she realized Landon was the wolf painted on her wall. He was the wolf her father had seen.

The wolf stepped closer and sat in front of her. She blinked back the moisture and fell to her knees. "You're so beautiful!" Wrapping her arms around his neck, she cried into his soft fur. "Don't you *ever* put that damned necklace on again."

The wolf laid his chin on her shoulder and placed his paw on her thigh. When she pulled back, he licked her face.

Kaitlyn laughed. "I know you can speak to me mentally. Stop playing the wolf role to the nth degree."

The wolf tilted his head and she heard his voice in her head. *The look of love on your face was worth every bit of torture I've put myself through. I love you even more for embracing every part of me.*

She sniffed back her tears and kissed his muzzle before she stood. Walking over to the window, she opened it wide then turned back to the wolf. "I know we're up a story, but I saw Caine jump from four stories just fine. Go and enjoy your last bit of moonlight. I'm sure come next month I won't see hide nor hair of you for three days while you make up for lost time."

The wolf stood and his entire body tensed. *Are you sure?*

Laughing, she swept her arm toward the open window. "Go. Quit wasting precious time."

The wolf took a flying leap, his powerful muscles stretching and flexing as he sailed across the room and right out the window. Kaitlyn rushed to the window's edge and smiled as she watched him dash into the woods.

Landon found his pack and ran with the other wolves for a while, but as the impending sunrise drew near, he moved to the woods closer to his cabin. He didn't want to be too far from Kaitlyn while he enjoyed his last bit of wolf freedom.

When he heard the sound of an animal crashing through the woods, he knew it was something large. A deer, maybe. Landon took off after the sound, bounding over large rocks and around trees as he hunted his prey. He moved quickly, knowing the sun was almost upon him.

As he barreled through the woods he nearly ran into the animal that was heading straight toward him. Landon's paws skidded in the forest underbrush at the sight of a smaller wolf flying through the air toward him. It had a gorgeous auburn coat just like—

The wolf slammed into him and knocked him onto his back. Kaitlyn's laughter entered his mind at the same time the sun peeked through the dense forest.

How is this possible? he wondered even as he felt his wolf form release and he shifted back to his human form. The rocks and sticks against his bare back pinched uncomfortably with a hundred-and-twenty-pound female wolf on his chest, but he didn't care. He held on to the wolf above him and waited for her to shift, but the red wolf just panted happily and then licked him all over his face.

"Stop that," he finally said and rolled out from underneath her. Alarm settled in his chest when the wolf pranced around as if she didn't have a care in the world. "Why aren't you shifting?"

The wolf stopped and sat, staring at him.

"Can you speak to me?" he asked, tension making his voice rough.

A slim red shoulder lifted and then dropped.

Landon went down on one knee and met her steady hazel-blue gaze. The wolf quickly licked his cheek again then pawed her muzzle. Landon frowned even as he ran his hand over her gorgeous pelt. "I don't know what you want? Help me understand."

The wolf walked up to him. Placing her chin on his shoulder, she tucked her neck close to his.

Landon's chest ached in fear and worry for Kaitlyn. He wrapped his arms around her neck and ran his cheek along her fur. "I love you, Kaitie."

The wolf began to shake and he felt human arms encircle his neck. Landon pulled her close and buried his nose in her neck. "You scared the hell out of me! I thought you were permanently stuck in wolf form like Andre."

Kaitlyn showered his neck with kisses, laughing heartily. When she drew back, her eyes were full of mischief. "I didn't shift back because I wasn't ready. I wanted you to hug me and love me in my wolf form, too."

Landon cupped her face and his heart raced. "You can control your shifting? None of the Lupreda can do that. How did this happen?"

She shook her head. "I felt a little strange when I removed my necklace. Then, once you left, it was like a part of me was gone, too." Shrugging, she continued, "Maybe I was able to shift because I'm a hybrid who was bitten by a very dominant Alpha wolf."

"That wasn't a wolf bite, Kaitlyn," he said in a harsh tone, even as his mind raced through the possibilities.

"But it was a *mating* bite. Just be glad you weren't there when I began to shift. After you left, all I did was wish I could be out here running in the woods with you, and suddenly pain unlike I've ever experienced rushed through my entire body." She grimaced. "Bones cracked and muscles made horrific snapping sounds. Once I realized what was happening, I was already in wolf form."

Landon stroked her face in amazement. "Maybe it was a combination of a couple of things. A wolf has never mated with a human before, let alone one with Lupreda blood. You've worn that silver necklace since you were a child. Taking it off may have allowed you to change." With Kaitlyn's ability to shift at will, who knew what powers their offspring would possess. A new era was dawning for the Lupreda. "Why didn't you talk to me mentally?"

"I don't know if I can." Her brow furrowed. "I tried, but apparently I wasn't successful."

He rubbed his chin and shook his head. "I heard your laughter in my mind, though. Maybe speaking mentally takes a lot more practice than wishing and the desire to shift does."

She kissed his mouth and smiled. "Maybe. Are you willing to teach a new wolf some old tricks?"

Landon laughed and nodded. He was elated and more than a bit humbled that his mate wanted to share every aspect of his life. "Do you want to know why I didn't acknowledge the wolf in you when I healed your wounds?"

She nodded and waited for him to continue. Landon brushed her hair away from her face, touching her cheek with reverence. "Because you tasted like one of my own, and I desperately wanted you to be a wolf, not because *I* needed you to be one, but because I thought you would accept me as I am, wolf and all. I thought my mind and senses were playing tricks, trying to convince me I was right."

Kissing his palm, her gaze held deep love. "This wolf is happy to be able to grant all your deepest desires."

A dangerous smile tilted his lips. "Is that a promise?" He lifted her in his arms and cradled her against his chest. "Let's get you back to the cabin."

"Insatiable man." She laughed and laid her head against his shoulder.

* * * * *

Be sure to watch for the next installment,
SCIONS: REVELATION,
to see how the prophecy is revealed,
coming only to Silhouette Nocturne this fall.

THOROUGHBRED LEGACY
The stakes are high when it comes to love,
horse racing, family secrets
and broken promises.

A new exciting Harlequin continuity series coming soon!
Led by New York Times *bestselling author Elizabeth Bevarly*
FLIRTING WITH TROUBLE

Here's a preview!

THE DOOR CLOSED behind them, throwing them into darkness and leaving them utterly alone. And the next thing Daniel knew, he heard himself saying, "Marnie, I'm sorry about the way things turned out in Del Mar."

She said nothing at first, only strode across the room and stared out the window beside him. Although he couldn't see her well in the darkness—he still hadn't switched on a light…but then, neither had she—he imagined her expression was a little preoccupied, a little anxious, a little confused.

Finally, very softly, she said, "Are you?"

He nodded, then, worried she wouldn't be able to see the gesture, added, "Yeah. I am. I should have said goodbye to you."

"Yes, you should have."

Actually, he thought, there were a lot of things he should have done in Del Mar. He'd had *a lot* riding on the Pacific

Classic, and even more on his entry, Little Joe, but after meeting Marnie, the Pacific Classic had been the last thing on Daniel's mind. His loss at Del Mar had pretty much ended his career before it had even begun, and he'd had to start all over again, rebuilding from nothing.

He simply had not then and did not now have room in his life for a woman as potent as Marnie Roberts. He was a horseman first and foremost. From the time he was a schoolboy, he'd known what he wanted to do with his life—be the best possible trainer he could be.

He had to make sure Marnie understood—and he understood, too—why things had ended the way they had eight years ago. He just wished he could find the words to do that. Hell, he wished he could find the *thoughts* to do that.

"You made me forget things, Marnie, things that I really needed to remember. And that scared the hell out of me. Little Joe should have won the Classic. He was by far the best horse entered in that race. But I didn't give him the attention he needed and deserved that week, because all I could think about was you. Hell, when I woke up that morning all I wanted to do was lie there and look at you, and then wake you up and make love to you again. If I hadn't left when I did— the way I did—I might still be lying there in that bed with you, thinking about nothing else."

"And would that be so terrible?" she asked.

"Of course not," he told her. "But that wasn't why I was in Del Mar," he repeated. "I was in Del Mar to win a race. That was my job. And my work was the most important thing to me."

She said nothing for a moment, only studied his face in the darkness as if looking for the answer to a very important question. Finally she asked, "And what's the most important thing to you now, Daniel?"

Wasn't the answer to that obvious? "My work," he answered automatically.

She nodded slowly. "Of course," she said softly. "That is, after all, what you do best."

Her comment, too, puzzled him. She made it sound as if being good at what he did was a bad thing.

She bit her lip thoughtfully, her eyes fixed on his, glimmering in the scant moonlight that was filtering through the window. And damned if Daniel didn't find himself wanting to pull her into his arms and kiss her. But as much as it might have felt as if no time had passed since Del Mar, there were eight years between now and then. And eight years was a long time in the best of circumstances. For Daniel and Marnie, it was virtually a lifetime.

So Daniel turned and started for the door, then halted. He couldn't just walk away and leave things as they were, unsettled. He'd done that eight years ago and regretted it.

"It *was* good to see you again, Marnie," he said softly. And since he was being honest, he added, "I hope we see each other again."

She didn't say anything in response, only stood silhouetted against the window with her arms wrapped around her in a way that made him wonder whether she was doing it because she was cold, or if she just needed something—someone—to hold on to. In either case, Daniel understood. There was an emptiness clinging to him that he suspected would be there for a long time.

* * * * *

THOROUGHBRED LEGACY
coming soon wherever books are sold!

Thoroughbred *Legacy*

Launching in June 2008

A dramatic new 12-book continuity that embodies the American Dream.

Meet the Prestons, owners of Quest Stables, a successful horse-racing and breeding empire. But the lives, loves and reputations of this hardworking family are put at risk when a breeding scandal unfolds.

Flirting with Trouble

by New York Times bestselling author

ELIZABETH BEVARLY

Eight years ago, publicist Marnie Roberts spent seven days of bliss with Australian horse trainer Daniel Whittleson. But just as quickly, he disappeared. Now Marnie is heading to Australia to finally confront the man she's never been able to forget.

The stakes are high when it comes to love, horse racing, family secrets and broken promises.

A new exciting Harlequin continuity series coming soon!

REQUEST YOUR FREE BOOKS!

2 FREE NOVELS PLUS 2 FREE GIFTS!

Silhouette®

nocturne™

Dramatic and Sensual Tales of Paranormal Romance.

YES! Please send me 2 FREE Silhouette® Nocturne™ novels and my 2 FREE gifts (gifts are worth about $10). After receiving them, if I don't wish to receive any more books, I can return the shipping statement marked "cancel." If I don't cancel, I will receive 4 brand-new novels every other month and be billed just $4.47 per book in the U.S. or $4.99 per book in Canada, plus 25¢ shipping and handling per book plus applicable taxes, if any*. That's a savings of about 15% off the cover price! I understand that accepting the 2 free books and gifts places me under no obligation to buy anything. I can always return a shipment and cancel at any time. Even if I never buy another book from Silhouette, the two free books and gifts are mine to keep forever.

238 SDN ELS4   338 SDN ELXG

Name _____ (PLEASE PRINT) _____

Address _____ Apt. # _____

City _____ State/Prov. _____ Zip/Postal Code _____

Signature (if under 18, a parent or guardian must sign) _____

Mail to the **Silhouette Reader Service:**
IN U.S.A.: P.O. Box 1867, Buffalo, NY 14240-1867
IN CANADA: P.O. Box 609, Fort Erie, Ontario L2A 5X3

Not valid to current subscribers of Silhouette Nocturne books.

Want to try two free books from another line?
Call 1-800-873-8635 or visit www.morefreebooks.com.

* Terms and prices subject to change without notice. N.Y. residents add applicable sales tax. Canadian residents will be charged applicable provinâal taxes and GST. This offer is limited to one order per household. All orders subject to approval. Credit or debit balances in a customer's account(s) may be offset by any other outstanding balance owed by or to the customer. Please allow 4 to 6 weeks for delivery. Offer available while quantities last.

Your Privacy: Silhouette is committed to protecting your privacy. Our Privacy Policy is available online at www.eHarlequin.com or upon request from the Reader Service. From time to time we make our lists of customers available to reputable third parties who may have a product or service of interest to you. If you would prefer we not share your name and address, please check here. ☐

SN08